# The Ghosts
# of Passchendaele

By

**Frederick Petford**

Published by The Claverham Press Ltd
London

Copyright ©
Frederick Petford
2021

ISBN 9798499279274

*Dedicated to the old places,*
*and to those who still know how to find them.*

Interested readers can explore more about the themes covered in
*The Ghosts of Passchendaele* on Facebook and Instagram at
**Frederick Petford**.

Come and join us!

# Contents

Chapter One .................................................................... 1

Chapter Two ................................................................... 13

Chapter Three ................................................................ 26

Chapter Four.................................................................. 40

Chapter Five.................................................................. 52

Chapter Six .................................................................... 64

Chapter Seven ................................................................ 77

Chapter Eight ................................................................ 93

Chapter Nine ................................................................ 107

Chapter Ten ................................................................. 123

Chapter Eleven............................................................. 138

Chapter Twelve ............................................................ 151

Chapter Thirteen........................................................... 161

Chapter Fourteen ......................................................... 181

Chapter Fifteen ............................................................ 197

Chapter Sixteen............................................................ 213

Chapter Seventeen........................................................ 226

Chapter Eighteen ......................................................... 239

# Prologue

*London, May 1919*

Gareth Evans, the editor of the *London Times*, took his seat in a rather shabby meeting room on Whitehall and waited for his fellow pressmen to settle. There were about thirty of them, he guessed, facing three formally dressed men sitting behind a table on a raised dais.

An expectant silence fell as the man in the centre cleared his throat.

'Good morning, gentlemen, thank you for coming. My name is Fabian Ware, and I am vice chairman of the Imperial War Graves Commission. I'm sure you recognise Rudyard Kipling on my left. On my right, and equally eminent in his own field, is Edwin Lutyens the celebrated architect.'

The two men smiled and nodded to the audience.

'This morning we are going to brief you and take questions on the Commission's proposals for the final interment of the empire's war dead, which were presented to the cabinet two days ago. Everything is embargoed until Wednesday morning and notes are available which you may take away at the end.'

He paused and appeared to gather his thoughts before continuing. 'Prior to the recent conflict, the greatest loss the British army had suffered in a single battle was at Waterloo where three thousand five hundred British combatants died. In stark contrast, by the end of the first battle of Ypres in November 1914 we had suffered nearly sixty thousand dead and wounded.

'At times in those chaotic early days of the war the number of casualties overwhelmed our capacity to deal with them, but in the years that followed we got much better at recovering and identifying bodies and great efforts were made to treat them with respect and dignity. Thousands are buried in temporary cemeteries close to the battlefields, but many men remain in hastily dug field graves where they fell. Now the hostilities are over the Commission has been charged with deciding what the final resting place of all the men will be, and ensuring those plans are delivered.'

Lutyens nodded gravely and watched a column of smoke rise into the still air as Kipling slowly stubbed his cigarette out in a glass ashtray.

'You'll bring them back, surely? The families will be expecting that.' The editor recognised the voice behind him. Warner from the *Evening Post*.

Ware's eyes ranged across the men as though assessing their mood, then said, 'No, we will not be bringing them back. The dead will all stay in France.'

A collective stir rippled through the reporters as he continued, 'The intention is to create a series of large military cemeteries where all the officers and men that we can locate and identify will be interred side by side. They will be transferred to these new permanent sites as quickly as possible, but it will take many months to complete the task. Land must be acquired from the French and Belgian governments, the cemeteries have to be designed and built, and various other arrangements put in place.'

'There will be an outcry, you know,' said Warner. 'The Americans are planning to take their boys home.'

'I cannot speak for the Americans. I would however ask you to consider the practical difficulties that repatriation presents. There are over half a million British dead in France and Flanders and the difficulty in returning so many bodies, many in an advanced state of decomposition, would be immense. Sadly it is also true that many local cemeteries in towns and villages would be overwhelmed. And that is before the war dead from the colonies are considered.'

The editor caught his eye. 'Evans from the *Times*, Mr Ware. Presumably if a body has been identified and the family wish to pay privately to have him brought back, that'll be alright though?'

Ware replied firmly, 'No, Mr Evans, that will not be allowed. We can't have one rule for those who can afford to do that and another rule for those who cannot. The men fought and died together. They will stay together. We are committed to the principle that every one of the fallen should be treated equally.'

'Who represents bereaved families on the committee, Mr Ware? Do you have a female voice speaking for grieving mothers for example?' the editor persisted.

'The committee membership is exclusively male. However, if the implication of your question is that we have only considered this from practical perspective, I would remind you that Mr Kipling lost his son at Loos, and Mr Lutyens lost five nephews in total. The matter is as personal to us as it is to everyone else.' The hardening in his tone was unmistakable.

'What are the roles of the two gentlemen alongside you, Mr Ware?' the man next to Evans asked.

'Mr Lutyens has been advising us on the design of the cemeteries. Not just the cemeteries in fact, we also intend to build monuments in France and Flanders which will record the names of those whose bodies have not been found. Ultimately we hope that every town and village in this country that lost men will have a war memorial dedicated to their memory.'

'Thank you, and Mr Kipling?'

'Mr Kipling has been working on the words that will form part of these structures, and also on the wording for the gravestones. The committee's view is that the stones should be uniform in design, with certain personalisation, of course, name, rank, regiment and so forth.'

A silence settled over the room as the implications of this sank in. Then Evans spoke again. 'So the government will be deciding what the headstones look like and what is written on them?'

'Correct,' Ware nodded and then added, 'of necessity the stone will be a non-religious design, given the variety of faiths of the deceased.'

Evans's eyes narrowed. 'So will the bereaved families have any say at all in how their dead sons are remembered?'

'They will be able to choose a short epitaph which will be inscribed on the headstone.'

'And that is it?'

Ware nodded again and then, seeming to sense the unease in the watching men, added, 'As I said, there is a strong feeling across the committee that the fallen should be treated equally, but we are also charged with building these cemeteries within a finite time. If it is left to families to commission, pay for, and place individual headstones there is a very real danger that the thing will drift on for years.'

Lutyens stirred and spoke for the first time.

'If I may, gentlemen, there's another factor at play here too. The sight of rank upon rank of identical monuments stretching across the landscape will send a powerful and enduring signal about the scale of the sacrifice this country has made. It is a vital part of the way we will remember the dead, not just as individuals, but also as a generation. A lost generation. I am certain that it is the correct decision. We cannot have these places looking like an enormous country churchyard.'

As he finished speaking Kipling looked across to him, then returned his gaze to the pressmen and nodded in sombre agreement.

Half an hour later Evans left the building and turned thoughtfully towards his newspaper's offices in Fleet Street. He wondered if the Commission's members realised how deeply proud of their fallen sons the bereaved families were. Or how angry many of them would be when the news broke.

There would be no funerals and no graves in Britain. If he was any judge there was trouble coming.

# Chapter One

Great Tew lay on a steep fold of ground in the valley of the river Cherwell. In winter when the white chalk bones of the land showed clear, its buildings and smoking chimneys were easily visible from the surrounding hills, but in May when lush green foliage ran riot across the Oxfordshire landscape the village all but disappeared, as though it had been absorbed back into the earth itself. Only the tall tower of St Mary's church and the roof of Langford Hall remained in sight above the tangle of woods, high hedgerows and sunken lanes that encircled the remote and ancient settlement.

And ancient it was. Great Tew could trace its roots back to the Saxons and the Langford estate took its name from a crossing place on the river for the old road from Worcester to Oxford. The gravel-surfaced main street was lined with an uneven mixture of cottages, houses, barns and shops, and halfway down the eastern side a wide gap in the buildings gave onto a pair of wrought-iron gates, painted black and topped with decorative gold spikes, that marked the main entrance to the estate. Beyond these, the red brick shoulder of Langford Hall was just visible through the trees.

The oldest part of the village was a grassy track called Stream Cross. From the high street it ran downhill towards a narrow wooden bridge that crossed By Brook, a tributary of the Cherwell formed by a spring in the churchyard that still supplied the village with its water. From there, the track wound its way upwards over Tan Hill before arriving at the hamlet of Little Tew, a mile west of the village.

Close to the bridge, Holly Cottage stood alone. The thatch was in good repair, and it had been recently painted pale yellow. As the bells of St Mary's chimed four o'clock, the housekeeper emerged from the kitchen door and addressed a young man sitting under the apple trees in the back garden.

'That's me for the day then, Mr Spense. There's cold chicken and potatoes for your supper in the larder.'

Edward Spense looked up from the book he was reading and raised his hand in acknowledgement. 'Thank you, Mrs Williams, I'll see you tomorrow.'

'My Bert's going after trout at Lath Pool later, so maybe I'll have one for you in the morning,' she said.

A brief laugh sounded from the man. 'Don't tell my brother.'

Mrs Williams chuckled and opened her mouth to reply, but paused as a tinkling bell sounded from the hall. 'There's the door, just a moment.' She walked through the kitchen and glanced briefly at herself in the hall mirror before opening the front door.

'Good lord!' Her exclamation of surprise was greeted with a small smile by the tall grey-haired man standing there.

'Indeed. Or so I believe, and I should know,' he observed, gesturing gently at his purple robe. His voice was firm and clear.

'I reckon,' she replied faintly.

'Good afternoon, Mrs Williams. I hope you are well,' said the man standing behind him on the narrow path. It was Jocelyn Dance, chief constable of the county of Oxfordshire and long-time resident of Great Tew.

'Good afternoon, Colonel. I'm fine, thank you.'

'I'm glad to hear it. This is the Bishop of Oxford. We've come to see Edward. Is he in?'

'Yes, he's in the garden reading.'

'May we go through?' the chief constable continued with a smile.

She hesitated for a moment, thinking to warn him, but the rank of the men before her was intimidating so in the end she stood aside and gestured. 'Straight along the hall.'

Nodding his thanks, the bishop strode through the doorway. As the colonel followed, he caught the housekeeper with a bright eye and gave her a wink.

It was a warm afternoon, and the back door was open, so the two men simply walked through it. Now regretting that she hadn't asked them to wait, the housekeeper edged past with a quiet, 'Excuse me,' and placed herself protectively between the men and her master.

'Visitors, Mr Spense,' she announced.

'Good lord!' This time the exclamation elicited an audible sigh from the churchman.

'Afternoon, Edward,' called the colonel, 'we've popped in for a chat. You've met the bishop before, I'm sure.'

Recovering swiftly, the young man put his book down and stood up. 'Yes of course. Good afternoon, my lord. Won't you both join me.' He gestured at the garden table and added, 'I'll find another couple of chairs.'

Five minutes later the three men were settled under the trees. The housekeeper was despatched to make tea for the bishop, 'And perhaps a biscuit if you have one,' the clergyman remarked, and to fetch a glass for the colonel, who had noticed the flagon of cider on the table and thought a bracer might assist with the conversation to come.

Like a wave retreating on a pebble beach, a gentle gust of wind hissed in the branches and released a flurry of apple blossom.

Edward glanced upwards and waited. He knew why they were there.

The colonel said, 'The bishop was just passing, and it occurred that we might take the opportunity to see how you were getting along.'

*Just passing Great Tew? Hardly*, he thought, but his tone was even as he replied. 'Well as you can see I am living a life of bucolic ease, my lord.'

'Please call me Sylvester, Edward, we are family friends after all. I used to see your father in Westminster regularly,' the clergyman replied.

'Yes, he took his duties at the House of Lords seriously. More so than my brother, I suspect.'

'Well your brother has to run the estate these days of course.'

'As did my father,' observed the young man.

Not encouraged by his tone the colonel interceded, his voice friendly. 'Edward, we are here to discuss your future. Specifically, whether you wish to resume your role as padre to the Oxfordshire Light Infantry. Since you left someone's been standing in, but the position is still yours if you want it.'

Edward nodded thoughtfully. The colonel had retired from the regiment and assumed his role in the police before the war, but he maintained close links and today's mission was probably at the request of the current commanding officer.

'The same is true of the living here at St Mary's, Edward,' added the bishop. 'When you joined up Reverend Tukes came out of retirement to hold the fort as you know, but now the war is over we need to start thinking about arrangements for the future.'

*For the future*, the phrase chimed in Edward's head. During the conflict no one had thought about the future very much. For families with loved ones in France life had been day to day, a crushing short-term existence dominated by news from the front and hopes for their safe return. The strain had been appalling and many in the village were still struggling to adjust to the new peace, even if their sons had come back.

Mrs Williams arrived with the tea and a large glass for the colonel, who watched with interest as Edward poured him a generous measure of cider. 'Black Horse or King's Head?' he asked. It made a difference.

'The Black Horse, Jocelyn. Cheers.' The young man lifted his glass and they both drank with pleasure. The bishop dropped a lump of sugar into his tea, stirred it, and picked up a biscuit. He had clearly made the wrong decision, he reflected gloomily, eyeing the enthusiasm with which the colonel smacked his lips as he tasted the pale yellow cider.

Edward put his glass down and addressed his visitors. 'I appreciate you coming to see me, but I must confess that I am not sure that my future lies in either the church or the army.'

'How are you feeling?' asked the bishop. 'Shell shock can be very debilitating, and I know you were in a bad way when they pulled you out of Flanders. After three years at the front, you'd certainly earned a rest.' He glanced around the peaceful garden. 'And this is surely the place to put body and soul back together.'

'I am better than when I arrived back here in 1917. The trouble is I seem to have left my faith in the mud of Passchendaele,' Edward replied.

The bishop nodded sympathetically. This was not the first such conversation that he had had with his fellow clergymen. The merciless slaughter had been enough to try anyone's faith in a benign higher power. 'You're not alone,' he said quietly. 'We were all tested.'

The young man's face tightened. 'I was expected to tell the soldiers that God was on our side and that we were going to win. I remember them all looking at me, as though I had some influence over their fate. But in reality they were simply lucky or unlucky.' He shook his head. 'There was too much suffering, too much sacrifice. By the end I was just an empty shell going through the motions.'

He looked at his visitors and added bitterly, 'And the men sensed it. I could feel their respect draining away.' He picked up his glass and drank deeply while the two men looked on in silence.

When the colonel spoke, his tone was sympathetic. 'Edward, the work you did was important, you know. It wasn't meaningless. Many died, of course they did, but at least they believed their cause was just. And they killed as well. Don't forget that. Our soldiers needed to know that God excused the taking of life.'

'I know you mean well but I don't believe any more, and that means a career in the church would be based on a lie.' He glanced at the bishop before adding, 'And I think I've done enough of that.'

The clergyman frowned. 'So you intend to leave the church completely? That would be a tragic shame, Edward. I remember when I first met you, the passion you had for the cause, your intellect and belief lighted us up. From an early stage you were marked down as a high flier. Think of the good you could do, even just here in the parish. There are many returning men who would benefit from counsel from a man who really understood. One who had been there alongside them.'

*Unlike you*, thought Edward, but his reply was scrupulously polite. 'The points you make are fair, Sylvester, but I cannot serve the church any longer.'

'Now the war is over communities need healing. Your faith will return as you carry out God's work, I am sure of it. He will redeem you,' the bishop persisted.

Edward smiled sadly and a trace of anger showed in his eyes. 'The biblical god of whom you speak does not exist.' The finality in his tone was unmistakable.

With a sigh of frustration the clergyman leaned back in his chair. He picked up another biscuit and chewed it thoughtfully. *He really means it*, he reflected. *We've lost him.*

Jocelyn Dance had known Edward all his life and something promoted him to ask, 'Is there anything else? Is something other than this faith business bothering you?'

Out of the corner of his eye he saw the bishop's eyes roll at his choice of words.

Edward stared at the two men, his face suddenly haunted. 'When I said I was much better I meant it, but a lingering problem remains. One that has followed me here from Flanders. Above all, it is the reason why I cannot serve the church any more. In fact I sometimes doubt my sanity.'

'Your sanity?' The colonel raised his eyebrows in concerned surprise. 'What on earth is it?'

'Since Passchendaele, I can see ghosts.'

*

Shortly after the dreaded whistles that marked the start of the British attack sounded in the trenches, a steady flow of grievously wounded men began arriving at the casualty clearing station in the shattered environs of Vieux Chêne farm, a mile west of Ypres.

In a roofless corner of what had once been a homely kitchen, Captain Edward Spense, military chaplain to the Oxfordshire Light Infantry, knelt by a man on a stretcher. He was holding his hand and talking to him as a medical orderly pressed a field dressing onto a cavernous wound below the soldier's ribcage. Their eyes met and the orderly gave a brief shake of his head.

'You're lucky, Randall, you've got a blighty. You'll be patched up and back home before you can say Great Tew,' Spense promised him, using the soldiers' slang for a wound that was bad enough to get you sent home but from which you would recover. The lie came easily, born of hard experience, but this time it was particularly painful. He knew the man well, a fellow resident of his home village and a star centre-forward in the hotly contested North Cherwell football league.

Randall's eyes were closed but he smiled faintly. As the two men waited for him to die the padre noticed the wall next to him was covered with green and blue floral wallpaper, which seemed incongruous in the bloody, noisy, chaos that surrounded them. He looked across the men lying on the ground. Some were ominously still but one man screamed and thrashed as a doctor and orderly bent over him. Beyond them, through a hole in the wall, he could see a steady stream of horse-drawn and motorised ambulances arriving at the back of the farm. A column of fresh troops was walking past them towards the front line, their faces set in stone as they eyed the straggly line of stretchers bearing wounded waiting to be evacuated.

'Hello, mother!' Randall's eyes suddenly opened, and a beautiful smile graced his face. 'Hello, mother,' he repeated in a clear strong voice, and then his expression slackened, his eyes closed, and his mouth fell open.

Spense looked down at him, thinking of the pretty girl in the white-painted cottage who would grieve at the news, but then was astonished to see an opaque, smoke-like stream emerge from the man's mouth. It rose into the air right in front of him, twisting and alive with vitality, before dissolving into a thin grey line that spread across the horizon and then shot away out of sight at an unbelievable speed.

At the same time Randall screamed. It was a barely human noise, full of pain and fury at the injustice of his fate. Wide-eyed and heart pounding, Spense stared down at the fallen soldier then looked at the medical orderly who was buttoning the man's uniform back together. 'Did you see that?'

'See what, padre?'

'That smoke that came out of his mouth.'

'Smoke? No, sir, I didn't.'

'But you heard him cry out?'

The orderly looked at him. 'He didn't cry out, sir, just slipped away. Saw his mum, he did. I've seen that before,' he added helpfully. 'But there wasn't no scream.'

Confused, Spense sensed someone standing over them. It was a tall, thin captain from the Royal Scots Fusiliers. Churchill's lot. They were the next regiment up the line, he remembered.

'He's lucky.' The officer's voice was resonant with the soft brogue of the Western Isles. Spense stared up at him aware that something was wrong, then, as he turned and set off across the room, he realised what it was.

*His mouth hadn't moved.*

He watched him go and saw to his horror that the back of his head was missing. It was a killing wound, exposed bone and brains glistening in the low sunlight of the early morning. Astonished that he was still standing, the padre hastened to his feet.

'That man, quickly, we need to help him.'

The orderly rose too. 'Which man, sir?'

Spense pointed to where the Scotsman was now standing, looking down at another wounded man. 'That captain in the Royal Scots.'

Doubt showed on the orderly's face. 'There's no captain, sir.'

'Of course there is, man, I'm looking right at him. He was standing next to us a minute ago. Dammit, he spoke to me.'

'Not that I can see, sir.' The orderly was looking at him strangely. 'How about a break and nip of rum? We've been hard at it.'

Spense glared back, anger rising. 'Not until we've helped that officer. Come on.' But when he looked back across the ruins of the kitchen his blood ran cold. The orderly was right, there was no one standing there, just the huddled forms of men crouched by the casualties.

Later that night he headed for his usual dugout behind the front line. He felt low and desperately tired. The attack had failed, and the darkness seemed remarkably peaceful after the appalling noise that had lasted all day. A private he knew from the Oxfords was just leaving as he approached the doorway.

'Any tea on in there, Rennie?' he asked hopefully. But the man just shook his head and made his way along the shadowy trench towards the casualty station. Finding himself alone Spense lighted a candle and sat down. With time for reflection at last, he was starting to wonder what on earth the events of the morning meant when a splash sounded outside, and a burly mud-stained sergeant appeared in the doorway.

'Room for a little 'un?' he enquired tiredly. Leaning his rifle on the bunk opposite Spense, he sat down. 'Alright, padre? A busy day for you, I imagine.'

'Yes, Sergeant, sadly so. It seems we took a pasting.'

'Aye we did. Dunno how I made it, to be honest. We got into their lines in the end, but there were so few of us left, they beat us back with a counterattack.' He grunted and unlaced his boots, then swung his legs up to lie prone on the stained blanket.

'I saw Rennie briefly. He was going out as I was coming in.'

The sergeant turned his head in the gloom. 'Oh yes? When was that?'

'Not ten minutes ago.'

After a slight hesitation the sergeant replied. 'With respect, sir, you didn't. Rennie was next to me this morning as we went through the wire. I saw him die.'

*

As Edward finished speaking a second drift of apple blossom fell towards the table. The visitors watched in silence as the younger man picked up his glass and carefully removed a single petal that was floating on its surface, his concentration absolute.

'What do you think you saw?' asked the bishop eventually.

'I think I saw Randall's soul leaving his body. There's little doubt in my mind.'

'Where was it going?'

'Good question, Sylvester,' Edward said wryly.

'What about the other men? The Royal Scots captain and Private Rennie,' the colonel asked.

The younger man smiled sadly. 'It wasn't just those two. I saw others. Made an embarrassment of myself in front of the men, frankly. I stood it for a couple of days, but when it became apparent that I was losing my mind I walked to battalion headquarters and told the brigadier that I couldn't do the job any more. To be honest I was expecting them to shoot me. Desertion and all that. In fact I was half hoping they might, it would have been a blessed relief at that point.'

'I am so sorry, Edward,' whispered the colonel, visibly distressed, 'what you have been through…'

'Anyway, they didn't,' Spense continued. 'It helps if you have a medal apparently. They told me I'd done my bit, then they cleaned me up, put me to bed, fed me some decent food, and a few days later they sent me back to Oxfordshire.'

The two older men exchanged glances before the bishop spoke again. 'Edward, you said that the problem had followed you home from Flanders. Are we to understand that these… apparitions, shall we say, have continued to appear to you in Great Tew?'

'Yes.'

'Good heavens,' the colonel interjected. 'Who? Where?'

'Do you mind if I keep that to myself, Jocelyn. I'd rather not risk ridicule.'

'Do they all communicate with you?' asked the bishop.

'No. The Fusiliers captain was a rarity. Often I'm just suddenly aware one is present.'

'Do they look different to normal people?' the colonel asked.

Edward sighed. 'Not really. Normally there's a strong acrid smell. Sometimes their clothes are out of place, but more often I just sense they are somehow not connected to the scene. As though an unscripted actor is standing on a stage. It's hard to explain.'

His friend nodded thoughtfully. 'Can I ask what you think they are?'

'I think they are ghosts of some sort. The captain told me Randall was lucky, but he'd just been killed so how could that be? Perhaps he went where he was supposed to be going but the captain was stuck in limbo, to use a religious term.' He shrugged. 'It all sounds so completely far-fetched. I'm sure you must think I'm only fit for the asylum.'

'You wouldn't be the first member of the church or the laity to see visions, Edward,' observed the bishop, although the doubt in his voice was hard to hide. 'In any event I think that your own assessment of yourself is fair. You are not at the stage where you can return to an active role as vicar of St Mary's.'

A smile passed briefly over the younger man's face. 'Amen to that, my lord,' he said.

After they left the cottage the two men walked silently back to the high street. Once around the corner they stopped as if by mutual agreement. Up the hill a large dray pulled by two heavy horses had stopped outside the pub and the carter and the publican were manoeuvring a wooden cask towards an open hatch in the pavement.

'What did you think about that, Jocelyn?' asked the bishop.

'It had the ring of truth about it to me,' he replied. 'There's no doubt in my mind that Edward was telling us what he saw.'

'What he believes he saw,' corrected the clergyman. 'But what are we to make of it? Either the fellow is seriously ill, or he is seeing ghosts. It's a thin choice either way.'

'Do you believe in ghosts?' asked the colonel, rather putting the bishop on the spot.

The man opposite hesitated, all too aware of his elevated position in the Church of England. 'Well put it this way, I believe in the human soul and it is not difficult to imagine that on occasions there are, shall we say, technical difficulties in its transmission to a better place. But to be able to see one? That is of a different dimension altogether.'

The colonel gave him a long look then nodded. 'A different dimension? Yes, I couldn't have put it better myself, Sylvester.'

The bishop looked up the street towards St Mary's. 'Will you walk with me to the car? My man's put it up by the church.'

'Would you mind if I don't? I must nip back to Holly Cottage. In all the excitement I forgot to ask Edward to supper. A distant relation of my wife's has just arrived with us for an extended stay and Eve is keen to introduce her around.'

'And the brother of the local squire is a good place to start?' The bishop smiled.

'Exactly. I just hope she isn't matchmaking. She has previous form in that area, I'm afraid.'

'Very well. Let's speak on the telephone then, although I cannot see that the situation is resolved from either of our points of view. Tukes must remain in harness for a while yet, and the stand-in padre will have to soldier on.' They both turned as a crash and loud shouting indicated the replenishment of the pub's beer supply was not going according to plan.

'In fact I'll just nip up and see Tukes now and let him know that his services are still required,' the bishop added.

The colonel smiled broadly, delighted by the clergyman's unwitting joke. 'Quite,' he said.

# Chapter Two

Eve Dance had rather a good feeling about Miss Innes Knox. The girl had arrived two days earlier from Glasgow, newly qualified as a doctor and with her deceased older sister's son in tow. The boy's widowed mother had succumbed to Spanish flu three months earlier and Miss Knox had bravely decided to, 'Raise him as my own, Mrs Dance.'

Young Jaikie was three years old and as bright as a button. The news that Marston House, a fine Georgian building that lay halfway down the high street, would once again be home to a youngster had galvanised the colonel's wife, Ellie the maid and Mrs Franks the cook in equal measure. A nursery had been prepared, toys and picture books had been purchased, and an exchange of letters had established the child's favourite foodstuffs. In short, the household was fully ready and a little overexcited when the diminutive flame-haired fellow strolled boldly through the front door, supremely confident of his welcome.

As for the daughter of her distant cousin, Eve liked her from the moment they met on the station platform at Oxford. The invitation had come about because young Jaikie, for all his outward appearance of robust health, had been hospitalised in Glasgow with a nasty lung infection.

'Fresh clean air, good food, plenty of outdoor exercise,' the paediatrician had advised, and once Miss Knox's elderly mother had remembered the connection to Great Tew and written to the colonel's wife, matters had been arranged with little difficulty.

It was a long way to come, and completely different to smoky industrialised Glasgow, but to Eve it seemed as though everywhere was in a state of upheaval as demobbed soldiers came back from France and women who had worked on the land or in the ammunition factories returned home.

Miss Knox was of medium height and wore her dark brown hair in a fringe and long French plait which Eve thought suited her very well. It was a pity about the ugly horn-rimmed spectacles which dominated her face, but she had a fine neat figure and an agreeable if slightly brisk manner which the older woman liked. She sensed she was a girl with character and ambition and in her view that was a good thing. This was confirmed during dinner the first night when it became apparent that her decision to accept the offer of accommodation in Great Tew was not just motivated by the health of 'the wean' fast asleep in the nursery upstairs.

'In my final year of study I specialised in psychiatry,' she informed the colonel and his wife. 'Diseases of the mind, if you will. I am more than happy to help out in the cottage hospital while I am here, but I believe my long-term career lies in that direction.'

'How very interesting,' remarked the colonel.

'I am glad you think so because my particular interest is in the field of criminal behaviour and the factors that underpin delinquency. The question that interests me is whether criminality is innate in some people, or whether they are driven to it by the life they have led.'

Unaware he was walking into a trap, the man opposite her said, 'That is an excellent question, Miss Knox.'

'Yes, isn't it? Actually I was hoping that you'd let me sit in on one or two of your investigations. As live research to support my studies. Would that be possible, do you think?'

'Ah.' He met his wife's eye and she smiled back in amusement.

'Well, Jocelyn? I fear you have been gently manoeuvred into a cul-de-sac.'

'We'll have to see, Miss Knox,' he said, making a mental note to treat her with caution in the future. 'We will have to see.'

Later that night the Dances had a conversation in the privacy of their bedroom.

Petite, attractive and lively, Eve knew that her husband's amiable personality and thick head of greying hair belied a fast and able mind. He was far more than the genial buffer he presented to the outside world, as the men under his command knew very well. In turn she was intuitive, capable and, when the occasion demanded, extremely resolute. When they worked together they were a formidable couple, and they played a full role in the life of the village and its wider setting.

The subject of the discussion was the meeting that afternoon with Edward Spense and the bishop, which the colonel related in detail to his wife.

Like her husband Eve knew the Spense family well. She was close friends with Edward's mother Claire, the dowager Lady Langford, who still lived in the hall. Her eldest son Piers was the current Lord Langford, having inherited the title on the death of his father in 1916, and her middle son Hugh had joined the Coldstream Guards and perished fifteen months later in May of 1918. Eve had shared the grief at this double blow with her friend and their bond was strong. She cared about Edward and wanted to help him if she could.

She also knew more than most about the secrets that lay hidden within the hills and valleys of north-west Oxfordshire. Even in 1919 the old religion was still practised around the village and certain families were known to have the Craft running in their veins, passed down from mother to daughter for generations. Things that might sound ridiculous in a sophisticated London drawing room seemed much more credible on a summer's night in Great Tew when the full moon threw deep shadows onto the landscape and timeless streams of energy ran hot and strong across the land.

'It's quite possible that Edward did see poor Phillip Randall's soul leaving his body and that, for whatever reason, some spirits are visible to him,' she remarked when her husband had completed his account.

'Agreed,' he replied. 'But, as I suspect Miss Knox would maintain, there is also a chance that the poor fellow's mental state is far worse than it appears. He may be suffering from delusions of a most damaging sort.'

Eve was silent for a moment, then said, 'You will write to the regiment and let them know that Edward will not be returning, I presume?'

'Yes.'

'Is there anything else we can do?'

'We can try to keep more of an eye on him. He's been living a hermit's life since he got back but at least he's coming here to meet Miss Knox so that will be a chance for you to have a look at him. Although obviously our meeting with the bishop will be off limits.'

'Yes of course,' his wife said. She sat down at her dressing table and began to brush her short blonde hair. 'It will be nice for Miss Knox to meet Edward. Perhaps he can show her around the area.'

Her husband met her eye in the mirror. 'Eve, as we have just discussed the man is hardly in a position to consider a romantic entanglement.'

'Oh no, of course not. Just platonic, you know,' she replied, which elicited a sigh from the colonel who had been down this road before and recognised the signs.

Later, as they lay in the darkness she said, 'Do you think Miss Knox is attractive, Jocelyn?'

Her husband had noticed her excellent figure and remarkably sensual mouth at their first meeting, but he paused as though giving the matter some thought for the first time. 'I imagine so, a little perhaps. Although I don't think those glasses do much for her.'

'No. I did wonder about those, it's almost as though she's concealing her face,' said his wife thoughtfully.

*

Lilly White, lady's maid to the dowager Lady Langford, made her way along the corridor on the first floor of Langford Hall.

She was carrying a breakfast tray that bore a single soft-boiled egg, two rounds of toast, cook's home-made marmalade and a pot of coffee. Her Ladyship was a creature of habit in these matters.

A copy of Wednesday's *London Times* lay next to the plate. Lilly was secretly amazed that the newspaper arrived at the hall at half past eight each morning, although as the first batch of them left Paddington station at five o'clock it was no surprise. Newspapers were the only way to know what was going on in the world, so their distribution was important.

She arrived at her mistress's bedroom door and entered without knocking. Lady Langford was sitting up in bed, her refined face caught in a bright ray of light that slanted through a gap in the curtains. 'Good morning, my lady.' The maid smiled and walked across the comfortably furnished room. She placed the tray on the eiderdown before picking up the bed tray and arranging both across her mistress's lap.

'And good morning to you, Lilly.' Lady Langford's voice was surprisingly low. When the young maid had started work at the hall she had assumed that her mistress was a smoker, but that was not the case, her unusual base tones were natural. She walked over to the window and drew the curtains. Light flooded through the diamond-leaded panes, throwing a chequerboard pattern onto the blue and yellow Turkish rug that lay at the foot of the bed.

'Sunshine, how lovely,' said Lady Langford with approval.

'Yes, my lady, it is a fine morning.'

Lilly lingered in the bay for a moment. The bedroom was at the back of the house and the view was spectacular. A large Elizabethan knot garden lay below the window and the geometric design of tightly pruned knee-high hedges and gravel pathways looked wonderful from above. On either side red brick walls guided the eye towards a flight of wide steps that led down to a lawn, edged with heavily planted flower borders. Croquet hoops protruded from the grass. Past the lawn, and lower again, were the pleasure grounds, a romantic tangle of paths, mature shrubs, statues and flowers.

Beyond the gardens lush tree-studded parkland dotted with grazing cattle ran flat for half a mile before disappearing steeply downhill towards the river Cherwell. On the far side of the valley a ridge topped with trees showed above the pasture and on the horizon Green Hill rose higher. On that tranquil May morning the landscape looked utterly timeless and unchanging. *Another summer is coming*, Lilly thought, as her eyes momentarily lost themselves in the far horizon.

All of which made the sudden cry of horror from behind her all the more shocking.

She spun round and stared. Lady Langford was sitting rigid, the newspaper clenched in one hand and tears were running down her cheeks.

'Whatever's the matter, my lady?' she cried. But instead of answering the older woman just shook her head and wept as misery contorted her face. Lilly rushed across to the bed. She scrabbled in her pocket for a handkerchief, *Clean, thankfully*, and dabbed gently at her mistress's cheeks. 'What on earth's happened, my lady?' she asked again.

Lady Langford held up the newspaper. She turned to Lilly, her eyes raw with pain. When she spoke her voice was barely audible.

'It's Hugh. My darling brave boy Hugh. They won't let me bring him home.'

*

Gareth Evans was in his office at the *Times*. It was teatime on Friday, three days after the news had broken about the War Graves Commission proposals. He was smoking a cigarette and had a cup of coffee on the desk in front of him.

Through the wide glass panels that rose from waist height to the ceiling he watched Wilkes sitting typing at his desk amongst his newsroom colleagues. When the young reporter had reported the arrival of hundreds of letters on the proposals he had asked him for a representative sample and had just finished reading them.

Nearly all were from grieving parents, the majority written by mothers. Working-class mothers. Some were fierce with outrage, but it was the others, polite, untutored, but redolent with quiet desperation that were particularly heart-breaking. It was a grim business, he mused. The nation's wounded soul had taken another blow.

He stubbed his cigarette out and picked one up to re-read. It was written in black ink on a single side of cheap lined paper torn from a pad, and the sender's address was in Barnsley. In his mind's eye he pictured a modest two-up two-down terraced house and a scrubbed front step that led directly out onto a street where everyone knew each other.

The writing was small and neat, a woman's hand without a doubt. He wondered if the faint outlines on the bottom of the paper were tear stains.

*Dear Sir,*

*I am writing to express my dismay at the news that the government has taken upon itself the decision that my dead son will not be returned to us, so we may grieve him properly. We are not even allowed a funeral.*

*How can this be? By what right do politicians in London choose the manner and location of my dear son's grave? He bravely volunteered to fight for King and country and died doing his duty. But now he will be buried where we can never see him and cannot choose the stone that commemorates him.*

*I am not alone. There are many like me in Barnsley that are angry and grieving all over again at this heartless decision.*

*The government took my son and now they must give him back.*

*Yours faithfully,*

*Winnifred Barret (Mrs)*

After a moment's reflection he reached out and picked up the telephone. 'See if you can get Ralph Almond at the House on the phone, would you?' he asked.

*

On Saturday morning Evans called Wilkes into his office.

'I met a friend of mine from the Foreign Office last night. He filled me in on the government thinking over Ware's proposals, off the record of course. It appears that just about every MP and many in the Lords are receiving sackfuls of letters of protest. They've never seen anything like it and some members with small majorities are getting jumpy. My friend said that Lloyd George is going to call a debate in the House and at present it's not at all clear that the government will win. Winston is undecided apparently.'

Wilkes nodded. 'I'm not surprised. In the pub last night there was a lot of ill feeling. Some people think it's the right thing of course, but many don't. "Nationalising death," one bloke called it. Let's say it was a lively discussion, sir.'

Ever the newsman, Evans jotted the phrase down on his blotter then continued, 'I also spoke to our esteemed owner. He thinks a major row is brewing and we should plot a middle course. I agree with him. If ever I saw a case where both sides have a justifiable position it is this one. The *Times* will sum up the arguments for and against but leave the decision to the consciences of those who have to make it.'

*

At seven o'clock on Saturday evening Edward Spense knocked on the front door of Marston House. The fine weather continued to hold and the sash window to the left of the door was wide open. Through it he could hear the delighted squeals of a small child and the noisy jolly rumblings of an older man.

It appeared that a tickling match was in progress on the rug.

Ellie the maid opened the door and bobbed a welcome then showed him through to the empty drawing room. Moments later a visibly perspiring colonel in his shirt sleeves and a loosened tie appeared with a wriggling red-headed little boy chuckling in his arms.

'Ah, Edward, lovely to see you. Please meet young Jaikie, or the wean, as he is known across his many domains.' He put him down. 'Jaikie, this is our friend Edward. Say hello and shake hands.' These instructions were followed obediently then the door opened, and

Eve Dance appeared followed by her guest.

'Edward, this is Miss Innes Knox, a relative of mine. In fact I should say Dr Knox, because Innes recently qualified as a medical doctor from Glasgow University. She intends to study psychiatry.'

'How do you do, Dr Knox,' he said formally and extended his hand.

'As Innes will be with us for an extended stay and, along with the wean, is rapidly become a much loved member of the family we have just agreed to be on first name terms. So if it is alright with you we will continue in that vein this evening.'

'Of course.' He smiled at the young woman. 'I am Edward Spense, Innes, but do please call me Edward.'

'They often call him Eddie up at Langford Hall, even the staff,' Eve observed, 'but we wouldn't dream of being so familiar.' Innes saw the look of warm amusement and affection that passed between the two of them and liked it.

*He could be a colonial, South African or Australian*, she thought. He was over six feet tall with a lean wide-shouldered frame and thick reddish blond hair that fell across his forehead. His eyes were brown, and his face was angular with a pronounced jawline. *Quite striking*, she considered coolly, *if one were looking for such a fellow*. She guessed he was in his late twenties and his tweed suit was worn but well cut.

She took all this in in an instant, then said, 'Well, Edward, this terror is young Jaikie. He is my deceased sister's son and I have taken him on.'

He raised his eyebrows in surprise. 'That is very creditable of you, Innes.'

'Unfortunately he has not been well, so when Eve and Jocelyn offered me a place here in the fresh air of the countryside I agreed straight away. I am starting work at the cottage hospital on Monday. They have two Spanish flu cases there already.'

'Well watch yourself. I gather it is young people in their twenties who are particularly vulnerable,' he said seriously.

'I have had it and recovered. A mild case only, unlike my sister.'

'Ah, I see. Well my condolences, Innes, I am sure that your stay here will be very pleasant. Jocelyn and Eve are quite the most delightful people in the village.'

'With that sort of flattery we'd better get you a drink,' the colonel butted in. 'Innes, what will you have?'

Sadly, after this promising start, the evening did not go as well as Eve had hoped.

The difficulties blew up out of nothing after the main course when Innes, displaying a perfectly reasonable curiosity, asked Edward where he lived and what he did. Clearly a little drunk, he fumbled the reply somewhat, saying he'd served in the war as a military chaplain and was now living in a cottage in the village.

Somehow it sounded weak, Eve thought defensively, *as though he hadn't done much.*

'So you do not live up at the hall?' Innes asked.

'No I don't.'

'Why is that?'

'When I got back from France I needed to be alone for a while.'

'But you are the vicar here at St Mary's?'

'Er, no, not at the moment.'

Innes screwed her face up in confusion. 'But I understood from Eve that you were the vicar before you went off?'

'I was, I studied divinity at Cambridge and came straight here.'

'But you have not resumed your post?'

'Not so far.'

'I see. When did you come back?'

'Eighteen months ago.'

'Do you mind me asking why you are still unemployed?'

Edward, feeling he was on the receiving end of a rather direct examination, took a long pull at his glass of claret. He was a little under the influence, having spent the afternoon drinking in the Black Horse. A thing he did too often as he was well aware.

'The truth of the matter is that I am struggling with my faith. I wonder if I would be much use to the people of Great Tew at present, Miss Knox,' he said.

Eve and her husband both noticed his reversion to formality and after a quick shared glance the colonel intervened. 'Edward had a long war, Innes. He joined up early and by 1917 he'd done his bit. You weren't in too good a state when they pulled you out, were you?'

'So they say, Jocelyn, so they say,' came the wry reply.

'I hope I will not cause offence if I venture the idea that the future of mankind rests with science not faith,' said Miss Knox briskly. 'As a scientist myself I can see the many opportunities that it brings to improve our lives. Practical things that will actually help people.'

'That's an interesting idea,' Eve observed, trying to calm the rather febrile atmosphere between her two guests. 'Tell us more.'

'I believe that science, not God, is the ultimate arbiter of mankind. In the end, it will prove more powerful than anything else. And it will certainly save more lives than faith.'

Edward stared over the table, slightly wild-eyed. 'Science gave us machine guns, barbed wire and poison gas, Miss Knox. Excuse me if I do not share your confidence in its power to heal. However, you will be reassured to hear that I no longer believe in God either.'

'Neither science nor faith, Mr Spense? A man adrift then and, if you will excuse me saying so, it shows.'

The colonel winced at this but to his surprise, Edward smiled. 'There are more things in heaven and earth, Miss Knox, than are dreamt of in our philosophy,' he said obliquely. 'But your assessment of me is tellingly accurate. No doubt you have a fine career awaiting you in psychiatry.'

Innes fell silent and Eve had a strong sense that she was regretting a familiar mistake, but before she could pour oil on the choppy waters that beset her dining room, Edward pushed his chair back.

'And now, after a delightful evening, I will take my leave.'

'Will you not stay a while longer?' said the colonel, also keen to patch things up.

'No. Thank you to you both. I'll see myself out. Goodnight, Miss Knox.' And with a smile that drifted between irony and contempt, he left. Seconds later they heard the front door close quietly.

There was a silence in the dining room. Then Eve heard Innes say quietly, 'Oh dear.' When she looked at her she could see a large tear making its way out from under her spectacles.

Like wind on the surface of a lake, a ripple of anger passed over the colonel's face. 'He won the Military Medal you know, Innes. For rescuing wounded men from no man's land.' His voice was quiet, almost as though he was thinking aloud. 'It needed a great deal of courage to go over the top holding a rifle. Imagine what it took to climb those trench ladders unarmed.'

She looked at him, her cheeks clearly wet. 'I am so sorry.'

*

In Holly Cottage Edward nursed a large glass of whisky and brooded. Innes Knox's abrasive manner had certainly irked him, but her observations made for uncomfortable reflection.

When he finally stirred and glanced at the clock on the mantelpiece he noticed it was twenty-five minutes past eleven. *Five minutes until his regular passer-by.* Resolved to action, he stood up, downed the last of his drink, and left the cottage by the front door. He walked unsteadily out into Stream Cross and waited.

Shortly afterwards an acrid smell filled his nostrils, and he spotted the familiar dark-clad figure walking silently towards him from the high street. As she got closer her features were revealed in the faint starlight. A grey-haired woman wearing a bonnet, perhaps sixty years old and dressed in Victorian clothing. Her head was lowered, and she appeared not to have seen him, absorbed as she was in her mission.

Heart beating he stepped out in front of her. She stopped six feet away and raised her head. 'Hello,' he said. 'I can see you. I see you every night walking by.'

Their eyes met and the expression on her face changed fractionally but there was no further acknowledgement, and no involuntary thoughts entered his mind. After a moment she moved to his right as if to go round him. Full of devilment he moved the same way, blocking her passage. She gave him a long look and he could see character and awareness in her eyes. She moved the other way, and he did the same, grinning, and curious to see what would happen next. Moments later he had his answer.

*Drunk.* The flat sardonic judgement was suddenly in his head. Then with a visible shrug she stepped forward and walked straight through him.

He felt as though he had been hit over the heart with a hammer, and an icy cold that seemed to suck all human warmth from his being flooded through him. As he dropped to the ground and passed out, his last terrifying thought was of reality falling away to leave him alone and screaming as he fell through an empty, echoing and limitless space.

# Chapter Three

Innes Knox was on Eve's mind as she climbed through thick woods a mile to the east of Great Tew. It was before dawn on Sunday morning and her destination was marked on the Ordnance Survey map of Oxfordshire with a small cross and a simple notation – *Standing Stone*. Eve knew it as the Beltane stone and the ancient monolith was one of eight widely spaced in the landscape around a smaller Neolithic stone circle called Creech Hill Ring on the Langford estate.

The three easterly stones aligned perfectly with the centre of Creech Hill Ring at sunrise on the summer and winter solstices, and on both equinoxes. A matching group of three stones to the west marked the sunset on those four days. The final two were located on the north–south axis and bisected the gaps between the two sets of three. Set more than a mile outside the inner ring, the stones were placed with remarkable accuracy along the radius of a perfect circle and a line drawn from any stone through the centre of Creech Hill Ring would, if continued, directly meet another on the opposite side.

The inner and outer rings had been built to mark the place where two of the energy streams that run over the surface of the earth collide, intermix, and then forge on again on their restless journeys around the globe. Thousands of years later it remained a place of extraordinary power, hidden in plain sight and capable of focussing energy like a magnifying glass gathering sunlight to ignite paper.

But this was the modern world of 1919. Ernest Rutherford had split the atom the previous year and as invention and industry drove human progress, such arcane knowledge had been long forgotten. If you suggested such a thing to a tourist who had stumbled across the solitary Beltane stone they would smile politely and then laugh about it with their friends when they returned to the city.

But Eve hadn't forgotten, and she wouldn't laugh.

Because Eve Dance was a witch.

She emerged out of the trees into the grey pre-dawn light and made her way to the stone on the summit of the hill. As she walked she looked around but could see no one else. Not that the presence of other locals would have mattered. Her actions would have seemed curious to the point of eccentricity to the tourist from the city, but to many in the village of Great Tew they would have been as familiar as the rhythms of evensong in St Mary's.

Using sticks from her bag she built a little fire at the foot of the stone and then poured the contents of a small bottle of pure lavender oil onto it. She struck a match and the wood blazed up immediately, engulfing the stone in fragrant smoke. Taking a decorative silver dagger from the bag she leaned forward, placed the blade in the flames, and started to chant. Her voice was low, and the words were not English, but they were delivered with a repetitive and compelling cadence as she slowly circled the stone, touching it with the heated blade four times as she completed the circuit. Then she retraced her steps in the opposite direction.

The ritual continued for some minutes as she used the dagger to connect the stone with the fire and then she finished by placing a handful of dried sage leaves on the dying flames. It flared up one last time as thick aromatic smoke twisted and writhed around the monolith. In the growing light an observer might have reflected that the smoke lingered longer than would have been expected on the airy hilltop, almost as though it was being absorbed into the granite.

Silent now, Eve stood with her head bowed and then walked round the stone to look to the east and the dawn. She sat down on the ground, stretched her legs out and leaned back, watching the silent orange sun as it rose above the horizon. The ridges of the Oxfordshire countryside caught the light as shades of deep blue lingered in the vales, and in the distance a long avenue of trees that led to Creech Hill Ring appeared – a bonfire built in the centre of the ring was visible from every one of the outer stones.

As the sun's rays reached her, she closed her eyes and put her hands flat on the ground, feeling the rough texture of the grass on her palms. With practised ease she let her mind rise high into the still air, carried by the energy of the charged stone at her back. An image of Innes Knox came to her, and she gently explored it and saw her hidden beauty and the bitter anger buried within. *Why was she angry?* Slowly she peeled away the layers and replayed the tense exchange between her and Edward Spense.

*Can I help you, Innes?* she asked. And she was given her answer. In a flashing moment of insight she realised the truth about Innes Knox. Questions floated through her mind as she drifted in the high white light above the Beltane stone. *Should she speak to the girl? What would be the purpose?*

Dawn had turned to full daylight by the time she reached a decision. She would say nothing for the moment. But if things developed between Edward Spense and Innes she would have to intervene.

*

From St Mary's church the main street ran gently downhill past the Black Horse public house and the baker on the left and the grocers on the right, before reaching the market cross a hundred yards away.

From this fine medieval edifice roads led in both directions. On the right Dell Lane connected the village to the outside world and passed the cottage hospital, the police house, and the bus stop before meandering through villages and hamlets and finally arriving in Banbury. To the left an unmade lane called Rivermead served farms along the Cherwell valley and ended at Beech Farm, the furthest of those that comprised the Langford estate.

Beyond the crossroads the blacksmith still supplied all necessary iron work to the area, but a new sign above the door now advertised mechanical services for motor cars. Mr Underwood had felt the wind of change and was branching out. The final building in the village was the King's Head public house, the rivalry between the two hostelries being celebrated through two enthusiastic though tragically denuded football teams. Beyond the pub the street petered out at a pair of gates that led to Home Farm.

From her position under the lychgate Innes watched as the final stragglers from morning church wandered down the street. A short while earlier she had noticed Edward Spense sitting on the low wall that enclosed the rear of the graveyard. For the few minutes since then she had dithered uncharacteristically, knowing that she had behaved badly when they met at dinner, but also aware that her company might not be welcomed – even if its only purpose was to deliver an apology. Nevertheless, she straightened her shoulders, braced herself and turned the corner to confront him.

There was no one in sight. With a sigh of frustration she walked over to the wall and looked out across the valley.

*My word, I'm a long way from Glasgow*, she thought.

From the churchyard the ground fell away down a slope that seemed to carry on for ever, ending in a line of mature trees that edged the river. A large group of cattle grazed peacefully close to the water. On the opposite bank she could see three farms and a hamlet surrounded by green pasture and woodland. They were all on the same level along the hillside and she thought it a curious coincidence.

When she turned she saw him standing twenty yards away silently watching her.

Irritated to feel her heart beat a little faster under his gaze, she said, 'Mr Spense, come over. I would appreciate a word.' Without answering, he strode across the grass. He was wearing a pair of battered brown corduroy trousers and a pale blue shirt with no tie and moved easily. *An athlete then.* 'Do you play football?' she asked without preamble as he came to a halt.

He seemed bemused. 'I have been known to turn out for the Black Horse if they're short.'

'Ah.' There was a brief pause, then she got down to the matter in hand. 'Mr Spense, I owe you an apology. Last evening at the Dances' I regret my behaviour was not all that it should have been. I was over direct and perhaps even rude. I am sorry. I have also apologised to Eve.'

He eyed her thoughtfully. 'Are you always like that?'

'Like what?'

'Over direct and perhaps even rude.'

Her mouth tightened below the horn-rimmed glasses. 'Well I am not some simpering girl whose only concern is her next amusing beau, if that is what you are asking.'

He raised his eyebrows and said nothing.

She sighed wearily. *Why was this so hard?* 'Mr Spense, I grew up in industrial Glasgow, as far removed from this rural heaven on earth as it is possible to imagine. Misogyny is the national pastime up there. It is as embedded in life as drizzle on the Clyde. I studied medicine at a university where every male thought I should be training to be a nurse and I fear that is where I acquired my spikey exterior. In fact I have a horrible suspicion that my fellow students' nickname for me was the hurcheon.'

'Hurcheon?'

'A hedgehog, Mr Spense. In the Scottish vernacular.'

He laughed, a spontaneous loud chortle. It suited him, she thought, that smile.

'Well if it is any conciliation, Miss Knox, at school my nickname was Tariff.'

'Oh yes? And what was the etymology behind that, I wonder?'

'It was stencilled on my travelling trunk. Edward Xavier Spense, sadly shortened to E X Spense.'

'That must have cost you dear,' she observed with a smile.

'Very quick, but not original, Miss Knox. And I got off lightly. Thomas Andrew Becket was universally known as The Turbulent Priest.' He smiled back at her. 'Your apology is accepted and I in turn regret that I turned up the worse for drink and may have been a little truculent. I have also made my apologies to our graceful hostess and received absolution.'

'Pax then? And back to first names, Edward?' She offered him her hand. As he took it he was surprised to feel a little thrill at her warm dry touch.

'Pax, Innes.'

They were still for a moment and then Innes said, 'The church was well attended this morning.'

'Yes, it is one of the three legs of rural life, the church, estate and public house. Some of the families who live here can probably trace their lineage back as far as ours. Mind you, like me, not everyone is a believer.'

'Oh? Why do they come to church then?'

'Insurance.' She smiled then realised he was serious as he continued, 'Will you join me for a glass of something at the Black Horse?'

The pub was set back from the road and a bench was placed below the front window. They sat down in the sun and Innes asked a question. 'The view across the valley from the graveyard is magnificent. I could see some houses and settlements on the far side, and they were all at the same level along the hillside. It seemed a strange thing.'

'They are built on the spring line, where fresh water emerges into the open air. So they know the water is clean. Once it's come through a field with beasts in that can't be guaranteed.'

She nodded thoughtfully, then said, 'The church tower must dominate the valley from over there. I imagine it can be seen from miles around.'

'Yes, that's true. It was a site of pagan worship long before a Saxon cleric decreed it was the right place for a Christian church and no doubt visibility was a factor. They liked the population to know the church was looking over them. On a calm day in winter its bell can be heard in Little Tew a mile away.'

'You are well informed.'

'Well I am an ordained minister.'

'Yes, one forgets,' she remarked offhandedly.

Edward felt a stir of irritation but before he could respond a statuesque figure appeared with a tray bearing their drinks, and he made the necessary introductions.

'Innes, this is Stanley Tirrold the landlord of the Black Horse,' he said. 'Stanley this is Miss Innes Knox. She is living with the Dances on an extended stay and starts work at the cottage hospital tomorrow.'

'Yes, I heard they had a visitor. A nurse are you, Miss Knox?' The publican's voice was a dark deep thing, well suited to his frame.

Edward was starting to recognise the tightening of Innes's mouth when she was displeased. 'No, Mr Tirrold, I am a doctor. Imagine that. A woman doctor.' The undercurrent in her tone was all too plain, but the publican was a match for it.

'Well that's a fine thing, I'm sure. And a Scottish lady if I recognise the accent?'

'Just so.'

'I took my wife to the Isle of Skye for our twenty-fifth wedding anniversary.' The landlord scratched his stomach ruminatively, then continued, 'Come to think of it, our thirtieth is coming round next week.'

'Oh really? And what are your plans for that?'

'Maybe it's time to fetch her back,' he replied, poker-faced. 'Enjoy your drinks.' He turned and walked back to the door with a heavy tread. Innes looked at Edward, who was leaning back on the bench rocking with silent laughter.

'Well really, I can see no reason why I should be the butt of his jokes,' she said tightly.

'He's testing you, Innes. Seeing if you are a fit and proper person to drink in his pub, or whether you should be eased down the hill to the King's Head. An inferior establishment in his opinion. And mine as it happens.'

'Did I pass or fail?'

'I would say the jury is out, but persevere, Innes. Laugh at the jokes, be patient, and try not to be too waspish.'

'Waspish? I am not waspish.'

'No, of course not. My mistake.'

A pair of ladies walked past arm in arm, took in every detail, and wished them good morning, and a horse and cart laden with bundles of wooden poles made its way slowly up the high street towards the church. The hooves sounded melancholy in the Sunday quiet of the street. They watched it pass in silence, the slouching carter giving them both a nod.

Innes took a sip of lemonade. 'Tell me about the estate. Is it very old?'

He smiled at her. 'Why don't I show you next Saturday? If Eve will take the wean for a couple of hours we can ride out and do a little circuit. Cover the tourist attractions as it were.'

She stirred uneasily. 'As I mentioned, I grew up in Glasgow. We did not canter down Sauchiehall Street, we took the bus.'

'You don't ride then?'

'I have never been on a horse in my life.'

*

The following Saturday Colonel Dance looked out of the study window to see Edward tying up two horses, one large and one small. 'He's here,' he called up the stairs.

In the master bedroom complications had arisen.
'Just a minute,' his wife's voice floated down. Grunting in acknowledgement the colonel opened the front door just as Eve opened the window above and called down. 'Morning, side-saddle or astride?'

Edward looked up. 'As she hasn't ridden before I thought astride would be easier.' He gestured at the conventional saddle on the pretty chestnut pony. 'Always assuming the indecency is permissible.'

'I agree. And I'm sure it is.' Eve's head disappeared.

Innes was in a state of semi undress and starting to regret the whole idea. 'Why can't we just walk?' she complained to her host.

'Oh no, it's too far to walk.' The older woman gestured at the jodhpurs lying on the bed. 'My daughter wore these on many occasions, I am sure we'll get you into them. And the jacket. Take off your petticoat.'

Twenty minutes later Eve and a rather nervous Innes appeared at the front door.

'Splendid,' murmured the colonel approvingly.

His wife smiled. The girl did indeed look splendid. The riding clothes set off her figure very nicely, while maintaining all necessary decorum. *Just the job for a pleasant ride* à deux *around the estate*, she thought to herself with satisfaction.

Aided by the mounting block next to the rail Innes carefully climbed aboard and, as Ellie appeared with the wean to wave goodbye, they set off slowly up the high street towards the gates to the hall. 'Don't worry about the horse, Miriam is as calm and friendly as can be. And she knows the way. You will be absolutely fine,' said Edward reassuringly.

'Oh really?' Innes replied faintly. But to her surprise, this confident assertion proved to be correct. Miriam behaved beautifully as they passed through the gates and made steady progress along the drive towards Langford Hall. She rather enjoyed sitting up high and found herself wondering what they looked like riding together as a couple. It was a curious thing to think, she reflected.

Langford Hall was a large and handsome three-storey Tudor house, built from weathered red bricks that had bled white in places. 'My old room.' Edward pointed to one of the spurs that pushed out from either side of the recessed main block. She looked up and saw a first-floor bay window, four panes wide with a heavy leaded diamond pattern on the glass. 'Mother and my brother Piers have rooms around the back.'

They continued past the side of the house and onto a grassy track that led out into open parkland. 'My word, it's very beautiful,' Innes said, as the view opened up.

Edward nodded with satisfaction, and she realised she had said the right thing. 'It's the result of nigh on a thousand years of human toil. That's Green Hill on the skyline and the standing stone on the summit marks the limit of our land. The hall sits roughly in the middle of the estate.'

'Good lord, you mean it extends that far in every direction?'

'Yes it does. We came over with the Normans and were given the land by William the Conqueror. During the civil war Sir Wyndham Spense was a royalist and led his cavalry alongside Prince Rupert. His wife Olivia defended Langford Hall for the king and famously held out for three months. When the place was finally taken, through superior firepower I might add, Cromwell was impressed enough to spare her life and she joined her husband in exile in France.'

'So the family lost the hall?'

'Yes, for some years, but when Cromwell died and King Charles the Second was crowned, the lands were given back to Sir Wyndham. And in appreciation of his loyalty, the king also handed over two estates next to ours that had supported Cromwell. Consequently the Langford estate became one of the largest in Oxfordshire.'

'How large, might I ask?'

'These days it's about twenty thousand acres, mainly let as tenanted farms that pay rent. Many of those have been in the same families for generations too, although some of the farms nearest to the hall are managed directly by my brother and Giles Stafford the land agent. We're famous for our beef, but we also raise sheep and pigs. The main pig farm is run by a Mr Trotter you will be pleased to hear.'

'How delightful.' She laughed and they continued along the track in silence as Innes considered what he had said. Then another question occurred to her.

'So you own the village as well?'

'Villages in fact. Four villages and numerous hamlets.'

'The family has a great deal of power locally then.'

'And responsibility. At the beginning of the war nearly five hundred people relied directly on Langford for their living, farm workers and their families of course, but also others like the shopkeepers and craftsmen in the village. The estate funds the cottage hospital and provides free electricity too. My father had a hydro plant built in a redundant water mill down on the Cherwell.'

He looked over to her and added, 'You are right though, Lord Langford is a powerful figure in these parts. But if the estate failed it would be disastrous for everyone, not just the family.'

'And he is your older brother?'

'Yes, he assumed the title when my much-loved father died. We were still feeling his loss terribly when Hugh our middle brother was killed. It was a bitter double blow, especially for my mother. Here we are…'

He broke off and nodded ahead. Innes saw they had arrived at one end of a wide straight ride, lined with mature trees. It ran level for half a mile, she guessed. 'This leads to somewhere I wanted to show you. It's a good surface so perhaps we might try a trot. What do you think?'

She hesitated. 'I'm really not sure. What is involved?'

'Give her a little kick and rise up in the stirrups. Then as you get going, move up and down in the saddle in rhythm with the horse. You'll know straight away when you've got it.' He clicked his tongue and called, 'Come on, Miriam.'

Feeling rather anxious, but determined to show him she could do it, Innes kicked in and rose as the horse accelerated. For the first twenty seconds she felt uncoordinated and ungainly then suddenly, more by accident than design, she found herself rising and falling in harmony with the pony's regular movement.

'That's it. We'll have you galloping before you know it.'

'No you won't,' she replied, glancing over to see her riding partner moving easily on his black horse alongside her. Nevertheless, by concentrating hard she managed to keep going and as the end of the ride approached she felt she had mastered the art reasonably well.

They passed between two high standing stones, and she realised they had entered a stone circle about fifty yards wide that lay on an exposed grassy outcrop overlooking the valley. Beyond the ring the ground sloped downhill on all sides and Innes could see the river Cherwell at the bottom of the hill to her right.

They both dismounted and the horses immediately lowered their heads and began to crop the grass. Edward said, 'This is Creech Hill Ring. It's Neolithic I believe…' He tailed off, his expression suddenly distant.

*That smell.*

But Innes didn't notice. 'Good heavens, look at that extraordinary tree.' Intrigued she walked towards an enormous, multi-trunked yew tree that stood alone at the end of the ride.

The acrid smell was all around Edward now, harsh, like burning newspaper. He saw the horses' heads come up as they stirred anxiously. Miriam whinnied and rolled her eyes. Suddenly cold in the morning sunshine, he knew what was coming and cast his eyes about, barely registering Innes's movements or chatter as she crossed towards the tree. Then suddenly the horses panicked and with a thunder of hooves galloped to the far side of the ring and disappeared over the slope. He barely noticed.

*There he was.*

With a shock he recognised the man standing midway between the two entrance stones. It was Christian Freeling, not back from France more than three weeks. He was wearing a collarless brown shirt, moleskin trousers, working boots and gaiters. Edward remembered that he was a farmhand at Beech Farm, the Atkins' place out on the far edge of the estate.

They stared at each other. An image of the Langford Yew flashed through Edward's mind. *A man hanging.* Belatedly he realised where Innes was and called out, 'Wait, come back!' but she had disappeared behind one of the great secondary trunks that grew around the original tree. Seconds later a cry sounded within the foliage. He ran over, meeting her as she emerged from the branches.

'Edward, there's a man hanging in the tree. He's dead.'

'I know. I'm sorry.'

'What do you mean you know?' She stared at him.

Edward didn't answer. He walked into the central court of the ancient tree. The original trunk was huge – at least ten feet wide. Four new trunks encircled it and rose high above his head. He walked towards the narrow gap that gave access to the hollowed-out interior. With his heart beating and the acrid smell almost overpowering him, he put his hand on the bark and looked inside.

*Dead. Dead!* The voice inside his head pulsed painfully.

Christian Freeling was hanging by the neck from a beam of wood placed across the top of the hollow trunk. His feet were five feet off the ground, his arms slack at his sides.

He was wearing the same clothes as his ghost.

*

Claire Spense sat at her desk in the morning room at Langford Hall and stared pensively out of the window. Her initial shock and grief at the war grave proposals had turned to burning anger, and the news that there would be a debate on the matter in parliament had stirred her to action.

She could see no reason why any bereaved mother should be forbidden from bringing her son home. The army did not own the bodies and in her view the government was punishing patriotic families unnecessarily. She had just finished writing a list of names that represented a potent cross section of the elite that ruled the country – politicians, diplomats, industrial figures, land owners and other men of influence.

There were one hundred and two in total and the formidably well-connected Lady Langford knew them all. And she was spoiling for a fight. She broke her gaze from the window and pulled a fresh piece of paper towards her. Picking up her pen she glanced at the name at the top of the first column, smiled to herself and began to write.

*Great Tew, Saturday.*

*My dear Pug,*

*How are you and darling Clemmie? I hope you enjoyed the ball at Sandringham as much as Piers and I did. You must come to stay at Langford again soon, do let me know when you are free. In the meantime, may I beg a favour from you regarding these dreadful war grave proposals?*

Two hours later a pile of letters lay on her desk, corresponding to neat ticks against the first ten names on her list. She crossed to the bell and rang it and shortly afterwards a footman arrived. 'Take those to the post office, would you?' She gestured at her desk. 'I'd like them to catch the post today. There will be more tomorrow.'

'Thank you, my lady.' The servant collected the envelopes and as he left the room he glanced down at the address on the top one.

*Private and confidential.*

*The Right Honourable Winston Churchill MP,*

*Secretary of State for War,*

*The House of Commons,*

*London W.*

# Chapter Four

It was late afternoon on Saturday and in the simply furnished front room of Well Cottage on Beech Farm the colonel and Constable Burrows were undertaking the grim task of telling Jane Freeling that her husband had taken his own life.

She was tearful but not surprised. 'To tell you the truth I was afraid something like this might happen, sir. He spent a lot of time sitting drinking and brooding, and he took his hand to me a couple of times which he hadn't before. Lord knows I loved him, but it wasn't easy.' She shrugged eloquently and added, 'I reckon there's a lot of men come back from France with their bodies whole and their minds broken.'

This perceptive observation hung in the room for a moment before the colonel asked sympathetically, 'How old was he, Mrs Freeling?'

'Twenty-four.'

'And no children yet?'

'No, not with him being away. We haven't been together that much, if you know what I mean.'

'Quite.'

The youthful Constable Burrows who had noticed Mrs Freeling's long blonde hair and fine features allowed his mind to drift in an unprofessional direction for a moment as the colonel continued, 'Well I'm sure that the Reverend Tukes will be over to see you after church in the morning. What regiment was your husband in?'

'The Gloucestershire's. His brother lived over there, and they joined up together.'

'Very well, I will write to the commanding officer to let him know. They should keep a record of these things I think.'

Mrs Freeling smiled in appreciation. 'Thank you, sir.'

'We'd better go and tell Mr Atkins at the farmhouse now and I'm sure he'll be down to see you straight away. Try not to worry, I don't doubt you will be looked after, Mrs Freeling. My sincere condolences once again.'

'Thank you, sir,' she repeated.

They took their leave and walked back up the track to the lane where they had left the colonel's car. Turning with some difficulty, driving not being his strongpoint, they drove the short distance to Beech Farm. The farmhouse was a large building with a whitewashed Georgian frontage. A group of mature beech trees in full leaf stood behind it and there were two well-maintained barns in the yard to the left. Everything looked tidy and well kept.

'Nice place, sir,' observed Burrows, clearly impressed.

'Yes, as I recall this is the largest farm on the estate and Clayton Atkins is quite the gentleman farmer. They attend church but beyond that we rarely see them socially in the village. He's a widower and it's just himself, his married son Isaac and his wife tucked away up here.'

The constable nodded, grateful for this local knowledge, and rang the bell. Half a minute later a young maid appeared and led them to the sitting room where Mr Atkins, Isaac and his dark-haired wife Nell were having a drink before supper. As they took their seats Burrows noticed a bulge on her slight figure and realised that she was pregnant.

The chief constable passed on the bad news. Like his grieving wife, the three of them were saddened but not surprised.

'Something wasn't right with the fellow,' observed the farmer. 'I'll probably see Lord Langford tomorrow at church, I'll speak to him then.' He was a quietly spoken man in his mid-forties. *A good-looking fellow in his way*, thought Burrows.

The colonel nodded. 'Yes, if you would. In addition to the shock of losing her husband, it won't be long before Mrs Freeling starts to worry about what's to become of her, so if you are able to offer some reassurance I'm sure she would appreciate it. Does she have family locally, do you know?'

'Her mother's in Banbury I think,' said Isaac.

'Not too far then,' the colonel replied and then turned to his wife. 'Well, some good news perhaps? I hope I am not speaking out of turn, Mrs Atkins, if I ask if congratulations are in order?'

She gave him a wide smile and slipped her hand over her belly. 'No that's quite alright, Colonel. I am with child, and we couldn't be happier.'

'I'm delighted for you. The great wheel turns, and life goes on.'

Shortly afterwards they set off back to the village. With the chief constable at the wheel it was not a journey that the young policeman was looking forward to. 'It's good news about Isaac and Nell,' the colonel shouted, grinning rather wildly as he piloted the open-top Austin at high speed along the narrow lane.

'Indeed, sir.' The constable closed his eyes and clung on as they swung round a blind corner.

'They've been married five or six years. I'd imagine they were starting to wonder if it was ever going to happen.'

'They must be very pleased, sir,' Burrows re-affirmed, raising his voice against the onrushing wind.

The colonel glanced in his direction. 'Are you walking out, Burrows, or got your eye on anyone? When did you arrive from Oxford? A year or so now, isn't it? The villagers like their policeman to be settled, if you know what I mean. And you've got the police house. A good-looking fellow like you, with prospects. I'd have thought you would be beating them off with a stick, eh?'

Burrows knew that as a single man he was lucky to be allocated the police house, which doubled as the police station, but the simple fact was there was no one else. The war had taken a heavy toll on police numbers and they were thinly spread across the county.

As the village constable for Great Tew and its surroundings he worked alone, reporting to the sergeant in Banbury eight miles away.

'No one's caught my eye yet, sir,' he said woodenly.

'Well don't wait too long. A sound wife is a career asset in the police… whoa, look out!'

The rear of a large cart had appeared around a bend less than thirty yards in front of them. It completely filled the road. With a sickening feeling the constable realised that a crash was inevitable and braced himself. He had however reckoned without the life-preserving instincts of his chief constable who cried, 'Hang on, Burrows!' hauled the wheel to the left and directed the Austin at a closed gate in the hedge bank. They hit it with a loud crash and the windscreen shattered, showering both driver and passenger with glass, then they were through and careering down the grassy slope at high speed.

'The brakes, sir! Apply the brakes!' Burrows shouted as he reopened his eyes to see a copse of poplar trees looming large in front of them.

'There seems to be some malfunction,' came the alarming reply. He looked over to see the colonel peering into the footwell and stabbing downwards with his foot. Without thinking he grabbed the wheel and pulled it hard. The car swung to the left, spent an extended and heart-wrenching period on two wheels, then finally fell back and came to a halt parallel with the slope.

'Blimey. Alright, sir?' the young constable said after a moment.

To his amazement the colonel was still looking into the footwell. 'I'm not sure what happened there. Anyway no harm done.' He looked round and saw a figure standing in the broken gateway. It was the carter. 'I say, come down and give us a hand, would you,' he called.

*

In the cool, dark, brick-lined cellar of the cottage hospital Innes Knox stood next to the body of Christian Freeling. She was alone and a single unshaded light dangled above her head, throwing a pool of light onto the corpse and casting hard shadows around the room. The official verdict of suicide had been reached swiftly. No note had been found, but that was unsurprising – like many farmhands the dead man had been barely literate – and as the bad news spread there had been widespread and sympathetic acceptance that the long reach of the war had claimed another victim.

But something was niggling away at the newly qualified doctor, and after church she had gone to have another look at the body. She pictured the moment when Edward cut him down and they slackened and removed the noose. He had been stone cold and there was absolutely no doubt he was dead, but she had had a clear view of his neck and it was this that was troubling her. *There should surely be more scarring*, she reasoned. Even if the poor man was resigned to death it was almost inconceivable that he would have simply hung there immobile. At the minimum there would have been involuntary movement in his legs which would have swung the body as he choked.

Leaning forward she peeled back the sheet that covered his face and saw a bruise on his cheekbone which she hadn't noticed before. She gently eased his shirt apart and looked carefully at his neck. There was an obvious furrow on either side of his Adam's apple where the rope had taken his weight, but no bruising to indicate any internal bleeding in the skin, or noticeable graze marks. The rope had been brought in with the body to frustrate any ghoulish trophy hunters and she picked it up. It was a rough one-inch farm rope with coir sticking out.

Thoughtfully she put it down then pulled the sheet onto to his thighs and bent over his hips and sniffed. He was still clothed and unwashed, but there was no indication that his body had vented *in extremis.* Had he done so it would have been a clear sign he had died in the tree. Its absence was not compelling, but it added to her sense that something was wrong. Finally she inspected his hands and removed his boots and socks. There was no indication of blood pooling in the bottom of his limbs, which would surely have occurred as he hung there after asphyxiation.

With a little grunt, she replaced the sheet and stood still, her arms folded. There was little doubt in her mind that the medical evidence suggested that Christian Freeling was already dead when he was suspended in the yew tree.

Tapping her foot she wondered what to do. There was also something else that was odd, she mused. When she had run out of the tree and called to Edward that there was a body hanging there, she was sure he'd said, 'I know.'

*What was she to make of that?*

\*

Three days later she saw Edward Spense in the high street and decided that she would ask him the question that had been playing on her mind.

It had been a busy morning. Dr Hall was out on his calls when she heard a commotion outside and went to have a look. A man was lying on his back in the road outside the police house and two large mongrel dogs were barking and snapping at the heels of a white-eyed rearing and kicking horse that was defying all attempts to calm it.

Constable Burrows appeared next to her.

'Mr Renton, get those dogs under control,' he bellowed as the horse and its baiters set off at high speed towards the main street. A rapidly building crowd followed and within moments Innes and the policeman were left alone with the fallen rider. He was sitting up and holding his arm across his chest.

'Come out of nowhere they did, bloody things,' he grimaced.

'Now then, Mr Bliss, ladies present,' said Burrows firmly as Innes gently examined his arm.

'I fear you have broken your collar bone, Mr Bliss,' she said. 'Let's get you up and inside and I'll have a proper look.'

She spent half an hour examining and binding the patient's arm and Burrows was quietly impressed with the efficient and sensitive way she dealt with the man. *An asset to the village*, he thought to himself. It was well known that Dr Hall's retirement had been delayed by the war and he wondered how long she was going to stay.

As Innes arrived at the corner of Dell Lane she noticed Edward sitting on the bottom step of the market cross, idly watching the slow-paced life along the village street.

'Good morning, Edward, how are you?' she asked as he noticed her approach and stood up.

'Very well, Innes. And you?'

'I've just finished dealing with an emergency. Mr Bliss fell from his horse outside the police house and broke his collar bone.'

He nodded. 'Ah yes.'

'You heard?'

He smiled. 'An event like that is round the village in fifteen minutes.'

There was a pause. Seeking inspiration Innes broke his gaze and looked down the hill. She could see the colonel's mud-splattered car parked outside the blacksmith. The bonnet was raised, and Mr Underwood's head was buried deep inside the engine.

She turned back to Edward and said, 'When we found Mr Freeling you didn't seem surprised. I called out that there was a body in the tree, and you answered, "I know." I must confess I have been wondering how you knew.'

'It was just a feeling I had.'

'That's odd because you sounded sure,' she replied.

'Not really, it was just a vague idea.'

'No, it was more than that. You weren't surprised.'

He shrugged, clearly uncomfortable. 'I don't know. A sixth sense perhaps.' He gestured defensively with his hands.

*He's dissembling*, she thought, irritated. 'I saw your face. You already knew something was wrong, I just want to know how.'

He gathered himself. *Those bloody glasses of hers.* 'Innes, you have a habit of turning a pleasant conversation into an interrogation. I'd be lying if I said I enjoyed it.'

'But aren't you lying anyway?' The words were out before she could stop them. *Take them back*, the voice screamed in her head as she saw the shocked expression on his face. But it was too late, and he gave her no time.

'Goodbye, Miss Knox. Enjoy the rest of your day,' he said tightly, and with that he turned on his heel and stalked off towards Stream Cross.

Anger flared inside her and she called out, 'I see you have thrown yourself upon your dignity, Mr Spense. Let us hope that it will bear your weight.'

He stopped and for a moment she thought he would turn and face her, but then he started walking again. Ignoring the staring villagers, she slumped down onto the step and leaned back. Tears of frustration welled up behind her glasses.

*Will you ever learn?* she wondered.

\*

As the end of May passed and glorious early June weather bathed Great Tew in benevolent sunlight, Innes and Edward saw very little of each other and had no conversations other than the most strained and polite exchanges when they were unavoidable.

The funeral of Christian Freeling was one such occasion. Innes was not going to go, but Eve intervened. 'It'll be noticed if you don't. With you being the one who found the body. I'm afraid they'll all want to have a gawp at you and relive the drama,' she warned and Innes, still learning about the social expectations of rural village life, duly obliged. And while what Eve said was true, she quietly admitted to herself that her main aim was to build a relationship between the girl and Lady Langford. They had been introduced at church and spoken briefly but that was all, so the funeral was another opportunity for casual conversation.

It was Lord Langford himself who had told the Reverend Tukes that the unfortunate man was to be buried in the churchyard – a consideration not normally offered to suicides. He had let it be known that in his view Christian Freeling had served his country and was as much a casualty of war as anyone who had been shot in the trenches, an opinion which had met with widespread approval in the village. As a result the service was very well attended, and many bereaved parents whose sons' bodies remained in France were there. They had all been denied a funeral and, as he sat in the church, Edward reflected that his brother's clear direction on the matter had perhaps enabled them to take some comfort from the service.

To Eve's disappointment there was only a brief nod between Edward and Innes in the crowded church. She knew there had been another falling out and reluctantly resigned herself to patience. *There's plenty of summer yet*, she thought as she moved over to pay her respects to Mrs Freeling. The poor woman had no clothes sense, she thought, the loose dress she was wearing did not suit her at all.

Later as the wake gathered pace in the Black Horse, Eve's husband found himself gently ambushed in the pub garden when he slipped outside to smoke a cigar. His wife disapproved of this indulgence and was inclined to lecture him, so he had concealed his generous frame behind a hedge. He was just staring up at the church tower and enjoying the first luxurious inhalations when Innes appeared, holding a pint of cider.

'I thought I saw you sneaking off, Colonel, and suspected your motives. I've brought you a glass to wash it down.' She passed it over with a smile.

'Guilty as charged, you've run me to earth. And thank you for that, it's Stanley Tirrold's finest barrel for a while, I would say.' He took a gulp, smacked his lips with pleasure and puffed away.

'Actually I was wanting a word, Jocelyn.'

He eyed her cautiously, unsurprised. 'Yes, I thought you might. Still keen on the police investigations?'

'Definitely.' As the sun caught her glasses he noted the firm set of her glorious mouth and sighed silently.

'Well it's difficult, Innes, in all honesty. I am guessing that it is serious crimes that you're interested in, and we don't get many of those out in the county. And more to the point, police interviews go by formal rules, and for good reasons. There's no provision for an amateur observer.'

Innes grimaced at this characterisation but soldiered on. 'It is actually the death of Mr Freeling that I have been thinking about.'

'Well it's tragic of course. He's not the only one at risk either. Damned shell shock, it's hollowed some men out. They seem fine, and then they suddenly just disintegrate.'

'What if it wasn't suicide? What if he was already dead when he was hung up in that tree?'

'Eh? What are you suggesting exactly?' For a split second he looked at her in surprise, then she saw understanding flash into his eyes. *This man is no fool*, she thought.

'I examined the body in the cottage hospital before it was cleaned and prepared. The rope had marked his neck, but not badly enough to indicate he'd died from hanging. And there were other things…' She went on to explain.

The colonel listened in silence, smoking and sipping. The church bell chimed five o'clock and the noise from the open back door of the bar steadily grew in volume as the drinks funded by the Langford estate took their toll.

*There were no funerals in the village for the men who died in France. It is almost as if this one is for all of them*, the colonel reflected unaware he was mirroring Edward's thoughts in the church, before refocussing on his companion.

'… so to my mind there are two possibilities. One is that Mr Freeling took his own life and was then hung up in the tree by someone else for reasons that are unclear. The second is that he was killed by another person and put there to make it look like suicide.'

'The latter being murder. Or possibly misadventure of course. These things do happen. If he died in some stupid accident and someone wished to avoid the blame,' said the colonel thoughtfully.

'Yes. Either of those would be a possibility.'

'Hmmm.' There was a long pause. 'Are you sure?' he asked finally.

'I'm only newly qualified and I'm not an expert in post-mortem studies, but the indications were quite strong.'

'Any signs of violence on the body?'

'No.'

'How did he die then?'

'I'm afraid I don't know.'

He fixed her with a look and said coolly, 'It's rather a shame you didn't mention this earlier, Innes. The poor man is in the ground now and we won't be digging him up, I can assure you of that.'

She coloured, uncomfortable under his gaze. 'I know. I was going to mention it to Edward but when I tried to, we ended up arguing again. Actually, I think he knows there's something wrong too. That was what we argued about. When I ran out of the tree and told him there was a body in there, he said, "I know." He looked shocked, almost haunted. I think he was expecting me to find Mr Freeling.'

A curious stillness came over the man in front of her. 'That's a strange thing to say,' he said carefully.

'He knew. I'm sure of it.'

The colonel puffed and considered what the young doctor had told him. Then a pleasing idea came to him, *One that would kill two birds with one stone*, he thought with some satisfaction.

'I'll tell you what, Innes. I can't just open up a public investigation into this. Piers Langford has decreed that the man is a war casualty, and the entire village has accepted that. The repercussions of a murder investigation would be considerable. I would need to be absolutely certain that there is a case to answer. You understand, I'm sure?'

'Yes, I can see that.'

'So find me the evidence. Use your psychiatry and your scientific skills. Put your theories to the test. If you can identify a suspected murderer and give me reasonable grounds, I'll open an investigation. If not we'll let sleeping dogs lie. How about that?'

'It's not quite what I was expecting.' She frowned.

'A challenge though, eh? Something to keep you busy. If questioned you may say you are acting at my behest, although I'll deny it of course.' He grinned at her, gave his cigar one final puff, and stubbed it out on the broad trunk of an oak tree. Then he drained his glass and with a nod and a smile he set off towards the back door of the pub, clearly in search of a refill. Halfway across the garden he stopped and turned.

'Get Edward to help you,' he called. 'He's a man in need of something to do. Good hunting, Innes.'

# Chapter Five

*An extract from the* London Times, *15th June 1919*

## Oxford Protest Meeting Over War Grave Proposals

*By Terence Wilkes*

*The inaugural meeting of the British War Graves Society organised by opponents of the plans for the treatment of the empire's war dead took place last night in Oxford. Speakers included the Rt Hon Sir Anthony Leaf MP, the Reverend Raymond Buller DD and the Dowager Lady Claire Langford, all of whom spoke powerfully about their objections to the news that the fallen will be interred in large military cemeteries in France and Belgium.*

*Particular anger has been caused by the announcement that all gravestones will be of the same non-religious design and that bereaved families will have little say in the words inscribed upon them. The fact that most will not have the funds to visit the cemeteries has added to their grief.*

*Lady Langford announced that she has started a petition to lobby the Prince of Wales, who is the War Graves Commission patron, and that further protest meetings are planned around the country. She read from letters her organisation has received and those attending were deeply moved by the heartfelt sentiments expressed by the correspondents. In one letter a grieving mother wrote, 'The country took my son, and the country should give him back,' eliciting a thunderous round of applause and cries of 'hear hear' from the audience.*

*Every attendee signed the petition and Lady Langford told me that her organisation has 3,000 members already. Lady Florence Cranbourne and the Countess of Somerset have publicly pledged their support.*

'That's fine, Wilkes,' said Evans as he put the first edition down on his desk. 'The mood of the meeting was strong then?'

The young reporter nodded. 'It was, sir. People are angry and some of the letters that Lady Langford read out were very upsetting. I really do think they've got a point.'

'Yes, well keep the reporting even-handed. Our owner rang again to tell me he has had a letter and two phone calls from Lady Langford pressing him to speak out against the proposals. The woman is remarkably well connected and appears to have been roused to deep anger from her slumber in rural Oxfordshire. And she's not alone. A lot of MPs with working-class constituencies continue to be inundated with letters of protest.'

'A strong upswell of opinion across the board then, sir.'

'Yes. This debate will be a fiercely contested affair and at present it looks as if it could go either way.'

*

Innes put the wean to bed and kissed him, then took a cup of tea out into the garden at Marston House. It was a beautiful place, developed by Eve over the many years that they had lived there. She walked over to a bench and sat down, placing the saucer on the seat by her leg. The sweet fragrance of an apricot-coloured rose on the wall behind filled her with a heady pleasure and she leaned back, closed her eyes, and let the peace of the place waft over her.

In the three weeks since the colonel's commission she had made little progress. *None in fact*, she admitted to herself. More cases of Spanish flu meant she had been busy in the hospital, but the simple truth was that frustrated by a lack of local knowledge and an absence of transport, she did not know how to start the investigation.

Clearly neither the colonel nor his wife was the murderer. Or Edward Spense, for that matter, although she had given the possibility some serious thought as she was still not at all clear how he had known the body was in the tree. But in the end she could not envisage him as a life-taker and had given him a clean bill of health, although the idea of working with him on the mystery was an uncomfortable one upon which she had not acted.

But the rest of the village and the population of the surrounding area were all potential murderers. It was an impossible task, and she needed some help. As her mind wandered, a long thin face with large ears and a rather lugubrious expression topped by a policeman's helmet swam into her vision. Her eyes popped open, and a smile appeared on her face.

*Constable Burrows. Now there was a thought.*

The following morning Great Tew's finest, if only, beat policeman found himself being hissed at as he left the police house to proceed on his rounds.

'Pssst, Constable Burrows, over here.'

He stopped and slowly turned to face the source of the summons, which proved to be the doorway of the cottage hospital. 'Miss Knox, good morning,' he said.

'Can you spare a minute? I'd like a word.'

Nodding, he followed her into the building. Once inside she sat him down, offered him a cup of tea, plied him with biscuits and presented her proposals.

Five minutes later she had finished speaking and in the ensuing silence he chewed slowly and stared at the floor. Although his outward appearance was not indicative of a fine mind, in fact the young man was acute and perceptive. He was also ambitious, and he was wondering what exactly the implications of an off-the-record investigation would be for his career if it succeeded. And, perhaps more pertinently, if it failed.

'You say this is directly authorised by the chief constable?' he asked.

'Better than that, he suggested it.'

Burrows chewed reflectively, like a cow on the cud, and then said, 'Are you sure about the medical evidence?'

'I am. Every indication is that Mr Freeling was already dead when he was strung up in the yew tree.'

'Murdered by person or persons unknown?'

'Correct. That is our mission, Constable. To unmask the perpetrators.'

He took another biscuit, his fifth, and crunched into it. 'And what evidence of murder is there, beyond the medical facts?'

'At this precise time?'

'Yes.'

'I'm not going to lie to you, Constable, as of this moment it is a blank page upon which we must write.'

'That is what I thought. Very well put, if I might say so, Miss. So it would be just the two of us?'

'The colonel suggested I rope in Edward Spense, but I'm not sure that would be a good idea.'

'Oh yes, I heard you'd had another row. Called him a liar, didn't you?'

Innes rolled her eyes. *Was nothing secret in this place?* 'There was a misunderstanding which has yet to be resolved,' she said primly.

There was another thoughtful pause, then the constable decided that he would opt for safety in numbers. 'If Mr Spense comes in then I'll help out too.'

'Really, Burrows?' Innes groaned. 'You would drive me to that?'

A trace of a smile, a rare thing, appeared on the constable's face. He wondered if he could extract a promise that the young doctor would stay in the village long term as well, but decided that would be over-egging the pudding. For the moment at least.

He met her eye. 'I'm afraid I would, Miss. That is my price.'

*

The following morning Innes braced herself and paid a visit to Holly Cottage.

Mrs Williams answered the door and a minute later she found herself being shown into a low-ceilinged sitting room with a long window that faced the street. Two settees, one yellow, one blue, were placed along two walls, while a large fireplace and a well-filled bookcase occupied the others. A Turkish rug lay on the floor. It was a simple and pleasantly masculine room, she thought.

Edward Spense was standing waiting for her. 'Miss Knox, this is unexpected. May we give you a cup of tea?' His tone was measured but not unfriendly, she thought, although the absence of the word 'pleasure' from his greeting was rather noticeable.

'Yes, thank you,' she replied. He nodded to the housekeeper who departed, closing the door quietly behind her.

'To what do I owe your visit?' he asked once they were settled.

'I've come to ask for your help, Edward. I am aware that yet again we seem to have fallen out, but I find myself commissioned on a task which I cannot fulfil on my own.' And then she stopped. In bed that morning she had calculated that this opening remark would elicit the question, 'What task is that?' allowing the conversation to develop along the lines she intended. However this was not the case.

'I see. I must say I am a little surprised to be your choice as helpmate, given the low opinion you seem to have of my character,' he remarked, with what Innes thought was an irritating lack of curiosity.

'Yes, well the nature of the thing means that my choices are limited.'

'I'm not sure that that is necessarily a compliment, Miss Knox.'

'The truth is I have already spoken to Constable Burrows, but he will only put his shoulder to the wheel if you agree to assist as well. That is why I am here.'

'So it is not you but Burrows who wants me involved?'

She sighed. 'No, Edward. I want your help and I also want Burrows to help. In fact it was the colonel who suggested that I petition you for assistance.'

'Jocelyn?'

'Yes, that's right.' She raised her eyebrows and waited but unfortunately Mrs Williams chose that moment to reappear with the tea tray and in the ensuing pouring and serving, the man slipped away again.

'Tell me, Miss Knox, how do you find village life?' he asked as the housekeeper closed the door.

'I am enjoying it. My work is useful, the Dances are delightful hosts and the wean is benefitting from the fresh air and exercise. We find it suits us well.'

'Your duties at the hospital are keeping you busy?'

'They are, although I do have time on my hands on occasions. Which is why I can undertake this commission on behalf of the chief constable.' She looked at him meaningfully.

'Ah the mysterious task. And at the colonel's behest, no less? Well I fear that I am unlikely to be of much assistance to you, Miss Knox.' He gestured towards a book on the blue settee and added, 'As you can see I am engaged in some improving reading which keeps me fully occupied.'

*For heaven's sake, he's sulking*, she thought. 'Look, Edward, can I just apologise for what I said at the market cross? For the record I think you were dissembling, but that is your affair. I know that I am sometimes impetuous in my remarks, but I am not asking you to like me, I am asking you to help me. They are different things. Will you not at least enquire what it is I am asking of you? Are you that incurious?'

*Now he'll surely ask what it is*, she thought confidently.

There was a long silence. Outside Innes heard two men walk past and cross the footbridge, their voices carrying through the open window. Something about fishing at Lath Pool tonight.

Edward smiled at her and nodded towards the window. 'Planning to poach my brother's trout,' he explained.

'Ah.' She smiled back, but then saw his expression change. When he spoke his voice was quiet but energised.

'Innes, your instincts are correct. I was dissembling about those moments when we found Christian Freeling and I suspect from your face a moment ago that you think I am unwilling to help you because I am cross with you in some childish way.' He looked at her pointedly before continuing. 'But that is not the case. I am reluctant to get involved because I am genuinely not sure of my sanity. I feel perfectly normal in every way, but something keeps happening that is abnormal. In fact abnormal does not cover it. Paranormal would be a better word.'

'Paranormal? As in not of this world?'

'As in unexplainable by science, certainly.'

She frowned and asked, 'What keeps happening?'

He picked up a packet of cigarettes and offered her one, which she declined with a brief shake of her head. Lighting one himself he blew smoke towards the ceiling and then started to speak, his eyes fixed on the fireplace.

'To answer that question I need to tell you about a place called Vieux Chêne Farm…'

Edward spoke quietly for ten minutes in a monotone, but the descriptions of the trenches and the hellish experiences he described painted a rich picture in Innes's mind.

He told her what he'd seen when Private Randall died at the casualty clearing station and about the mortally wounded captain from the Royal Scots who had disappeared before his eyes. He described meeting Private Rennie outside the dugout and then being told that he had died in no man's land ten hours earlier. And how there had been others after that, and the appalling realisation that he was going insane. He told her about walking to the battalion HQ and expecting to be shot, and the warmth and security of the hospital and how nice the nurses had been. Then about coming back to Great Tew and the desperate need he'd had to be alone.

Then he described the acrid smell and the sight of Christian Freeling standing between the great entrance stones of Creech Hill Ring, even though the man was already dead and hanging in the Langford Yew. And the woman who walked over Stream Cross bridge every evening at half past eleven, leaving the same smell hanging in the air.

At last he finished and looked at her.

'So as you can hear, Innes, I fear I am not an ally that you can rely on. There is a real danger that I'll be carted off to Oxford Asylum at any moment.'

Innes sat silently, her tea untouched. She desperately wanted to say the right thing and to avoid the spiky misunderstandings that seemed to flare up out of nowhere between them. In the end she just told the truth.

'Edward, I am most terribly sorry for what you have been through. I can barely conceive what it must have been like,' she said quietly.

'We were all in it together over there. A lot of it's not an uncommon experience, apart from the ghosts, that is.'

'So you believe that what you saw, what you are continuing to see, are ghosts? For want of a better word?'

'The majority of me does. I really do think that when Randall died I saw his spirit leave his body and that caused something unfathomable to happen which means I can now see dead humans. But deep inside, a small part of me is screaming, "This is insane. You are insane."'

He gave her an ironic smile and added, 'It's hard enough to deal with the living and the dead as it is. It becomes impossible when you cannot tell which is which.'

She pursed her lips in sympathy. 'Have you told anyone else?'

'The colonel knows. And the bishop. I told them so they understood why I cannot go back into the church or army. But that's it.'

'Has Christian Freeling appeared to you again?'

'No.' He shrugged. 'Perhaps now he's been discovered he can go on his way. Something tells me he's not close any more.'

She was silent for a while, then remarked, 'There's a new school of thought in psychiatry that suggests if you believe something to be true, then it is true. The idea being that it becomes true because you act upon it. I don't think that's right, incidentally. There are also recorded incidents where patients have hallucinated when under extreme stress, almost as though in those situations the mind starts inventing a new reality to escape the truth.'

He nodded slowly, clearly thinking about what she had said. 'Yes, I can see the argument for both of those. Does medicine allow for people who can really see ghosts?'

'I've not seen a textbook on it.'

He laughed, a short sharp chortle. 'No, perhaps not.'

'Edward, my interest is in psychiatry, the science of what happens when the mind starts to malfunction. But what you've told me is just so credible that I really don't know what to say. In Scotland, especially in the outer islands, there is a long tradition of people having "the sight" and such things are considered normal. To be honest I am at a loss as to how to advise you.'

'I'm not sure I am seeking advice, Innes, although your instincts do you credit. In the main I told you because I am sure I can trust you and I want you to understand what's behind my reluctance to say I will help you. I live each day not knowing what will happen on the next.'

'Will you at least let me tell you what I have been asked to do?'

'Of course, fire away. Actually on second thoughts, shall we walk? The lane over towards Little Tew is a pleasant stroll.'

She agreed and they set off shortly afterwards. Edward glanced up at the sky. 'We may have a shower, but we can risk it.' He pointed up towards the high street and then swung his arm past the cottage and towards the footbridge thirty yards away. 'This is the route my regular lady takes in the evening. The acrid smell is very strong afterwards.'

'What is she like?' asked Innes, curious.

'Victorian I'd say by her clothes. In late middle age. I've stood at this gate a couple of times, and she looks at me and makes eye contact. I think she knows I can see her, but she doesn't slow or turn, just paces over the bridge and disappears into the darkness. There is no sound of footsteps. On one occasion I played the fool and stood in her way. She just walked through me. I passed out immediately and didn't regain consciousness for four hours.'

Innes shivered. 'Good lord. I wonder where she's going?'

'Who knows? Shall we?' He pointed towards the bridge and they set off.

Over the next ten minutes she related to Edward what she had told the colonel and Burrows. He didn't interrupt. At the end she concluded with, 'So I find myself with a task from the colonel which he clearly thinks will keep me off his back regarding other police investigations. If you join us we will muster three, of whom only Burrows has the slightest idea of what to do next.'

'Oh I think that's obvious,' said Edward.

'Oh really? Do tell, Mr Holmes.' She gave him a smile.

'We must make enquiries about Freeling's mental state. Speak to people who saw him or worked with him, question his wife and his friends, see if a picture emerges that indicates he was suicidal. That sort of thing.'

'We?'

'Well I am sure having something to do won't do me any harm. Consider me in on the case, as it were. But be warned, I drink too much and am inclined to see spirits as well as imbibe them.'

'Don't worry, I'm sure Constable Burrows will keep you on the straight and narrow.'

'He's very good at seeing me home, so I suppose that's a start.'

*

A week later Lilly made her way along the first-floor corridor of Langford Hall carrying the breakfast tray. 'Good morning, my lady,' she said as she entered the bedroom. There was a stirring beneath the blankets of the four-poster and a gentle groan emerged.

'Is that you, Lilly?'

'Of course, my lady.'

'And are you bearing aspirin along with the usual jentacular delights?'

'There are some in your bathroom cupboard. Would you like one?'

'I would like the entire bottle.'

Lilly gave a little laugh, recalling her mistress's condition when she had attended to her the previous evening. 'Oh dear, it was rather a late night at Lady Mulford's.'

'I fear I tarried too long and allowed Lord Mulford's hospitality to ambush me. I really should know better, he does it every time. My recollection of being driven home and put to bed is rather vague,' came the muffled reply.

'He is famous in the area for his…' Lilly hesitated for a moment then finished with, 'exuberance.'

With a sigh Lady Langford's tousled head emerged from the bed covers. 'Well there's not much of that about this morning, I can tell you.'

Lilly retrieved a couple of aspirin and placed them on the tray with a glass of water, then arranged the whole thing over her lap, before drawing the curtains. 'Perhaps the headline in the newspaper will lift your mood, my lady,' she said.

'Oh really?' Lady Langford picked it up and moments later a cry of satisfaction echoed around the bedroom as she smacked the front page with the back of her hand. 'Aha! The debate is set for the 7th of July, before they rise for the summer. I've written a hundred letters, Lilly. It's surprising how many people of influence one knows. And how many secrets, if you get my drift. Even Alfie Harmsworth who owns this mighty organ stuck his head over the parapet once I'd had a chat with him.

'It is excellent news, my lady.'

'It certainly is. I'd celebrate with a bottle of champagne if I could face it. Perhaps at dinner. Anyway, Lilly, we will attend the debate in the Strangers' Gallery, along with some members of the

War Graves Society. Jamie Lowther the Speaker was at school with my darling husband, he'll make sure we have spaces. It won't do any harm for those who speak for the bill to have thirty or forty bereaved mothers staring down at them.'

'I'm sure not,' Lilly answered, delighted that she would get the chance to sit high above the debating chamber and watch the proceedings. She glanced at her mistress and added, 'You wouldn't be planning anything untoward would you, my lady?'

'Untoward? No, I can assure you whatever happens will be entirely in keeping with the sentiments of the occasion.'

And with this rather vague reply, she cracked the top of her boiled egg and set about it.

# Chapter Six

The first meeting of the investigators took place at Holly Cottage a few days after Innes had told Burrows that they were now officially three in number and, in a naked power grab that made her Glaswegian background all too obvious, Innes appointed herself chief convenor.

'We need a leader, and it is I who must bear ultimate responsibility for the success or failure of the mission, so I nominate myself. All those in favour please raise your hands. Put your hand up, Burrows,' she added with a dangerously warm smile as the two men remained motionless, 'there's nothing to be afraid of.'

'Shouldn't I be in charge? Being the policeman and all?'

'I am reluctant to burden you with the heavy responsibility of command when you have so much to offer in the field, Constable. It would surely be too much for one man, even one so capable,' she replied smoothly.

This remark had Edward hiding a smile behind his hand. Although their relationship to date had not been the smoothest, there was no doubting the woman's intellect. 'I'm sure that will be fine, Innes,' he said. 'Burrows and I stand ready to contribute what little we can. As you're in charge perhaps you can tell us what that will be?'

Innes was not enthused by his tone. 'Edward, clearly this is going to be a team effort, I am merely suggesting that if we are ever divided I will have the casting vote. Your earlier suggestion that we talk to Mr Freeling's friends and family to establish his mental state would be a good place to start. Do you not think so, Burrows?'

The policeman nodded sagely. 'I do, Miss. The Oxfordshire police instruction manual states that when gathering evidence one is looking for two things – either confirmation that a witness statement is correct by virtue of its similarity to others, or new lines of enquiry that emerge where there is a difference between accounts.'

In the short silence that followed this remark the other two stared at him.

'By Jove, Burrows, you really know your stuff, don't you?' said Innes.

'I do take time to study the manual, Miss Knox. If truth be told I am ambitious and hope to get on.'

'Nothing wrong with that,' Edward said. 'I'm sure we will need to consult the manual again before we're finished.'

With that they fell to detailed planning and a division of labour was agreed. Innes would pay a visit to Nell Atkins at Beech Farm on the pretext of checking the progress of her pregnancy and to see what the family had to say. Edward would take her there and speak to Jane Freeling at the same time. Burrows would make enquiries amongst the people in the village who knew Mr Freeling.

Edward borrowed an estate car when he needed a vehicle and he offered to teach Innes to drive so that she would be able to transport herself around the area. She agreed to purchase a driving licence from the sub-post office and, as there was no driving test, they could start immediately.

The following morning he called in to Langford Hall to see his mother and found her in the knot garden. 'Hello, dear, how nice to see you. When are you moving back in?' she asked him brightly, in what had become a standing joke between them.

There had been no rift. He saw her regularly and was on friendly terms with his older brother as well, but when he had come back from France, exhausted and hollow-eyed, the prospect of living in the great house with its servants, house guests and the need to maintain appearances in the upper echelons of Oxfordshire society had been overwhelming. It was Piers who had suggested Holly Cottage and volunteered Mrs Williams, and Edward was grateful to him for helping his mother to understand his need for solitude when her every instinct was to care for him and keep him close.

'Not yet, but you'll be pleased to hear I am steadily getting better.' Standing close to his mother he sensed an energy about her which he hadn't seen since he had returned from France. 'You look well,' he remarked.

'Our campaigning over the war graves is keeping me fully occupied. The debate in the House of Commons is getting nearer and I really think we have a good chance of blocking these dreadful proposals. The British War Graves Society has five thousand members, and our petition has attracted eight thousand signatures so far. Eight thousand, imagine that!' Pride and purpose showed in her face as she beamed at him.

Privately Edward thought that the Commission's proposals were right, a view which was widely shared by the men he knew who had served in France, but he smiled and said, 'That's marvellous, I wish you all the luck in the world. I'll pop in for dinner one night this week but for now I was hoping to borrow the Alvis this morning.'

'I'm sure that will be fine, just ask Fenn, although you might have to prise the thing out of his hands, it's very new and he loves it as a knight loves his charger.'

Edward laughed. The chauffeur was notoriously proprietary towards estate vehicles. 'I'll nip over to the stables then. The Austin would be alright too if necessary.' He made to move but his mother was too quick for him and placed a restraining hand on his arm.

'Where are you off to?' she enquired.

'I'm taking Innes Knox, Dr Knox I should say, over to Beech Farm to check on Nell Atkins. She's pregnant.'

'Yes, I noticed when I saw her at church.' She eyed him speculatively. She had met Innes Knox once and received a favourable impression apart from the horrendous spectacles, and

Eve Dance had been singing her praises. 'Miss Knox took on her sister's child, didn't she?'

'Yes, the little chap has been ill hence the extended stay in the country air.'

'Do you know her well?'

'I really do not. It's just a favour.'

'Well bring her to dinner when you come. In fact come on Thursday, it'll just be Piers and me. I have guests for the weekend, but they are arriving on Friday.'

'Alright I'll ask her.' He smiled and added, 'But before you indulge in motherly speculation I am not looking for a romantic entanglement. And neither is she.'

'Eve Dance tells me she is delightful.'

'Yes well, she is also stubborn, forceful and highly opinionated. We have had our disagreements.'

A slight smile passed across Lady Langford's face. 'Is that so? Well I shall look forward to getting to know her better. You can go now.'

With the required information extracted, she removed her hand and watched him leave. *Perhaps I'll have another word with Eve*, she reflected.

*

Like Constable Burrows, Innes was impressed with the general air of prosperity that surrounded Beech Farm as she and Edward pulled onto the sweep of gravel at the front of the house.

*What it is to have money*, she thought, finding the comparison with her own upbringing in Glasgow very stark. Her father had been a school teacher, but they had lived amongst the tenements that provided the workers for the dockyards and she had witnessed poverty and hardship on a daily basis. Bitter disabled men injured in the accidents that plagued the works, habitual drunkenness, and violence that flared out of nothing, were all part and parcel of life in the industrial heartland of the empire.

With Glasgow on a war footing even at night the city had echoed to the sounds of industry, grinding on like a single great machine, the foundries churning out black smoke and cast iron as the rivet guns sounded over the Clyde. There had been a constant sense of innovation and urgency, driven by the needs of the western front. But buried in this sleepy part of north-west Oxfordshire where a hundred shades of green stretched away to the horizon, the sense of timelessness, of there having been no real change for hundreds of years, was overpowering at times. And to her surprise she liked it very much.

'The Atkins family have been here for seven generations,' Edward remarked after she commented on the house. 'Clayton Atkins lost his wife four years ago, but he's not remarried. They had around ten farmworkers at the beginning of the war and most volunteered. The land girls stepped in of course, Piers told me there were over two hundred on the estate. They really did play a huge role in keeping things going.'

'Have they gone home now?' asked Innes, curious.

'The majority, yes. The men who returned got their old jobs back, but we're still very short of labour even though Piers has done his best to mechanise with steam tractors and so on. Things like that are shared across the whole estate now. We lost an awful lot of working horses to the war as well.'

'It must be expensive to buy new equipment.'

'Yes, and when my father died we had to pay heavy death duties. No one seemed to consider that Langford has many livelihoods reliant on it. In the hall there are gaps on the wall where a Gainsborough and a Reynolds used to be.'

'Good morning, Mr Spense, that's a fine motor car.' A voice cut across their conversation and Innes looked over to the front door, which now stood open.

'And good day to you, Mr Atkins. Yes, a new Alvis which I had great difficulty prising away from Fenn,' Edward called back.

The man in the doorway smiled and nodded. 'You did well there. And this is Miss Knox I believe. Good morning, I saw you at church, but we weren't introduced. Will you come in?'

They climbed down from the open car and crossed to the door.

'We were out for a run and Miss Knox thought she would pop in and see Mrs Atkins. Just to check that she is in good health, with the happy news and all,' Edward remarked as they walked into the stone-flagged hall.

'Of course. She'll be glad to see you, I'm sure. Come on into the parlour and I'll give her a call. May we offer you a cup of tea?' The charming and handsome farmer created a very favourable impression on Innes, and she wondered why he hadn't remarried. There would surely be plenty of interest, she reflected as she took a seat in the comfortably furnished room.

Edward said, 'I tell you what, Mr Atkins, I'll leave Miss Knox here for a few minutes and walk across to Mrs Freeling to see how she's doing.'

The farmer glanced at the maid who had appeared. 'Winnie, run over to Well Cottage and tell Jane Mr Spense is dropping in. I'll just give our Nell a call, then you can have your lady's chat, Doctor. Before you go can I just have five minutes with you, Mr Spense, about the steam engine? There's something to mention to Lord Langford, if I might ask you.'

'Of course. Innes, I'll see you in half an hour or so.'

With that the two men walked back outside and a minute later Nell Atkins came in and introduced herself.

*

Like Burrows, Edward was struck by what an attractive young woman Jane Freeling was. Her long blonde hair was freshly brushed and hung loose, framing her delicate features and only her strained smile gave any indication of the grief she must have been feeling. They sat on a bench in the back garden and had a glass of cider. In the far distance Edward could just see the top of St Mary's church tower seemingly rising straight out of the middle of a wood.

'What a pleasant place to sit, Mrs Freeling. I didn't realise that you could see the church from your cottage.'

'Yes, I used to sit here when Christian was away at the war and think about being together again when he got back. But I'm alone now.'

'I am dreadfully sorry. To lose the poor man when he had survived the carnage over there – well it must make it particularly difficult to bear.'

'That's right enough, Mr Spense. I'm at a loss in every way.' She grimaced and distractedly smoothed her hands over the loose blue dress that stretched over her knees.

Fearing an outburst of tears Edward hurried on. 'Have there been any discussions about arrangements for the future?'

'Well this is a cottage for a farm worker, so I can't stay here, but Mr Atkins says his cook is thinking about retiring and going to live with her sister in Banbury. The suggestion is that I become cook and housekeeper up at Beech Farm.'

'I see. How do you feel about that?'

'Well beggars can't be choosers and I don't see any other offers appearing, so I'll be doing that I reckon.' *She doesn't sound happy about it*, Edward thought, but at least she was thinking practically.

'Well it will give you security and something to do while you recover from your grief,' he said. She nodded silently and stared out over the fields as he continued, 'Tell me, Mrs Freeling, did you have any inkling that your husband was considering suicide? I hate to ask but it might help us to spot any others who are vulnerable. If we know the signs, as it were.'

'He was happy enough to be back, but I could see a change in him. He was quick to rile, and he drank too much. He seemed to be raging about something inside. I asked him about it, but he wouldn't talk to me.' She looked at him. 'Imagine that.'

He nodded sympathetically. 'If it's any consolation, Mrs Freeling, I understand what you have just said exactly. I was there too, as you may know.'

She nodded. 'I heard you were in a bad way, living on your own and all.'

Edward smiled. 'I see the native drums beat as loudly as they ever did. They call it shell shock.'

'Shell shock, yes,' she nodded slowly, 'that's what did for my Christian. The day he disappeared I thought he'd just gone off to work in the fields as normal. It was only when Colonel Dance and the constable turned up that I had any inkling something was wrong.'

'So he must have walked to Creech Hill Ring and hung himself that morning? Miss Knox and I found him about half past eleven, well before lunchtime.'

She shrugged. 'Looks like it, yes.'

'But he seemed normal when he left?'

A flash of irritation crossed her face. 'No, Mr Spense, he weren't normal. That's what I've been saying.'

'No, I understand that. I'm sorry, Mrs Freeling, what I meant was, normal compared to the way he'd been since coming back from France. Not especially upset or angry?'

'I made him one of my rabbit stews the night before to cheer him up and he was better for a bit. But by morning he was very down.' As she continued Edward could see the anguish on her face. 'I ain't told anyone else this, but he had the rope with him when he left. Said he needed it. I didn't think anything of it at the time. Why would I?' Her face cracked and a great heavy sob emerged. 'I mean, how was I to know? Him walking off to kill himself and me giving him a kiss and a wave.'

She shuddered as the tears flowed, leaving long wet streaks on her beautiful face.

Edward said gently, 'There would have been other trees along the way. Can you think why he walked all the way to the Langford Yew?'

Mrs Freeling produced a handkerchief, and her voice was muffled as she spoke. 'He loved that tree. When we were courting we used to meet there at night.'

'A special spot for you then?'

'He believed in the old ways, and he thought it was a powerful place, especially with the ring up there too. I reckon that's just where his feelings took him when he decided he was going to do it.'

They continued to talk for another ten minutes until Edward rose and said his goodbyes. He felt desperately sorry for the woman. The thought that her husband had survived the war only to perish at home was appalling. And her final remark was heart-breaking.

'I sit here at night thinking, how could you have let him do that? Walk off with the rope over his shoulder. But I did, Mr Spense. That's what I did. I'm not much of a wife I reckon.'

He left her to her grief and walked back to Beech Farm. Innes was also ready to leave so they departed.

'We'll go back to Langford Hall, and you can have a go at driving along the ride towards Creech Hill,' Edward suggested. 'Where we had a trot before. It's straight and flat, and we should probably have another look at the Langford Yew. Just in case there's anything to notice.'

'Yes, good idea,' Innes agreed.

As they drove back to Great Tew he asked, 'How was Mrs Atkins?'

'She seemed fine, if a little shy. She didn't want me to examine her, but she appears perfectly healthy.'

He nodded. 'When is it due?'

'She says she's roughly four months gone, so it'll be in the late Autumn. But I can't be sure as she wished to keep her dignity intact. In fact she seemed determined to make as little fuss as possible.'

He laughed. 'That's country folk for you, Innes. They've been having babies in the shade of the trees for a thousand years around here and, "I don't need no doctor," is very much the prevailing view.'

'But surely if there's a problem…'

'To be honest they'd be as likely to call one of the women who are known for their knowledge of such matters.'

She was silent for a moment, eyeing the lush countryside they were passing through. 'What, like a wise woman. A witch?'

*No, witches are for other things, Innes,* he thought, before replying, 'There is a long tradition of natural medicine around here. Knowledge gets passed down through the female line in families.' *Like the witches.*

She sniffed. 'Well modern science offers much better care, I'm sure of that.'

'You may be right but let's not reprise that conversation. Shall we stop at the Black Horse for a sandwich before going on to Creech Hill?'

'Yes, I'm hungry. I'll tell you what the Atkinses told me about Christian Freeling, and you can tell me all about your sleuthing with Mrs Freeling. She's a very attractive woman, they say,' she added offhandedly.

'Really? Can't say I noticed,' he lied.

*

It transpired that the Atkins family had little to offer in terms of additional intelligence about Christian Freeling's mental state.

'I asked Mrs Atkins about how he had been, but she said she'd not really seen him, and I suppose she wouldn't, being up at the farmhouse most of the time. Clayton Atkins said that he'd been uneasy about him. He'd been moody and short-tempered apparently. "I had to handle him with kid gloves at times," was the phrase he used,' Innes reported as they sat at a table in the corner of the pub.

'I got the impression that his wife felt the same way,' Edward agreed.

Innes nodded. 'People under strain often have very short tempers. It can feel as though they are on a hair trigger all the time.'

Edward remembered Jane Freeling's tear-stained face as he left Well Cottage. 'You know I do wonder if we are doing the right thing investigating this. His wife is grieving deeply but she is resigned to his suicide and everyone at Beech Farm is coming to terms with it. We do run the risk of stirring up more suffering.'

'But the medical evidence suggests he was murdered, and we owe it to his wife to find out who did it.'

'Are you really sure about the evidence, Innes? The whole village is convinced that he killed himself. His wife saw him leave the cottage with a rope, for heaven's sake. Both she and the Atkins family have told us he was depressed and, it's fair to assume, suicidal, and my brother Piers has announced unequivocally that he is a casualty of war. You are new to Great Tew, and I must confess that I think you are taking on a great deal here.'

The horn-rimmed spectacles glinted as she remarked pointedly, 'Justice must be done. Burrows and the colonel understand that, even if you don't.'

Edward frowned. 'I really don't think that is a fair thing to say. It's not that I don't care about justice, it's just that I don't want anyone to suffer more than they need to. The family has a long tradition of caring for the people on the estate and I feel protective towards them.'

'Christian Freeling worked on the estate too. What about caring for him?'

*She is merciless*, he thought, irritated that she was refusing to acknowledge his point of view. 'Well I suppose we will have to agree to differ. And hope that in satisfying your curiosity we don't end up doing more harm than good.'

Her mouth was set in a thin line as she inhaled and made to answer, but thankfully the appearance of Stanley Tirrold making his stately progress across the bar to the table curtailed the burgeoning row. He was carrying a tray with two rounds of beef sandwiches and placed them on the table.

'Thank you, Stanley,' said Edward.

'You're welcome. Good day, Miss Knox,' he said formally.

'Hello, Mr Tirrold. That is a fine-looking sandwich.'

'Mrs Tirrold is a marvel in the kitchen. I do the beer and cider and she looks after the grub. It's a very satisfactory arrangement.'

'She's back from Scotland then?'

A ghost of a smile showed on the publican's face. 'Indeed she is. It was a joyous reunion.'

'Have you had the place long?'

'It's been in the family for years. My grandfather took it over, then my father and then me.'

'What's happening then, Stanley, any news?' asked Edward.

'Very little. Laura Bessing has still got her eye on Constable Burrows and he's still blissfully unaware, but I can see her getting there in the end. Smart girl that one.' He turned and nodded back towards the bar.

Innes glanced over. A young woman with a sunburned freckled face and curly dark hair was polishing glasses. 'Is that her, Mr Tirrold?'

'Yes, she was a land girl on the estate and stayed when the others went back. I had a vacancy, so she moved into the room over the stables and works here now. She's a good girl, as far as they go,' he said carefully. 'Not too flighty. We used to have a bit of trouble with one or two of them, when the men had had a drink. I blame the full moon.'

'Ah,' said Innes, smiling, then to her surprise she realised he was serious.

The publican continued, 'Funnily enough the last time I saw Christian Freeling there was a bit of trouble in here. He was having a drink and laughing and joking with some of the regulars. Then a row flared up. It happens sometimes, someone makes a remark, someone else takes exception, you know the sort of thing.'

'I grew up in a poor part of Glasgow, Mr Tirrold, I know exactly what you mean. So was Mr Freeling involved?'

'Yes. He and Tommy Harman squared up to each other and had a couple of drunken swings. I had to ask them to leave.'

'What was it about?' asked Edward, smiling to himself. He'd seen the large-framed publican ask people to leave before, and knew he wasn't averse to backing up his words with action.

'Laura, over here for a minute if you please,' Mr Tirrold called across the bar. When she had joined them he asked, 'Remember when Christian Freeling and Tommy Harman had that fracas? What was it about?'

She looked embarrassed. 'Well, me in a way, Stan, although not as though it was my fault.'

'Go on.'

'Tommy made a remark about me, and Christian didn't like the sound of it. Said he should take it back, although to be honest I'd seen him giving me the eye himself once or twice. Anyway I told both of them it didn't matter and to behave, but Tommy said something else, and then Christian warned him again and next moment they're at it.'

'So who threw the first punch?' asked Edward.

'Tommy. For sure. I can picture his face now, flushed and angry he was, and he got a sneaky one in and almost put Christian on the floor. Next minute he's back up and they're going at it. Then Stan's pushing past me with the chief inspector in his hand…'

'The what?' Innes thought she'd misheard.

'The chief inspector. That's what he calls the truncheon he keeps behind the bar. Anyway, he wades in and the next minute they're both out on the pavement. I could hear them shouting and threatening each other. It went on a bit out there too I think.'

Innes glanced at Edward and their eyes met. 'And when was this, Laura, can you remember?' she asked.

'Oh I can. It was two nights before you and Miss Knox found Christian in the Langford Yew.'

# Chapter Seven

After lunch Innes took the wheel of the Alvis and drove along the ride to Creech Hill Ring. To Edward's surprise she was a natural and quickly mastered the controls. They halted at the end of the ride, and she turned the engine off. In the ensuing silence they could hear it gently ticking as it cooled.

'How far are we from the hall?' Innes asked.

'About three quarters of a mile,' he replied.

In front of the car the two great standing stones that marked the entrance to the ring stood resolute and impassive. Beyond them the ring itself, roughly fifty yards in diameter, was encircled by smaller stones, each the height of a man.

'Forty stones in total,' said Innes after a moment.

'That's right,' confirmed Edward. 'Although you did well to count them. It's supposed to be very difficult and there's a local legend that says if you manage it you'll fall pregnant within a year. Whether you want to or not.'

'Really?' Her glasses glinted in the sun as she turned towards him and the undertone of irritation in her voice was clear as she continued, 'And tell me, what befalls the men who manage this challenging task. Do they get off Scot free?'

'I've never asked.'

'What a surprise.' With a sigh she climbed down from the car. 'Shall we have a look at the yew?'

He joined her, and they walked towards the great tree which stood to the right of the entrance stones. 'Here we are then. The Langford Yew. It's as famous as the stones and about the same age.'

She stopped and stared at him. 'What?'

'Really. The stones are late Neolithic, about four thousand years old, and it's believed the tree was a sapling around the same time.'

'That's astonishing, I can barely believe it.'

'When the Romans landed in Britain, this yew tree was already two thousand years old. Staggering, isn't it?'

'Remarkable. It must be one of the oldest living things on the planet.'

'The professor who dated it told me there are older trees dotted around, especially in America. It's amazing to think of what it must have witnessed, not least in this ring.' Innes walked around it, studying the four trunks around the central core, as he continued. 'Mrs Freeling told me that they used to meet up here when they were courting. She thinks he did it here because the place meant something to him.'

They slipped through the gap in the hollow trunk. Innes looked around. 'It was just luck I discovered him really. He was completely hidden in here. I just wandered in out of curiosity.'

'Lucky the crows hadn't found him,' said Edward.

She shuddered. 'Quite.'

'And as I told you, I saw him by the entrance stones. I knew he was dead, so I think we'd have found him anyway.' She looked at him. *I am choosing to believe you, but I still have my doubts*, was written in the conflict on her face. 'The cross beam is still there.' He pointed to a thick stave of wood that was propped against the inner wall. 'If it was suicide he must have put this across the open gap up there, then slid off it, or lowered himself. He'd have climbed up from the outside I suppose.'

She looked at Edward and said firmly, 'Except that he didn't. That is not what happened. We should be looking for evidence that he was strung up by someone else.'

He crossed over to the stave and slowly turned it. 'Like this, do you mean? Look, there's a clear mark around one side where the bark has been rubbed away. If the body had been on the ground here and someone threw the rope over the beam and hauled him up, then that would produce a mark like that I'd say.'

'Wouldn't it just. Well spotted.'

'Although I suppose that's also true if he'd killed himself. He'd be swinging and the rope would have marked the wood in the same way.'

'But as I told you, Edward, he wasn't swinging. There was insufficient bruising on his neck. You can't have it both ways. If the rope was under enough strain to mark the wood in that way, then his neck would have been a mess. And it wasn't. Ergo, he was dead when he was strung up.'

Her mouth was set in a resolute line. They were standing close together, facing each other and he noticed how finely shaped it was. *Almost perfect*, the thought came to him unbidden. They looked at each other for a long moment.

'Will you believe me now, Edward?' she asked quietly, her face turned up to him. In the dim light her eyes were completely obscured by the faint tint in the lenses of her spectacles.

'Yes,' he replied. 'I will.'

*

The investigators reconvened in the garden of the Black Horse, at a table a safe distance from any eavesdroppers. Burrows was out of uniform and Edward had just returned from interviewing Tommy Harman, who still lived with his parents in a semi-detached cottage not far along Rivermead.

'He's open about the fact they had a barney and he's clearly not grieving for Christian Freeling. He says the man chased him down the high street. "Always was a mad bugger," were his exact words,' Edward reported.

'Did he say what caused the fight?' asked Burrows.

'He admits he "might have been a bit lippy" about Laura Bessing, but he said that Freeling was no angel with the ladies either. To be honest it doesn't sound like any more than a pub fight to me. Not the sort of thing to go back to in the cold light of day. And certainly not a killing issue.'

'It does explain why I saw a bruise on his face when I examined him though,' said Innes. 'But we're saying it doesn't seem to lead any further, yes?'

Both men nodded and there was a brief pause as they raised their glasses in unison. Innes took a sip of hers. She was trying the cider for the first time and was enjoying it, rather to her surprise. She put her glass back down and summarised.

'His nearest and dearest say he was depressed and moody and are not surprised he took his own life, however the medical evidence, backed up by our observations at the tree, suggests he was murdered. So we have a divergence as outlined in your manual, Constable.'

Burrows nodded and cleared his throat. 'If I may, I'd like to make some observations about timing and opportunity.'

'By all means, the floor is yours.' She smiled at him.

'We know that Mr Freeling left Well Cottage at his usual time of seven o'clock in the morning. We also know that when you found him at half past eleven or so, rigor mortis was present. That's what you said wasn't it, Miss?'

She nodded. 'Yes, that's correct. It normally commences about three hours after death.'

'Yes, so it says in the manual. Now it is an hour's walk from Beech Farm to the yew, so we can assume that he went straight to the yew without hanging around, if you'll pardon the expression, because according to the rigor mortis he must have been dead by half past eight at the latest.'

'Yes, good thinking, Burrows,' Innes said approvingly.

'The point is, Miss, knowing that, we can start to find out what people were doing between eight o'clock and half past, because that's when he was killed. He must have been killed at the yew, or close to it, and whoever did it was smart enough to use the rope he had with him to make it look like suicide. Correct me if I'm wrong, Miss, but there were no signs of violence on the body were there?'

'Not that I saw. He certainly hadn't been stabbed or beaten on the head.'

'So how did he die? How did the murderer actually kill him?'

'Ah, good question. Any ideas, Edward?' Innes glanced across the table at the lean suntanned man sitting opposite.

'Poison wouldn't leave a mark,' he suggested. 'But it would require a fair amount of preparation which seems a bit unlikely given the timescale. Freeling had only been back from the war for three weeks. Surely we would have heard if there had been an incident so serious that it resulted in a carefully planned poisoning.'

'No I agree, Mr Spense. There would be gossip. I would have heard.' Burrows raised his eyebrows meaningfully and played his trump card. 'However there is one other possibility. The manual states that if a person is choked to death with a soft cloth, say a loosely rolled-up scarf for example, it only leaves faint traces on the victim's neck. And if the murderer then used the rope to string the body up those would be obscured by the marks from the noose.'

He picked up his glass, took a lengthy swig, and leaned back with some satisfaction.

Innes looked at him in admiration. 'You are a one-man detecting machine, Burrows. We are advancing in leaps and bounds. Not only do we now have a time for the murder, but you have also almost certainly identified the modus operandi of the heinous perpetrator. I'd tip my hat to you if I were wearing one.'

'Thank you, Miss. We now have to find out if the killer simply saw an opportunity and took it, or if Mr Freeling was lured to the yew by person or persons unknown, acting with malice aforethought.'

'And what are your feelings on that, Mr Holmes?'

'I'd suggest that it was the latter, Miss, mainly for the simple reason that Mr Freeling was not on Beech Farm land and had no reason to be up at the yew that we are aware of.'

'So you think the whole thing was planned, contrary to Edward's feelings about the timing?'

'It looks like it, although perhaps we should check that Mr Atkins didn't send him there for some reason. He might have been going to help on another farm.'

'Very true, Burrows, that sort of thing happens all the time. It's quite likely in fact,' Edward observed.

'In which case it might be an opportunistic killing. At this stage both remain possibilities,' Innes said. There was another pause while they sipped their drinks and pondered their conclusions. 'Anything interesting from your discussions around the village, Burrows?' she asked.

'Nothing of note, Miss,' he responded.

'How shall we continue our enquiries then? What gems of insight does the manual offer?'

'I think we need to establish why Mr Freeling was at Creech Hill Ring. Was he sent by Mr Atkins or was he meeting someone else? Once we know that, we can rule a lot of things out, one way or the other.'

'And our best method of doing that?'

'Let's ask him if he knows why he was there.'

Edward watched Innes as she turned this over in her mind. Her body was tensed and leaning forward, and a slight smile played on her lips as she considered the suggestion from Burrows. *A huntress.* Finding himself smiling with her, he asked, 'Well, dear leader, what is it to be?'

'We might as well ask the question, just to be sure. Mr Atkins always comes to church on Sunday, why don't you have a word after the service. The conversation can be a little more casual then. Don't you think?' Both men nodded, seeing the sense in her suggestion.

'Very well, I'll speak to him then and see what he says,' said Edward.

*

At seven o'clock on Thursday evening Edward walked round to collect Innes from Marston House. As they strolled up the high street in the warm evening sunshine he was amused to see the villagers straining to take in every detail while appearing not to see them at all.

Innes was rather preoccupied and didn't notice. Despite repeated reassurances from Eve, she was feeling nervous about the invitation to the hall. The prospect of mixing socially with such an historic and aristocratic family was daunting to a girl from the Glasgow tenements and she hoped she wouldn't let herself down. When she was nervous she became confrontational and a repetition, or anything even close to it, of her first encounter with Edward would be her worst nightmare.

So when she spoke her voice was unusually hesitant. 'Eve told me that you don't normally dress for dinner, so I hope this is alright,' she said. She was wearing a bronze-coloured cocktail dress and had borrowed a string of pearls from her hostess. Her hair was in its usual French plait and fringe, and her spectacles were firmly in place.

'You look splendid, Innes. If we have guests of rank then the whole hall makes an effort to turn on the style, but mother's general approach is informal and the household arrangements are firmly in her domain.'

'Your brother has never married?'

'No. He claims he's not found the right girl, although Lord knows the queue was long enough to stretch down the high street.' He gave one of his pleasing chortles. 'I fear he is a life-long bachelor and my mother's palpable desire for grandchildren will be thwarted for a few years yet.'

'An heir and a spare?' Even as she said it, Innes wondered where on earth she'd dragged the phrase from.

Out of the corner of her eye she saw Edward smile thinly. 'Since Hugh's demise I am my mother's last hope, as she is fond of reminding me. But seeing all the grieving war widows on the estate with their lives in tatters, I do wonder – I mean, why put yourself through that? Is love really worth the risk?'

Innes was silent for a moment and then said, 'Well hopefully there won't be another world war.'

'It's hard to imagine there would be much appetite for it. Not after the last four years.'

They arrived at the ancient iron-studded front door and Edward rang the bell. As he was family Innes wondered why they didn't just go in at the back door but a glance upwards at the towering three-storey façade was a powerful reminder, if it were needed, that they didn't do things the Glasgow way around here.

Half a minute later the door opened and an elderly grey-haired man in a butler's coat appeared before them. 'Good evening, sir, good evening, Miss Knox. Welcome to Langford Hall, please come in.'

He stood aside and Edward gestured for her to go ahead into the wide high-ceilinged entrance hall. Innes had a brief impression of a polished oak floor, a grand staircase, yellow walls and oil paintings. As she came to a halt she noticed an elephant's foot umbrella stand holding a collection of walking sticks and umbrellas and a single cricket bat. Next to it a coat stand was festooned with a range of garments and beyond that a crowded shoe rack bore a collection of outdoor shoes and boots.

*This really is a home*, she thought. The idea seemed incongruous somehow.

'This is Mr Leonard Dereham our butler, Innes. The finest old retainer in the county of Oxford. And I do mean old, he started work here when James the First was on the throne.'

'Very droll, Mr Edward. I trust you are still enjoying the rather limited delights of Holly Cottage and Mrs Williams?' The butler cracked a smile and Edward grinned back. Innes could see there was real affection and understanding between them and she realised that the butler would have seen all three Spense boys grow up.

'It serves, Dereham. Peace and quiet and all that,' Edward replied.

'Your mother wants you back, you know.'

'I am well aware of that. She rarely mentions anything else when we are together.'

'And is Bert Williams still poaching Langford's trout?'

Edward nodded. 'I fear I had one for supper the other evening.'

'My lips are sealed, sir. Lady Langford and Mr Piers are in the drawing room if you will step this way, Miss.' He led the way along the hall and then turned left down a short corridor that ended in a door, which he opened and announced, 'Mr Edward and Miss Innes Knox.'

Both men stood aside. Innes glanced at the butler who gave her a reassuring smile and with her heart beating wildly she walked through the doorway with her escort close behind.

'Evening, mother, hello, Piers,' Edward said as two people rose from a settee. 'Innes, you've met my mother at church I believe, and this is my brother Piers, otherwise known as Lord Langford.'

'Good evening.' Innes smiled at both of them as Piers stepped forward and shook her hand. He was of medium height, plump and saturnine. His dark suit was well chosen and fitted him perfectly. *An intelligent man*, she thought as their eyes met.

'It's a pleasure to meet you, Miss Knox. Welcome to our home. Tell me, what would you like to drink? Mother and I are having a brandy and soda, would that suit?'

'Thank you, that would be very nice.' Her host nodded to the butler, who Innes realised had followed them into the room.

'And for me,' Edward added.

'Do sit down, Miss Knox,' Lady Langford said in a surprisingly low voice. Innes smiled her thanks. The older woman was about her height and wore a bright yellow dress that reached to just below her knees. Discreet diamonds sparkled at her neck and ears and her grey hair was beautifully styled high on her head. Her fine-boned face showed both character and resolution. *A face that smiles easily*, she thought.

Both Lord Langford and his mother were beautifully turned out and it occurred to her with a slight shock that they probably had a lady's maid and valet taking a professional pride in ensuring that that was so. It was another reminder of the different world these people lived in.

She sat down next to Edward on a matching settee opposite their hosts and looked around. 'What a beautiful room. It really is lovely.'

She was being truthful. The room was large and square with double-aspect windows that looked out over gardens towards the parkland at the back of the house and across a lawn studded with mature trees to the side. The walls were painted pale blue and three were covered with fine paintings, while a handsome marble fireplace and overhanging mirror dominated the fourth. In deference to the continuing fine weather the fire was not lighted.

'Thank you, Miss Knox,' said Lady Langford. 'This is the drawing room, and I redid it five years ago when my husband was still alive. It's a strange thing living in a big house. One inherits everything, including the furniture and paintings and the opportunities to make one's own mark can be limited.'

She paused and then quite pointedly put her hand to the side of her mouth and said in a stage whisper, 'Especially with these incredibly old families, you know. Rather set in their ways.' She rolled her eyes theatrically.

'For heaven's sake, mother, you were living in a castle when father proposed,' Piers said with a smile.

'Not a very big one though, dear,' Lady Langford retorted. Innes smiled gratefully. She realised that they were all making an effort to put her at her ease, and she liked them for it. They chatted easily for half an hour before Dereham announced dinner and led the way into a small dining room next door.

'As we're just four this evening we'll eat in here I think,' Lady Langford said as they took their seats on two sides of a polished walnut table.

Dinner was simply cooked and delicious. Vegetable soup, cold trout, roast estate beef and trifle, all served with silent professionalism by a footman while the butler announced the dishes and served the wine. Her thoughts drifted back to her parents and friends in Glasgow on more than one occasion as the meal progressed. *If they could see me now.* The idea brought a smile to her lips.

'Tell me about your childhood,' Lady Langford asked as they waited for the main course. So Innes did. She explained about growing up in the shadow of the Glasgow tenements and how her father, as a school teacher, had been a figure of some note in the neighbourhood. She also told her host about the drunkenness, the injuries, the theatre of the shipyards at night, the poor diet, ill health, and the indomitable nature of the families who lived often ten or more in a two-room apartment with a shared bathroom along the corridor.

She spoke for some time, becoming aware that Edward and Piers had ceased the conversation they were having about beef prices and were listening silently.

'Thank you, dear, that was very interesting. Hearing you describe the city so candidly, I do wonder what you must think of us,' said Lady Langford quietly when she finished speaking.

Innes smiled. 'Glasgow is a hard-edged, unforgiving place, made of noise and smoke and steel and stone, but here the landscape caresses you, like folds of green silk. I am starting to like it very much. Edward explained that many people rely on you for their livelihood and from what I have heard the Langford family is well liked and respected hereabouts. That's more than can be said for many of the factory owners where I come from.'

'We take our responsibilities very seriously, but I think all of us would agree that we were born lucky,' Piers acknowledged.

'What was the estate like during the war, Lord Langford? Were many changes forced upon you?' Innes asked.

'I'll answer your question if you'll address me as Piers and Lady Langford as Claire.' He glanced to his side. 'Is that alright with you, mother?'

'That'll be fine I think.' Lady Langford was starting to form a rather favourable impression of this no-nonsense girl. Eve Dance was right. She was bright and tough and, if only she'd take those dreadful spectacles off, Claire guessed she was also very attractive. She certainly had a striking mouth and fine complexion. 'I hope we will be seeing more of you, Innes, so formality need not be maintained. In any event I believe that the war has changed the way we will do things in the future.'

Piers nodded in satisfaction. 'Good. In answer to your question, Innes, yes there were many changes. We accepted them willingly of course, all pulling together and so on, but I'll not pretend it was easy. A lot of estate men volunteered or were called up and we had to give up many of our working horses. In return we got land army girls who I would make a point of saying did a fine job of keeping the farms running, but there were barely enough of them either. There was well-paid work in the munitions factories in the cities too, and we were competing with that.'

'Where did they stay?' asked Innes, intrigued.

'They were billeted throughout the estate. We had forty in the hall,' said Claire. 'Imagine that. They filled up the spare servants' bedrooms upstairs to begin with, then spilled out into the empty rooms we had on the first floor. It was the most tremendous fun, if truth be told. Such a jolly lot. There was always some rag going on between them.'

'They must have been disruptive to your normal existence though,' said Innes.

'Oh we got off lightly. My friend Lady Mulford had Chase Abbey, her place near Banbury, requisitioned and turned into a convalescent hospital. They had no choice in the matter. They had to put a lot of the furniture in storage and fill up the main rooms with beds.'

'Mother was in her element, weren't you. Busy with your VADs.' Piers smiled.

'Yes. They needed nursing assistants you see, Innes, for the men. They went to proper hospital first and then on to places like Chase Abbey to convalesce. Chase was for gas victims.' Her face clouded. 'Some of them were going to be bedridden for life, it was just awful. Their lungs were damaged you see. And they were so young.'

'Mother galvanised old Reverend Tukes into action and they set about recruiting for the Voluntary Aid Detachment in Great Tew. They were quite merciless. Any woman found loitering or without gainful employment was shanghaied and dragged off to training. Terrible stories abound. It was like a modern day press gang. By the end of the war there were two charabancs going daily to Lady Mulford's place, fifty women in total,' Piers said with a laugh.

Innes looked at him. She could see the pride in his face. *She did what she could, and she did it well.*

'They needed us, dear. The men needed us. And we had more than one marriage out of it,' Claire added, glancing at Innes.

The conversation drifted pleasantly on until they finished eating. Then Lady Langford stood up. 'As we are being informal this evening we'll all just go back into the drawing room for coffee.' There was a general standing up and with a quick smile at Dereham which was generously reciprocated, Innes followed her hostess through the doorway, with the two brothers behind.

'That was a delicious meal, Claire, thank you,' she said when they had resumed their positions on the settees. 'It's wonderful that rationing is over, but I imagine you weren't too restricted by it here.'

'Well yes and no I'd say. Everyone was registered with the butcher and baker and once the cards were introduced there were no shortages, but to be honest with an estate like this where we produce food to sell…' She shrugged and smiled at the obvious conclusion to be drawn.

'Yes thank you, mother, anyway. It was a lot better than the rations in the trenches,' her younger son remarked.

Innes very much wanted to hear more about Edward's experiences in France and seized her cue. 'I'm sure. Tell me, Edward, what was the food like over there? We've had a delicious meal this evening. How does it compare to food in the army?'

He laughed with genuine amusement, then said, 'To be fair when I first went over to France the food wasn't bad at all. There was a lot of meat and many of the men who signed up from poorer areas were better fed in the army than they would have been at home. My job was welfare, so I was told all about it. The allowance was four thousand calories a day plus a big slug of rum or whisky and free cigarettes. In fact there was plenty of booze around, the main problem was getting clean water. If you were in the forward trenches you were always thirsty, and the water tasted foul. It was often brought up to the men in old petrol cans.'

'Yes, practical things like that just don't occur do they, unless you are experiencing them,' Innes observed.

He shook his head. 'No, very true. Every battalion had two huge cauldrons and everything was cooked in those including the stew, which became ubiquitous I might add, and even the tea to drink. The food got steadily worse and by the time I left there were a lot of complaints amongst the men. Machonochie's tinned stew, pea soup and Huntley and Palmers iron-hard biscuits are etched in every soldier's memory. The stew and the soup were just about edible hot, but cold they were man killers.' He smiled grimly.

'How much time did you spend in the trenches, were you in there constantly?' Edward's mother asked, her face absorbed and interested.

*He hasn't talked about this before*, Innes realised.

He shook his head. 'Not at all. Regiments were rotated in and out all the time from the reserve camps. In any given month we would spend about ten days in the trench system and about three or four in the front line. It was hellish up there, soaking, cold, constant shelling and sniping and a real struggle to get hot food and drink. The men wouldn't take it for more than a few days at a time and the commanding officers knew it.'

There was a brief silence around the table.

'I suppose it was the same for Hugh,' said Lady Langford in a small voice.

Edward looked at her. Innes saw his face crease with sensitivity and when he spoke his tone was soft. 'It would have been, yes. Officers and men lived together in the trenches. Someone told me that two hundred generals were killed overall. They were right up there with the men a lot of the time.'

'It is just hellish that so many men died. The worst ever war they say,' she replied.

Piers stirred and spoke. 'Of course the casualty numbers are appalling, and we've suffered as a family. But one of those history fellows from Oxford who was looking through the Langford archives told me that as a percentage of the population, the casualties during the English civil war were double what we've just been through.'

'My word, that makes you think doesn't it,' said Claire.

'Doesn't it just. It was family against family you see, village against village. The slaughter was terrible.'

'Do you know the story of Lady Olivia Spense and her redoubtable defence of Langford Hall against Cromwell's roundheads, Innes?' Claire asked.

'Edward mentioned it, but I don't know any details.'

'Well it's quite a tale. What happened was…' and with a smile Lady Langford moved the conversation along. An hour later they took their leave and walked slowly back along the drive towards the high street.

'That was a most pleasant evening, Edward. Your mother is delightful, and I liked Piers too, very much,' Innes said.

'I'm glad,' he replied. And he was he realised. For some reason it was important to him that she had a good impression of his family. *Odd*, he mused silently.

As they came to a halt outside Marston House Innes looked at him. 'I noticed that none of you thank the servants when they do things for you, opening doors, serving drinks and so on.'

'No. The servants do so much around the house that if they were thanked for each and every thing it would start to get ridiculous. My mother would be saying thank you all the time. So it's understood that thanks are only for special services that go beyond the call.'

She nodded, seeing the sense in what he was saying. 'Yes of course.' There was a pause but as Edward said nothing, she finally added, 'Well good night then. Thank you again.' And with that she walked through the gate and up the path, feeling his eyes on her all the way.

'Good night,' he said as she reached the front door. 'I enjoyed it.'

She turned and looked at him in the moonlight. 'So did I.'

Upstairs in the darkened bedroom Eve lay in bed and eavesdropped unapologetically as this exchange floated up through the open window. She nudged her husband and whispered to him.

'That sounds as if it's gone well.' The only response was a sigh and slight snore from the slumbering form, but that didn't stop her smiling to herself in the darkness. Like Constable Burrows, she had reached the conclusion that Miss Innes Knox was an asset to the village and should be persuaded to stay.

But unlike the young police officer, she had a plan.

# Chapter Eight

The following morning Eve called in at the hall and invited Lady Langford for a walk. The weather was bright and sunny, with a strong breeze moving towering white clouds across the sky, and Eve shivered with pleasure as she felt the energy running over the land.

*On days like this you can feel the great engine at work*, she thought.

As they made their way across open parkland towards a group of Devon reds grazing peacefully by a copse a quarter of a mile away, Eve linked arms with her friend and asked, 'How is everyone?'

'Oh all well I think, in their way,' Claire replied. 'Edward is still insisting on maintaining his independence at Holly Cottage. I do see a fair amount of him, although perhaps not as much as Mr Tirrold at the Black Horse.'

Eve laughed. 'Mrs Williams is very reliable. He is in good hands, albeit not the best.' She gave her friend's arm a gentle squeeze to reinforce the point she was making.

'I know, but I'd be happier if he was back with us.'

'Well the crucial thing is that you are on good terms and in each other's lives.'

'True.'

They strolled on chatting comfortably, two small figures in a big landscape, as the Cherwell valley opened up before them and the whaleback ridge of Green Hill filled the horizon.

'How was your evening with Innes Knox?' asked Eve.

'She was nervous and it showed, but to be honest I rather like her. She seems to have got Edward to open up a little about his experiences in France. He didn't say anything personal, but it was the first time he's spoken about what they went through over there. I don't know if it is Innes's influence or just a sign he's getting better, but either way I was glad to hear it.'

'What did you think of her spectacles? Awful, aren't they?'

Lady Langford grimaced. 'She can't help having weak eyesight, but yes they are most unfortunate. Surely she could obtain a more complementary pair. It almost feels as though she's hiding herself behind them, although I can't imagine why.'

Eve thought this was a very perceptive remark but simply said, 'She's a pretty girl underneath, I suspect. And she must be bright and quite resolute to have qualified as a doctor.'

They walked on in silence for a minute or two, each busy with their own thoughts, then reached the brow of the steep slope that led down to the river. They stopped and stared out across the airy space.

Claire asked, 'What are her plans, do you know?'

'I think her stay with us is open-ended. Great Tew seems to be suiting her and Jaikie. If she decides to make it a permanent move she'll have to think about getting a place of her own I suppose, but it's not necessary for the moment, and I enjoy having the wean around. He's a breath of fresh air and Ellie and Mrs Franks adore him. The fellow has a dangerous charm about him.'

Claire laughed out loud. 'Well we shall have to see what happens, but I have no objection to her seeing more of Edward if that is what they both want.' She calmly met her friend's eye and an unspoken moment of understanding passed between them.

Eve nodded, pleased. 'Well the summer stretches before us. Who knows what the next few months will bring?'

With the main business of the walk concluded she moved on to other things.

'Tell me about your War Graves Society work. Are you ready for the debate in the Houses of Parliament?'

'Oh yes. We will muster thirty on the day and I've bludgeoned the speaker into giving us all tickets to the Strangers' Gallery. Happily, I am aware of a most unfortunate indiscretion perpetrated by his youngest son while up at Oxford and have turned the screw. The man is putty in my hands.'

Eve laughed delightedly. 'Oh, Claire, you are incorrigible.'

'Perhaps,' came the reply. And then she added in a steely tone, 'But I am also deadly serious.'

*

After church on Sunday Edward managed to position himself next to Clayton Atkins as the chattering congregation passed through the door and out into the graveyard.

'Good morning, how are you?' he greeted the man.

'Very well, thank you, Mr Spense, you too I trust?' The farmer's handsome face cracked into a smile.

'Getting better all the time, thank you. And how is Mrs Freeling getting on? I heard that you have offered her a place at Beech Hill Farm.'

'Yes, we'll have to let her cottage to another worker so she can't stay there, but we're keen to help if we can. The cook's retiring so we have a vacancy and with Nell being pregnant it'll be another pair of young hands to help out when the baby arrives.'

'Of course. I'm pleased. We do need to rally round. Actually, on the subject of the Freelings, I was wondering if you had asked Christian to go to the Langford Yew the morning he was found? To meet someone perhaps or to do some job that needed doing?'

The man looked surprised by the question and scratched his head thoughtfully. 'Well no, the tree isn't on our land, and he wasn't on a commission on mine. I saw him go that morning. So did Isaac and Nell. He passed the kitchen window when we were having breakfast. I just assumed he was going to the fields as usual. Why do you ask?' he added.

'Oh idle curiosity really. Mrs Freeling said he set off with a rope and I just thought he might have had it for some different purpose.'

The farmer nodded. 'Yes, we saw the rope. From what I know I'm afraid it was a decision he'd already come to. During the night perhaps.' He shrugged. 'To be honest, Mr Spense, we're trying to put it behind us. The poor man is in the ground, and life goes on, doesn't it? Farmers know that better than most.'

'They do indeed. And how is that new steam tractor working now you've made those adjustments?' The conversation moved on to other things and shortly afterwards they parted.

The next day Edward reported back to Innes and Burrows.

'Well that has ruled out two lines of enquiry,' observed the constable. 'We now know he wasn't sent to the yew by Mr Atkins. And because he died by murder and not suicide, we can also safely assume that he wasn't going to the tree to kill himself.'

'Agreed,' said Edward. 'The idea that he went to the tree with the intention of committing suicide but was then murdered before he could carry out his plan is stretching credibility too far, I'm sure.'

'Yes. So we have to assume he went to the tree that morning to meet someone. Freeling thought he was going to help with some task for which a rope was required, while his opposite number had murderous intent. And he had planned it carefully, right down to the fake suicide. Getting the poor man to bring his own rope suggests a very cool head indeed, wouldn't you say?' asked Burrows.

'It does. Which raises the question of motive. We haven't thought about that yet, have we?' observed Innes.

'No, Miss, but we need to,' the constable replied. 'Someone wanted him dead so badly that they arranged to meet him and then took a great risk by strangling him in broad daylight. And it was almost certainly someone in the village, or on the estate. The question we must answer is why? What had Christian Freeling done to deserve that fate?'

The day of the debate had arrived and Evans and Wilkes were already in the press seats when the War Graves Society's members filed into the Strangers' Gallery. The editor was amused to note that the front two rows were reserved for them. 'Friends in high places,' he said out of the corner of his mouth as some MPs down in the Commons looked up and waved as Lady Langford assumed her place in the centre of the front row.

Sitting next to her mistress, Lilly was thrilled to recognise some of the politicians from newspaper photographs as she watched and listened, completely captivated by the drama of the occasion. Mr Asquith, who had lost a son in the war, opened the debate and spoke in favour of the proposals and Mr Churchill also spoke powerfully for the motion, emphasising the huge practical difficulties involved in the repatriation of over half a million bodies.

But others disagreed. In his speech Sir James Thame said, 'I am sure I speak for many when I say that the dead are not the property of the State or of any particular regiment. The dead belong to their own relations.'

At this a burst of applause and cries of 'Hear Hear' sounded in the Gallery, and Lilly cringed as Lady Langford stood up and called out, 'That's the spirit, Jimmy,' resulting in a delay until order was restored.

Another speaker made a pointed reference to the fact that the War Graves committee members were exclusively male. 'Bereaved mothers are not represented, which is surely a glaring omission,' he concluded. This produced more noisy support and resulted in the Speaker calling out, 'Order Order,' and warning that he would ask the sergeant at arms to clear the Strangers' Gallery if there were any further disturbances.

When everyone had spoken Lilly heard a cry of 'Division' and there was a general movement on the benches below. At the same moment, like two ranks of troops coming to attention, Lady Langford and the women with her stood up.

Evans turned to Wilkes and muttered, 'Here we go, hang on to your hat.'

'Gentlemen, a moment of your time!'

Lilly stood rigid with embarrassment as her mistress's compelling cry rang out across the House of Commons. It produced a shocked silence down below and she found herself staring at a sea of upturned faces as Lady Langford continued, 'Before you vote, remember the bereaved mothers. Here they are. Look upon them.' She raised her arms and gestured before continuing, 'We gave you our sons and now you must give us our sons back. The government does not own the bodies, the families do. You have no right to nationalise death. And here is a message from those many loyal and patriotic families who think the same way. We say give us them back!'

With that she held up a large paper bag that had appeared from nowhere and tipped its contents over the railing. The other women in the front rank did the same and a thick cascade of bright red paper discs each the size of a penny fluttered downwards.

'And here is more. Don't have their blood on your hands.' Resupplied by their compatriots behind, another volley of paper shrapnel fell towards the benches.

As cries of 'Shame' echoed around the chamber and the mood became increasingly chaotic, Lilly heard the Speaker call, 'Sergeant, clear the Gallery.'

A final flurry of red paper descended as a door to Lilly's left burst open and three burly men in House of Commons livery entered, their purpose only too clear. Neutral observers in the Gallery scuttled for cover as Lady Langford's dramatic cries echoed out into the air above the benches.

'Our voices are being crushed. Resist them, ladies! Gentlemen of the press, look how our suffering is compounded by this brutality!'

Evans and Wilkes watched spellbound as the seething frustration of the grieving mothers suddenly found a target. There was a spurt of crimson as the leading man took a solid blow across the nose from an umbrella.

'That's blooded him, ladies, tally ho!' Lady Langford surged to the front of her troops as more men piled through the door.

Lilly saw the Speaker of the House of Commons staring upwards in horror as the scene descended into chaos, with groups of cursing men and shrieking women struggling violently for supremacy.

Feeling an exhilarating rush of sisterhood, she climbed onto the bench and leapt onto the broad back of a uniformed official. Clinging to him like a monkey she pulled his hair and screamed in his ear as a stout woman with powerful forearms and a Yorkshire accent belaboured him with her umbrella.

As they spun round she saw her mistress succumb, pushed to the floor by the sheer weight of combatants and with their leader *hors de combat* the women were slowly subdued. Lilly was pulled firmly off her mount by unseen hands and corralled in the corner with the others. They were in a sorry state, some bruised and bleeding, some crying and many hatless and with torn clothing.

She found herself next to the Yorkshire woman who grinned at her and said breathlessly, 'Now that were a good scrap, lass. A few of us needed that.'

'They will remember us now, ladies. I am proud of you all,' called Lady Langford, still struggling as she was lifted bodily out of the door by two grim-faced officers of the House.

*

The following afternoon Evans and Wilkes met in the editor's office to review the events of the previous day. Well pleased with the article that his young reporter had written, Evans had worked hard himself to produce a measured and reasonable Leader that balanced sympathy for the women's cause with the absolute need for national democracy to take precedence over individual opinions.

And in his view it had. The bill for the proposals had passed and was on its way to becoming law. The great military cemeteries in France and Flanders would be built and the officers and men who fought and died together would stay together, equal under death.

'What happened to Lady Langford, Wilkes, did you manage to find out?'

'She was taken to Westminster police station along with her maid. They spent a night in the cells and appeared before the magistrate this morning. Both bound over to keep the peace and fined three pounds apiece. I believe Lord Langford travelled up to view the proceedings.'

Evans laughed. 'It must have been an interesting train journey back to Oxfordshire. Imagine a son ticking his mother off for her behaviour. It's the other way round normally, eh?'

Wilkes joined in with a smile. 'Indeed, Mr Evans. Seeing your mother up before the beak with the press taking notes must be a sobering experience.'

'They showed some spirit though, didn't they? I think some of those ladies were spoiling for a fight, you know. It makes one quite proud in a way.'

'They felt ignored and their frustration boiled over,' agreed Wilkes. 'But the die is cast now, and I imagine the whole thing will slowly die down.'

'Do you think it is the right decision?' The editor realised that he had never asked Wilkes what his personal opinion was.

'I think it probably is. It's a very raw thing for many bereaved families now, but with the passing of time…' He shrugged and then reached for his shorthand notebook. 'Did you hear what Churchill said during the debate. Yes, here we are,' he read out the quote.

'*There is no reason at all why, in periods as remote from our own as we ourselves are from the Tudors, the graveyards in France of this Great War, shall not remain an abiding and supreme memorial to the efforts and the glory of the British Army, and the sacrifices made in that great cause.*'

He looked at Evans. 'Time will be the judge, sir, but I suspect providence will show that the decision is the correct one.'

\*

Lady Langford's brush with the law had not gone down well with her eldest son.

Lilly witnessed the short and painful exchange that took place in public on the pavement outside Westminster magistrates court, where Lord Langford gave his mother the benefit of his views. She travelled third class on the train back to Oxford so did not know what happened during the journey, but after Fenn picked them up the ride back to Great Tew passed in frozen silence, and the tension emanating from the back seat was all too apparent.

'I am going to my room,' her mistress announced when they arrived at Langford Hall. 'Lilly, I will take my supper up there. Please tell cook.' With that she swept across the hall and up the grand staircase. On the half landing she paused momentarily and glared down at her son. 'When you are ready with your apology, I will consider receiving you,' she informed him and then disappeared from sight, head held high.

'She's not sorry is she, Lilly,' murmured her son, staring after her.

Brave as a lion she replied, 'Begging your pardon, my lord, but none of us are.' And with that she scuttled for the servants' door, leaving Lord Langford standing in the hall.

In the privacy of her bedroom Claire could at last give vent to the hollow misery that had engulfed her ever since she had learned that the bill had passed. She slumped in an armchair and stared sightlessly out of the window, seeing four-year-old Hugh giggling with delight as she chased him around the knot garden. She remembered him at sixteen, cantering his hunter across the wide parkland, his joyful athleticism so obvious. And she pictured him so handsome in his brand new Coldstream Guards uniform standing on the gravel outside the hall, kissing her goodbye with a lopsided grin and promising to be back for Christmas.

*But her darling boy wasn't coming back. Not now. Not ever.*

With a keening wail of pain she leaned forward, raised her hands to her face and let the tears flow.

*

The final week of July passed, climaxing with three violent storms one after another that battered the ripening hay and sent the Cherwell into flood down in the valley, but by early August warm weather settled in and the river returned to its benign normality. The nights in particular were very fine, as a waxing moon threw dark shadows in the sunken lanes and bathed the ancient fields and woods in silver light.

And on one such night Bert Williams went poaching.

He took his folding rod and blood-stained canvas bag and moved quietly and by discreet pathways upstream to Dipper Pool, half a mile from Beech Farm. Named after the charismatic little birds that hunted underwater along its banks, the pool was deeper than a man in places and the shadows under its tree-lined western edge were a favourite resting place for big trout.

It was also a favourite place for the estate's gamekeeper, who was known to sit quietly in the woods waiting for the flurry of splashing as a fine specimen was landed. A ripple of shot in the trees overhead and a frantic heart-pounding chase in the dark often followed and Bert was well aware that he was on his last chance with Lord Langford, the local magistrate whose trout they undeniably were.

He approached the pool with extreme caution, drifting like a wraith through the woods. As the sheen of water appeared in front of him, he crouched in cover at the edge of the trees staring silently across the water, every instinct alert. Fifty feet away on the far side of the pool a patch of gravel shelved gently into the water. The deep bank where the trout lay was just below his feet, but to cast at it he had to get across the rapids below the pool and onto the little beach opposite.

If the gamekeeper caught him halfway across the river, then he'd be doing a month in Oxford prison without the option of a fine, as Lord Langford had made abundantly clear.

A cloud drifted slowly towards the moon. With a silent prayer of thanks he watched and waited, eyes combing the bank opposite for any sign of movement. Then the light level suddenly dropped as though a thick lace curtain had been drawn across the scene. And Bert moved. Rod and bag slung over his shoulder he crossed the narrow grass bank, eased forward into the water and set off, moving as fast as he dared over the slippery stones. The depth varied between a few inches and a couple of feet and once he went in up to his thigh but flailing silently, he managed to keep his balance.

With a grin of relief he reached the other side and disappeared into the trees. He emptied his boots then took the folding rod out of its case and assembled it. Once he was ready he crept to the edge of the trees and looked out across the pool with an experienced eye.

Below the far bank the deep water was rippled with silver and black, and he pictured the stunted flat cast that he would use to put the fly in the right place. Then with his mind made up he returned to his bag and removed a roll of material. Unwrapping it he took his favourite fly, Reid's Assassin, from its place amongst the others and tied it on, his hands working by habit in the darkness.

The sudden sharp crack of a branch snapping froze him to stillness. Bert knew the night-time sounds of the countryside and animals did not break branches underfoot.

The keeper was coming.

Completely motionless he stared through the trees and saw a shadow moving in the gloom twenty feet away. The man's dog would find him any second, he reflected glumly, wondering what the food was like in Oxford prison. But to his surprise there was no bark or challenging shout and moments later Bert saw a figure appear on the beach. Risking discovery he crept forward, placing his feet with agonising delicacy until he had a clear view of the open gravel and the rippled water beyond.

To his astonishment it was a woman on her own. A woman he rarely saw but recognised vaguely, standing staring out over the pool. He could see her clearly in the bright moonlight. But before he could wonder what she was doing there, she raised her hands to the front of her dress and started to unbutton it.

Bert smiled silently in the darkness. *Well, well, a midnight swim, is it?*

She stepped out of her dress and Bert saw that she was naked underneath and with a noticeably swollen belly. Without further delay she waded smoothly into the water and pushed out towards the centre of the pool. Bert stood silently for ten minutes as she swam in the silver-lighted water, and watched her emerge, the droplets shining in the moonlight as they cascaded off her body. Still soaking wet, she pulled her dress over her head and slipped her feet into her shoes.

And with that she was gone.

*A ripe little river nymph. What am I to make of that?* he wondered. But not for long. He wasn't supposed to be there, and he certainly wasn't going to tell his wife that he'd behaved like a peeping Tom. He put the incident to the back of his mind, retrieved his rod and stepped down to the water's edge. Casting expertly he dropped the Reid's Assassin just above the deep water and watched it drift downstream.

Two hours later with three good trout in his bag he recrossed the river and disappeared into the woods, making his way back to Great Tew by little-known and barely discernible paths.

As he slipped across the deserted high street, Constable Burrows stepped out from behind the market cross.

'Well, well, Bert Williams, out for a stroll at…' he turned and looked at the clock on St Mary's tower, 'half past two in the morning. Can you account for yourself?'

'Ah, Constable, always a pleasure,' Bert leered hopefully at him. 'You're right though. It's a lovely night so I thought a walk would do me good.'

'With a rod case and bag no less. And what is in the bag?'

'The bag? Well that's, er…' The older man tailed off and there was an all too obvious pause before heavenly inspiration arrived on flighted wings. A beauteous smile spread across his face and he continued, 'I've been fishing, if you must know.'

'Fishing? So you admit it?'

'Oh yes, three nice trout from Dipper Pool.' He paused again and then added, 'Just like Mrs Sutton asked for.'

'Mrs Sutton the cook at Langford Hall?'

'Yes, that's right, Constable.'

'Mrs Sutton your wife's sister? The widowed Mrs Sutton with whom, if the rumours are to be believed, you are on intimate terms?'

'Well maybe, but that would be irreverent,' replied Bert with a note of outrage.

'Wouldn't it just,' observed Burrows dryly. 'Let me see.' He nodded at the bag and the poacher duly produced the fish and laid them out on the bottom step of the market cross where they glimmered in the moonlight.

'Nice eh?' said Bert with satisfaction.

'So your claim is that you were fishing Langford waters at the request of the Langford cook, in the middle of the night?'

The man next to him shrugged. 'Best time for it.'

This time it was the police officer's turn to pause. He looked at the trout, then looked at Bert, who had adopted an air of innocence that a choirboy would have been pleased with, and finally glanced up the road to where the gates to Langford Hall stood open.

'Mrs Sutton has a room over the stables, doesn't she?' he said after a moment.

'Yes,' Bert replied cautiously.

'Fine, let's go and ask her. Put the fish back in the bag and give it to me.'

'But it's the middle of the night, Constable. We'll be disturbing her,' Bert protested, the anxiety in his tone all too apparent.

'The alternative is a night in the cell, and me having a word with His Lordship in the morning,' said Burrows, who was well aware that such a conversation meant Mrs Williams would be living in splendid isolation for a month.

They set off up the road and ten minutes later arrived at the cobbled stable yard where the cars were kept, along with the estate's riding horses. A line of windows above the garage indicated accommodation and at Bert's direction they climbed an outside stair to a door.

'This it?' enquired the constable.

'Yes,' Bert replied rather tensely.

'I will knock, and I will ask the questions. You will say nothing, or you will be in the cell before you can say dry fly. Do you understand?'

But before Bert could reply, the door opened to reveal an attractive blonde woman in her mid-forties wearing a woollen dressing gown and slippers. She was holding a lighted candle.

'Oh hello, Bert. I couldn't sleep and was just making a cup of tea when I thought I heard voices,' she said, a note of surprise in her voice.

'I was just explaining to the constable that I've brought the fish you asked for.' The words tumbled out in a rush before the policeman could intervene.

'I said say nothing,' Burrows muttered furiously, glaring at him, then turned to the cook. 'Mrs Sutton, did you request that Bert obtain some fish for you?'

A pregnant silence fell over the little tableau at the top of the stone steps.

'Sorry, what did you say?' the cook asked after a moment as her gaze moved from one to another.

Burrows sighed, all too aware that the element of surprise had been lost. 'Mr Williams has some fish that I believe he has poached from the estate in his bag. His defence is that you asked him to get them, in your position as cook to the Langford household. Lying to a police officer is a very serious offence, Mrs Sutton, so choose your answer carefully. Is what he says true or not?'

'Oh yes. You were going to bring them round in the morning, weren't you, Bert.'

As the poacher nodded vigorously Burrows stared at her with narrowed eyes. 'I have a list of people I keep a special eye on, Mrs Sutton. You have now joined it. I'd watch my step if I were you.' With that he dropped the bag on the top step, pushed his way past the grinning poacher and descended to the yard.

'You won't stay for a cup of tea, Constable?' To his fury he could hear the amusement in her voice as the invitation was extended.

'I will not.' He stalked off in silence, his bitterness compounded by a second, unmistakably honey-toned invitation which he heard as he rounded the corner.

'You'll come in for a bit though, won't you, Bert? As you're here. Don't forget the fish.'

# Chapter Nine

A grim atmosphere had settled over Langford Hall and day after day drifted by with no sign of any change.

Lady Langford spent most of the time sitting in her bedroom staring silently out over the park. She was barely eating, all visitors were refused, and some days she did not bother to get dressed, which was unheard of. Increasingly worried, Lilly raised it with Mr Dereham, and it transpired the butler had already discussed it with His Lordship.

'It's grief. The decision about the bill has brought all the pain back in a second wave and we'll just have to hold on until it starts to ease,' he told her.

'But she knew Mr Hugh was dead, didn't she?' Lilly replied.

'I think she was holding on to the hope that she would be able to bring him back for a funeral at St Mary's, but now…' he pursed his lips, 'well you can see it's been a crushing blow. No final parting and no grave that she can visit easily. She won't be the only one going through this agony up and down the country.'

Lilly nodded. 'Yes, I know. I saw them.'

'Let's keep our chins up, be attentive and respectful and let time pass. That's really all we can do.'

And this policy did seem to bear fruit because a week later her mistress requested a hearty breakfast, got dressed, and headed out of the front door with something of a spring in her step. She was feeling better. The long days of despair and desperation were starting to pass and there was a vigour and purpose to her movements that had been absent for a long time.

Put simply, Lady Langford had made a decision.

As she entered the pleasure grounds anyone following her movements would have assumed that she was wandering at random. The narrow pathway twisted and turned through a sunken stumpery thick with gnarled roots and ferns, then forked around a clump of widely spaced beech trees before coming together again on the far side. From there it climbed to a little knoll where a bench backed by azaleas gave a fine view out over the parkland.

She stood there for a long time letting the breeze ripple her hair as she sensed the atmosphere. *Was this the place? Perhaps.*

She carried on downhill between luxuriant flower beds where hollyhocks, delphiniums and foxgloves flourished in front of tall, clipped hedges. Again she wandered seemingly without purpose, before pausing at the junction of two paths. To her right a grassy hedge-lined ride led to a privet arch fifty yards away.

On impulse she walked that way, passed under the arch, and emerged onto a grassy hilltop outside the cultivated gardens. Looking back the way she had come the view was very fine. At the end of the ride three long tiers of stone-backed rose beds climbed the slope to the house and the old red-brick walls provided a perfect visual backdrop to their glorious summer display. Smiling, she turned and looked in the other direction.

If the view towards the house was delightful, the airy prospect out over the Oxfordshire landscape was magnificent. Down and to her right she could see the parkland where she and Eve often walked and in the distance the line of trees that led to Creech Hill Ring. Immediately below her the ground fell away towards the river Cherwell in a jumble of woods, rich pasture and thick hedgerows before climbing to Green Hill.

Walking to the lip of the slope she folded her dress around her knees and sat down, letting the sun shine on her face as she stared out across the landscape thinking about the many generations of Langfords that had gone before. Her husband was safely buried in the vault below the altar in St Mary's but the agony of losing him and then Hugh had changed her, she knew that. The idea she was now resolved to enact would at least go some way to helping with her grief.

She sat there for three long hours, letting the place wash over her, *making sure*, and then with a sigh of satisfaction she climbed to her feet and made her way slowly back to the house.

*

At four o'clock two days later Lilly arrived at Holly Cottage. Mrs Williams had left for the day but fortunately Edward heard the tinkle of the bell and answered the front door.

'Hello, Mr Edward,' Lilly said. 'Your mother has sent me to say she'd be pleased if you would call on her.'

'Now?'

'I believe so, sir, yes.'

'I see. Is she feeling better?'

'I think so. The last weeks have been dreadful but just recently she's been in the garden a lot, and I've seen her talking to the head gardener.'

Edward raised his eyebrows. 'Oh really? Well that sounds encouraging, perhaps she's planning some changes. A project would be just the job, I'd have thought.'

Lilly nodded firmly. 'Yes, I think you're right there.'

'Very well, I'll just tidy up outside and then follow you back.'

The maid bobbed and turned and Edward made his way back into the garden to collect his book from the table. The weather looked fair, but a sudden shower could never be ruled out.

He was gloriously unaware of the hidden storm that was approaching.

His mother was waiting for him in the library when he arrived. He kissed her cheek and they sat and talked over a cup of tea and a plate of Mrs Sutton's renowned shortbread biscuits.

'How are you feeling now?' he asked her. 'You've lost weight, you know.'

'A pound or two, yes. I'm afraid the news about the debate rather knocked me for six and I've been in purdah for days.'

'Have you made your peace with Piers?'

Her face tightened. 'I have not. He has not apologised for his outrageous remarks outside the magistrate's court, and I have declined to withdraw the observations about his character that I made in response. A state of armed truce exists between us. Or to put it another way, we are avoiding each other, which is not difficult in this house. He really is quite intolerable at times.'

Edward hid a smile. They were both sulkers. It would pass. 'You were the talk of the village, you know. I've never seen such a well-read copy of the *Daily Sketch* in the Black Horse. "Lady Langford's Legionnaires" they called you all.'

She smiled, her eyes creasing in pleasure. 'I rather like that. I really do. Perhaps we should re-mobilise in support of women's emancipation? What do you think?'

'Well it would be another popular cause in many quarters.'

'Yes, I will give that some thought.' She picked up a biscuit and crunched it delicately. 'Have you had enough tea?'

'I have, thank you.' He drained the last mouthful in his cup and put it back on the table. 'Was there something in particular you wanted to see me about?'

'Yes, come into the garden, there's something I would like to show you.'

Pleased that his mother was taking an interest in life again he happily agreed, and they walked through to the entrance hall and out of the front door. 'This way,' she said, linking his arm and leading him round the house towards the croquet lawn.

'What have you got in mind?' he asked curiously.

'You'll see.' They crossed the manicured grass as she continued, 'Have you seen anything of Innes Knox?'

He hesitated fractionally then decided not to mention the fact that they were working together on trying to unmask a murderer. 'Once or twice. I called round to the Dances' when she was there. Nothing beyond that. Why do you ask?'

'Oh no reason. She seemed like a nice girl. Quite bright and attractive too, wouldn't you say?'

'She's alright. As I remember telling you before, she has a waspish manner and is inclined to strong opinions.'

'Better than being inclined to strong drink,' his mother remarked with a meaningful glance.

'Yes, well, I am aware that I probably spend more time in the Black Horse than is good for me.'

'And will you do something about it?' she gently persisted. 'Don't you think it's time you found something to do? You know Piers would welcome your help with the estate and I'd love to have you back at the hall.' She gave his arm a squeeze and turned the screw. 'Speaking as your mother.'

He looked at her and smiled but didn't reply, and they strolled on in silence. She led him along the long ride with the privet arch at its end and they emerged out onto the open hilltop. To his left a stand of beech trees provided some shelter from the prevailing wind but the rest of the hilltop was open to the elements.

He released her arm and walked to the top of the slope. 'I'd forgotten how beautiful it is here. That view. I haven't been here for ages.'

She joined him. 'I'd like to have a memorial stone for Hugh up here, something that celebrates his life. I've been speaking to the head gardener about building a little bower where we can sit in any weather and imagine him as he was. I like the thought of that.'

'It sounds lovely,' he agreed and slipped his hand into hers. 'What sort of thing have you got in mind? A cross, perhaps?'

'No, a plain white marble stone will be fine. A gravestone in fact.'

'A gravestone?' His surprise was obvious, but he softened his tone and said gently, 'But Hugh's grave will be in France, the matter has now been decided. You know that.'

She looked at him, her eyes alight with purpose. 'Oh no, dear, his grave will be here.'

'Here? What do you mean, his grave will be here?' he said slowly.

'Oh it's simple enough. Hugh must be at Langford. I want you to go and get him, Edward.'

*

Eve had been feeling restless for some days.

Like a soldier hearing gunfire carried on the wind, she knew danger was coming but could neither discern its shape nor measure its substance. *What was the threat? To whom and when?* In an effort to see more clearly she rose in the middle of a sleepless night, took her bag and quietly left the house. In the street outside she paused for a moment then made a decision and set off for Stream Cross.

As she turned into the lane she was seen by Bert Williams who was also abroad in the darkness. He watched her pass from the shadows, saying nothing. He knew her ways. She crossed the little footbridge and climbed the track that snaked up Tan Hill. On the summit was another of the great monoliths that formed the outer ring around Creech Hill.

She crossed the cropped grass and spoke a quiet greeting to the stone she knew as Litha, then sat down and leaned back against it. Far below, trees, hedges and fields merged and then reformed in changing shades of purple and black as clouds slowly moved huge shadows towards the distant hills.

Like a questing vixen Eve raised her head and smiled with satisfaction.

*The right place. It was a good choice to come here.*

She lifted her gaze to the stars, closed her eyes and let her mind rise upwards. Familiar feelings of connection and awareness flowed through her as she drifted in the airy infinite heights. She pictured the people she cared for, floating from one to another like a ghost moving through a crowd. *Her daughters in London, Jocelyn, Claire, Edward, Innes, Jaikie...*

A thrill of alarm ran through her. *Edward and Innes.* She went back to them and focussed hard, trying to see. *There was a shadow. Not close yet but present at a distance.* She studied it then suddenly shivered with shock and opened her eyes, forcibly breaking the contact.

Left with a lingering, sickening sensation Eve stared pensively out over the darkened landscape.

She had seen violent death and it was coming.

*

As Eve sat silently at the Litha stone, Edward lay in bed and replayed the conversation with his mother that afternoon repeatedly in his mind. He could just about remember every word.

'What! Bring back his body? It can't be done.' His reaction had been a mixture of alarm and astonishment. 'It simply can't be done,' he repeated, his eyes creasing in sympathy as a single tear rolled down her face. Instinctively he stepped forward and embraced her hard, thinking how frail she felt. 'The idea is madness,' he said quietly, 'we'll never get permission to bring him back. The only alternative would be grave robbing.'

Even as he said the words he felt a prickle of alarm. *Was that a faint acrid smell?*

She stiffened and pushed him away. 'No, Edward, not robbing. How can you steal something that already belongs to you? He is my son, and he needs to be here in Langford. And I am asking you to go and get him.' Given the enormity of what she was suggesting her voice sounded remarkably matter-of-fact. They stood and looked at each other for a moment then he broke her gaze and walked back to the lip of the slope.

*The acrid smell was definitely there. Was Hugh watching and listening? From France?* His mind reeled at the thought.

His mother slipped her arms around him from behind and pressed the side of her head between his shoulders as he stared out across the landscape. 'Sometimes it feels like he's here already. In spirit if not in body. I just want the two things brought together again. To make him whole,' she said.

'What's that, a mother's instinct?' he managed to say.

'A mother's love, Edward. The same as I have for you. Please go and get Hugh, my darling.' She squeezed him. He sighed and continued to stare at Green Hill, turning things over in his mind. The idea was insane in every respect. An appalling image came to mind of a shadowy figure digging in a French graveyard at night. The wooden clunk of a shovel as it hit the coffin and then harsh shouts as men in helmets with torches and rifles ran towards him shouting, 'Grave robber!' The very worst of crimes.

'I'm sorry but it can't be done,' he said flatly.

'Don't say that. We just need to find a way. Or rather you do. Your father would have done it, you know that.' It was a low blow, but undeniably true. His father would have moved heaven and earth to get his son back and if it could not be done legitimately he would have had no qualms in finding other methods.

'Think of the difficulties, mother. The complications are appalling.'

Safely hidden behind him she smiled in quiet triumph. 'You're right of course. And you can't do it alone. We will have to find you an accomplice. Someone trusted. From the estate I imagine. Does anyone spring to mind?'

He turned and looked down at her and smiled wearily. 'I know what you're trying to do. But I have not agreed to do this. The absolute most I am prepared to do is think about it.'

'Oh yes, dear, thank you.' She smiled winningly up at him.

'Do not make the assumption that I will agree. If I were a betting man I'd say the odds were a hundred to one against me going.'

'A hundred to one? Not too bad at all.' Lady Langford deployed the devastatingly charming grin that formed one of the many weapons in her armoury. She took his arm and they started to walk back towards the privet arch.

*I'll take those odds for the moment*, she thought. *Plenty of time yet.*

*

In search of a motive for Christian Freeling's death, Innes had travelled to Gloucester to meet his brother and she reported the results of the conversation to Edward and Burrows in the parlour at Holly Cottage.

'He doesn't believe that his brother killed himself. He said Christian loved his wife, was grateful to have got out of France intact and was looking forward to settling down and starting a family. There was nothing to indicate that he was suicidal, quite the reverse in fact,' she said.

'What did you tell him?' asked Burrows.

'To justify my interest I did say there was some doubt about the cause of death, and could he think of anyone who might have wished his brother harm. Something that had happened out in France within the regiment for example. Or anything he'd mentioned about Great Tew.'

'And?'

'And nothing.' She shrugged eloquently. 'He said they were close and if there had been anything of a magnitude that warranted murder he was sure he would have known about it.'

'So you've drawn a blank then,' Edward said.

'So I thought, but as we were parting he did say something. Apparently his brother's wife was much sought after. "A right good-looking lass, with a glad eye," was how he described her, and she had another suitor in Great Tew who was very angry when Mr Freeling won her hand.' She raised her eyebrows meaningfully and sipped her tea as the two men digested this.

'So your suggestion is that he was murdered by a defeated love rival?' Edward asked, a note of scepticism in his voice. 'Even though they'd been married for eighteen months by then.'

'Don't forget he'd been away in France. And the murderer didn't waste much time when he got back, did he? He could have killed him for revenge, or even to clear the field so he could have another crack himself,' Innes pointed out.

Burrows nodded sagely. 'It wouldn't be the first time. Such things do happen.'

'So who is this fellow?'

'He never knew his name, his brother just mentioned it in conversation, that's all.'

'Any idea, Burrows? Anyone spring to mind?' Edward turned and looked at him.

The constable shook his head. 'Nope. They were married by the time I arrived in the village, so any rivalry was over.'

Edward nodded. 'I was away in France so I've no idea either. It shouldn't be difficult to find out though. I'll have a word with Stanley Tirrold. Publicans always have their ear to the ground. He'll be able to point us in the right direction, I'd have thought.'

And so it proved. A conversation with the landlord of the Black Horse elicited the name of one Jack Wright, a labourer at West Lea Farm on the edge of Little Tew.

'Was it much of a rivalry?' asked Edward.

'Jack was sweet on her for sure, mind you all the village lads were. She was the kind of girl that always let you think you were in with a chance. I think she quite liked the idea of them fighting over her. One of those she was, if you know what I mean. Anyway the field narrowed to the pair of them and in the end Christian carried the day. Jack was upset. He's got a temper on him, and he kicked off in here a time or two. I had to send him down the road in the end.'

He stared meaningfully at Edward as he imparted this doleful final remark, like a judge handing down a sentence from the bench.

'Oh dear, not the King's Head, Stan?'

'We have our standards here and I uphold them,' the landlord replied majestically.

'Quite right. So Jack Wright is still at West Lea Farm?'

'As far as I know, yes.'

At this point Laura Bessing, who had appeared behind the bar, interjected. 'Jack Wright? I know him. All of us land girls soon learned to steer clear of Jack.'

'Oh yes? Why was that?' Edward asked.

'He's all sweetness and charm until he gets you on your own, then he's overly pushy, if you know what I mean. Doesn't like taking no for an answer. One or two of the girls fell foul of him. I think they all escaped with their virtue, but the word went round among the land girls. When Jack Wright was about you walked home from the pub together.'

There was a silence and through the open window Edward heard Mrs Dale the greengrocer over the road calling to her daughter, 'Ada, don't forget the eggs.' A distant acknowledgement echoed back in reply.

'He's a bad lot then, this Jack Wright?'

'It's his temper. He'd buy a girl a drink then think that bought him certain other rights as well. When it didn't, things could get difficult. That's what the others said anyway, not that I ever got involved.'

'Saving yourself for Constable Burrows aren't you, Laura.' The landlord smiled.

'Cheeky, Stan,' she replied.

Edward grinned. 'Does he know?'

She rolled her eyes ruefully. 'I've given him enough hints, but I don't think he's cottoned on yet.'

'Maybe you should get yourself arrested,' he replied, still smiling.

'Yes, then he'd have to take down your particulars,' Stanley Tirrold said, rather pleased with himself.

The barmaid's eyes flashed, suddenly alluring, and she smiled thoughtfully. 'Now there's an idea, Stan,' she said.

The unwitting object of Laura Bessing's affections paid a visit to West Lea Farm the following morning. The weather remained fine, and he rode his police bicycle there, passing Holly Cottage and crossing By Brook before the steady climb over Tan Hill. From there his effort was rewarded with a pleasing freewheel downhill into Little Tew.

As its name suggested the village was smaller than Great Tew, with a population of around a hundred people. And it was famous locally because Little Tew was a Thankful Village, one of only thirty in the country. It had sent nine men to war, and they had all come back. And although this was joyful for the families involved it also threw into sharp contrast the suffering wrought upon other settlements. In the village of Great Rissington over the border in Gloucestershire, William and Julia Souls had lost five sons.

However on that particular morning the constable's thoughts were occupied with other considerations. He cycled through the village and turned onto a tree-lined track that led downhill to West Lea Farm. The farmhouse was tidy and well kept but did not display the prosperity he had seen at Beech Farm. His appearance in uniform caused the usual momentary anxiety but his reassurance that he, 'Just wanted a word with Jack Wright,' produced a sigh of weary recognition in the farmer's wife.

'He and my husband are up at Long Field, mending the fence. It's straight along the track then turn up to the right at the second gate and climb the slope. Best leave your bike here. Knock on the way back and I'll brew a pot of tea before you cycle back.'

Nodding his thanks he set off. It was a pleasant walk; the hedgerows were thick and green and the verges lush with summer flowers. A steady hum of bees underpinned the gentle noises of the countryside and he noticed thick growths of wild parsley on the banks of a little rill that ran along a ditch under the hedge on his left.

Arriving at the second gate he let himself through and looked up the hill. On the far side of the next field a line of trees marked the edge of a wood, and he could see two figures working on the fence. It took him five minutes to reach them.

'Good morning,' he called cheerfully. 'Jack Wright, is it?'

Both men turned at his greeting and the larger of them nodded, his face expressionless. 'Yes that's me.'

With a nod to the farmer, Burrows continued speaking. 'Well I'll just have a word, Mr Wright, if you don't mind. Sorry to interrupt your work.'

'What about?' He was a big man with an uncompromising slab-sided face that seemed to be hewn from rock. His hair was noticeably thinning on top and the constable guessed he was in his mid-thirties. *Those girls did well to get away*, he thought, having heard Edward's report from Laura Bessing.

'I'm checking one or two details about events leading up to the suicide of Christian Freeling. Just so we have all the facts, you understand. I'm told you were sweet on Jane Freeling at one time yourself, sir. Is that correct?'

A shadow passed over the other man's face. 'I'll not deny it. She led me on and then said she wasn't interested.'

'And how did you feel about that?'

'I wasn't happy. She played me off against Christian Freeling. I see that now. Used me to make him keener I reckon.'

'He wasn't keen himself then?'

The big man uttered a short and bitter laugh. 'Oh aye, he was very fond of all the ladies. And she's a looker. Any bloke would be glad to walk her up the aisle.'

'Including yourself?'

'I've told you, I was interested but it turned out she wasn't,' he replied, his tone shortening noticeably.

'Were you jealous of Mr Freeling then? With him winning the day as it were?'

Wright broke eye contact and looked out over the valley for a moment. In the field opposite three horses were chasing each other and the noise of their drumming hooves carried to the men. When he replied his voice was softer and the constable could see a sadness in his eyes.

'Yes I was. I loved Jane Freeling in my way, and I hated him for a while, I'll admit that. There was a scene in the pub and I got kicked out.'

'How do you feel now?'

'Now? Well he's dead isn't he. I don't feel anything.'

'It's just that Jane Freeling's on her own again isn't she? After a period of mourning, well…' Burrows shrugged and left the question hanging in the warm air.

At this point the farmer interrupted. 'What exactly is the reason for your questions, Constable?'

'As I said, sir, just clearing up a few details, nothing to worry about.'

'Sounds to me like you're sniffing around for some kind of motive,' he replied.

The farmhand stared at the constable. 'Is that it? You think I was involved in his death somehow?'

'The morning he died, it was the twenty-fourth of May just to jog your memory, what would you have been doing, Mr Wright?'

'Bloody hell. You are sniffing round. I'm not having this.' He paced over to the policeman and confronted him, raw anger suffusing his face.

'Steady now, sir,' said Burrows more calmly than he felt. If it came to a scrap he wasn't at all sure he would emerge the victor. 'I'm just wondering if you saw anything, that's all.'

'Why would he?' the farmer's voice came over his shoulder. 'He'd be here with me and the others. No reason to be over at Creech Hill.'

Burrows turned and eased away from the vibrating labourer with some relief.

'You're sure about that are you, sir?'

'Of course I am. He works to my orders. And he works here on West Lea Farm.'

Burrows wasn't entirely convinced. It seemed to him the farmer had stepped in to take the pressure off his workman. But he decided for the moment enough was enough. 'Well that's fine then.' He turned back to the big man. 'Apart from yourself, did Mr Freeling have any brushes with other blokes in the village?'

'I told you he liked the ladies. Before Jane Freeling started to take an interest he'd chase anything in a skirt, including other men's women. And some of them liked him too. It didn't matter if they were walking out or even married. If they gave him the eye he'd be straight after it.'

'Well that would cause trouble, I'd imagine.'

'Oh he was clever. Never got caught to my knowledge. There's one or two prim and proper married ladies in Great Tew with a guilty secret, I can tell you that.'

'Oh really?' *Now we're getting somewhere*, the constable thought. He pulled out his pocket book. 'And who would that be, sir?'

Ten minutes later he made his way back down the track to the farmhouse in search of his mug of tea and well satisfied with his morning's work. He called out and an answering cry directed him to the back of the house where a fine selection of vegetables was growing in neat rows up against a red-brick wall.

'You're lucky living here. Being on the farm you must have been able to supplement your ration card with what you produce. Although thankfully we've seen the back of all that now, with the coupons ending in May,' he said as he removed his helmet, took his mug, and sat down on a bench conveniently placed by the back door of the farm.

'Yes, finished and unlamented. Queuing up for bread and meat in the countryside. I ask you. But yes, you're right, we did put a little aside from time to time. Only a little, mind.' The farmer's wife smiled down at him.

'I'm sure. Even just along the track there I saw fresh parsley growing by the rill. I enjoy a nice parsley sauce with a bit of boiled ham.'

She looked at him with amusement. 'I don't think you'd enjoy that, my love. It might look like parsley, but it isn't. It's hemlock, bless you, and deadly poisonous. It grows in abundance around here. My husband cut it all down a couple of weeks ago and what you saw was the new growth coming back through.'

'Oh right. I'm not a local you see. Oxford born and bred.'

'No. Well don't you go near hemlock. I'm not lying when I say it's deadly.'

# Chapter Ten

After three long weeks of agonising, Edward told his mother that he wasn't going to go to France. His refusal cut her to the quick and as they walked in the Langford gardens she pleaded tearfully with him to change his mind, but he held his ground.

'You have asked for the impossible and I don't think I should be blamed for refusing,' he insisted. Nevertheless, her parting words spoken quietly and with profound emotion were excruciating.

'You are my son, Edward, and I love you. Nothing will ever change that, but I deeply regret that you cannot find it in your heart to bring your darling brother home. I fear it has changed my opinion of you for ever.' And with that crushing blow delivered, she turned and walked into the house without looking back.

Torn between rage at the injustice of her remark and despair at the consequences of his decision he stared after her for a long moment then, with a face like thunder, he stalked around the corner of the house and down the drive to the high street. He called in to the Black Horse and bought a flagon of strong cider and a bottle of brandy. Stanley Tirrold and Laura Bessing exchanged glances as the door swung shut.

'Taking trouble to someone, Stan,' the girl observed.

The landlord sighed. 'Only to himself, Laura. And I thought he was getting better.'

As his purchases indicated, Edward got very drunk that evening. He did it quietly and on his own, in the parlour of Holly Cottage.

He felt deep anger towards his mother, whose request had put him in an insufferable position. *Damned if I do and damned if I don't*, he thought as the fierce exhilaration of drunken rage vied with aching self-pity. He swigged repeatedly from the brandy bottle, desperate for the release that oblivion would bring and when at last it came, his final thought was of Innes Knox speaking to him over the dinner table at Marston House.

*'A man adrift then, Mr Spense, and if you'll excuse me saying so, it shows.'*

\*

Hours later he stirred and slowly came awake. He was lying full length on the yellow settee, the back of his hand resting on the floor next to the empty brandy bottle. He realised with a shock that he could smell burning and his first thought was that the cottage was on fire. But even as he groaned and sat up a second realisation hit him.

*That acrid smell again.*

He looked at the window and saw it was wide open. The Victorian woman must be passing, he thought confusedly, his mind thick with cider and brandy. But the clock on the mantlepiece showed five past four in the morning. *It's too late. It can't be her.*

And the smell was getting stronger.

A feeling of self-disgust overcame him, and he wondered what on earth getting drunk would do to resolve the rift with his mother, as scenes from his childhood with Hugh flickered through his mind.

Hugh running laughing through the attics where they played on wet days. Or climbing trees in the pleasure gardens in the endless summers. His patient teaching as they cast for trout and swam together in Dipper Pool. Sledging in the park in the winter, their breath cloudy in the chill air. His face creased into a gentle smile as he remembered his best friend, his mentor, his brother. Piers had been older and a little aloof, but Hugh and he had been as thick as thieves.

But as the memories became more and more intense, he started to feel uneasy – it was as though some outside agency was filling his head with a random kaleidoscope of images that exploded in his mind like fireworks as they vied with each other in their urgency to be seen.

Unnaturally so.

From nowhere a great wave of love flooded into the room. An overwhelming, heart-searing sensation that washed over him so strongly that he slumped back against the settee as though he had been pushed. Electricity crackled in the air as pins and needles pulsed through him and every hair on his body stood on end.

His waist muscles tightened involuntarily, and he was pulled up into a sitting position. To his astonishment he realised that he could no longer see the fireplace because an opaque glittering haze had appeared. A haze that became brighter and denser as he stared. Buried in the dancing glow a darker shape slowly defined into a human form. It was his brother, dressed in military uniform and bathed in light, standing smiling at him with his familiar lopsided grin.

'My God, Hugh,' he whispered open-mouthed. 'Is that you? Are you here?' The loving sensations that engulfed him were answer enough and the pulsing voice in his head was unmistakable and undeniable.

*Home, Eddie. Home.*

*

The colonel was a sound sleeper, so it was Eve who heard the urgent knocking on their front door.

With a muttered, 'Who on earth is that?' she climbed out of bed and crossed to the window, glancing at the clock as she did so. It was half past four in the morning and a faint coral pink light was showing in the sky. She lifted the sash fully open and leaned out. Below her, alerted by the sound of the window opening, Edward stared upwards, his face drawn and hair ruffled.

'Eve, I'm sorry to disturb you. Is Jocelyn there?'

'Of course he is, Edward, it's the middle of the night. What's wrong? Is there an emergency?' He stood and looked at her then just gestured hopelessly with his hands and in the faint light she realised his cheeks were wet. He was crying.

'Wait, I'll come down.' With a brisk shove on her husband's shoulder and a cry of, 'Wake up, something has happened to Edward,' she pulled on her dressing gown and walked quickly along the landing and down the stairs.

Opening the front door she ushered him into the parlour. Ellie appeared in her dressing gown, obviously wakened by the banging on the door and Eve told her to make some tea before she could fully realise the state of their bedraggled caller. He had clearly slept in his clothes, but it was his shocked, fearful eyes that really caught her attention.

*He's scared. Something's happened.*

Before she could ask him anything footsteps sounded on the stairs and the comforting figure of her husband, resplendent in an eccentric green and red Chinese silk dressing gown, courtesy of his time in Hong Kong, appeared in the doorway.

'Edward?' Eve saw a flash of intelligence cross his face as he quickly summed up the situation. Closing the door he crossed the room and sat down opposite their visitor. 'What's happened?' he said simply.

Edward stared at the floor for a moment, seemingly lost in thought, then he looked up and spoke quietly. 'I've had a visit from Hugh.'

They both stirred in surprise. 'What do you mean, a visit?' Eve asked.

'I mean he appeared to me in a light haze in the cottage,' Edward replied, his voice flat and unemotional. 'And he had a message.'

'A message? What was it?' She leaned forward, her eyes intense with interest.

'Did Jocelyn tell you about my other experiences? In France and here in Great Tew?'

'He did, and I have no doubt that human spirits exist and that they walk among us on occasions. Although I wasn't aware they engaged in international travel.'

He smiled, appreciating her effort to lighten the mood. 'In order to explain I need to tell you about a confidential discussion my mother and I have been having. She has asked me to do something, and I have refused, because I believe it is impossible and because the consequences of failure would be appalling. I suspect she thinks my refusal is cowardice, and in my innermost thoughts I wonder if she is right. It is an issue that has caused us both great personal distress.'

He shrugged and then added in a bitter tone, 'Incredibly, it now appears my dead brother has an opinion on the matter as well.'

With a sudden movement he leaned back and covered his face in his hands. A low moan of pain emerged. 'Ye gods, I really think I must be going insane.' He stared at them wide-eyed. 'A message from a dead man? Tell me I'm not bound for the looney bin please.'

Eve made to say something but at that moment the maid reappeared with a tea tray and further discussion was suspended as she placed it on a table.

'That's fine, Ellie. Back to bed now and quietly please, don't wake Miss Knox or the wean.' Eyes agog at the drama the girl bobbed at her mistress and departed. Eve poured the tea and handed Edward a cup as though it was a pleasant Sunday afternoon. Then she sat down next to him and took his hand.

'Look, Edward, I am certain you are not going to end up in an asylum. For some reason you have been given this extraordinary ability to see what others cannot. It may be temporary, or it may be permanent, but it is not insanity. I really am sure of that. Now, do you feel able to tell us more about this row and its bearing on Hugh's message?'

He nodded. 'I'm going to have to tell someone. Not least because if I carry out my mother's request I will need help. It cannot be done alone. In fact it almost certainly cannot be done at all. The very idea is madness.'

'What on earth is it?' The colonel's voice sounded in the silence that followed.

Edward looked at them. 'She wants me to steal Hugh's body from his grave in France and bring him back to Great Tew so he can be buried on the estate.'

'Bloody hell!' The older man's muffled expletive was masked by the gasp of surprise from his wife.

'What?' she said simply, her face frozen in shock.

He smiled dryly at her. 'That is the matter between us. She has asked most forcefully. I have declined with equal robustness. Hugh has now declared in her favour. The message was unequivocally that he wants to come home. He wants to be buried at Langford.'

*

That afternoon the colonel and Edward took a long walk through the estate. Their path led them past Creech Hill Ring and down into the valley before looping round Dipper Pool and turning back towards Great Tew.

And as they walked they talked, largely about the practicalities of exhuming Hugh's body in secret and bringing him back across the English Channel.

'Do you even know where he is?' the colonel asked.

'Yes, we do. Two months after the telegram notifying us of his death we received a letter advising us that his body had been recovered and he was interred at a temporary cemetery at a place called Rouville, south-west of Cambrai. The Coldstream Guards were in action there in the latter stages of the war. From what we know Hugh was killed as they attacked the village.'

'Well I'm glad they found him,' the colonel replied.

Edward nodded. 'The casualties were relatively light I think, and the ground was taken quickly, meaning that they were not struggling in a sea of mud. And the battle was a fairly recent one.'

'Yes, I can see that would have made things easier.'

The younger man shuddered at the memories that crowded in on him. 'When we weren't in the trenches we were involved in searching for bodies in land that had changed hands several times. As a padre I was expected to help recover, and identify the men, whatever their regiment.'

The colonel blew out his cheeks in sympathy. 'How did that work then?'

'We were divided into squads of twenty and allocated a patch of the old battlefield five hundred yards square. Some of the bodies had already been recovered – where there were marked field graves and so on. We were looking for the others. But when thousands of soldiers had gone over the top and been mown down by German machine guns and blown up by shellfire the work often bordered on impossible and was deeply disturbing for the men who carried it out.'

They passed through an open gate and stopped and watched as a pair of roe deer that had been feeding in the grass at the edge of a field raised their heads and bounded elegantly away across the parkland.

'It must have been awful,' his friend remarked soberly.

Edward sighed. 'It was. The men were volunteers and were paid an extra half-crown a day and it was terribly important work, but it was a grim business, Jocelyn. The bodies were rotting and many of the volunteers only lasted a day or two. But those that stayed on developed a bit of a knack. If a pool in the mud had an oily sheen on it there would probably be a body at the bottom of it. Or a brighter patch of green where the vegetation had started to recover. Often identity tags were the only things we could realistically recover. Sometimes we used paybooks or personal effects, even letters to identify people. Everyone did their best, but the truth is that many bodies will never be found and many more will never be identified. They'll probably keep turning up for a hundred years. Especially when the farmers finally start ploughing again.'

The colonel nodded silently, his mouth set in a firm line and they walked on, each deep in their thoughts. When they reached the banks of Dipper Pool he spoke again, and his question was a simple one.

'Will you go?'

Edward sighed. 'My personal belief is that the government has made the right decision in accepting the War Graves Commission proposals. It would be better if Hugh stayed in France with his comrades. Much better. Most men who served think that.'

The man next to him grunted his agreement as he continued, 'But I know my mother will not back down, which means the profound rift between us cannot be resolved unless I acquiesce – whatever my inner doubts and fears. To be frank we need each other and it's not just important for us personally, it's important for the estate and everyone who relies on it. We can't have a permanent split at the top.'

'And now your dead brother has weighed in with his opinion as well.' The colonel couldn't help smiling in sympathy at the position his friend found himself in.

'Quite.' Edward found himself smiling too. 'If I don't go he'll probably haunt me for the rest of my life.'

'And beyond,' the colonel observed, then added, 'I'll come too of course.'

Edward stopped and stared at him. 'Really? Are you sure?'

'If you are going, yes. It will be a desperate business and you will need someone you can rely on. And I think we'll need a third. Some of the work will be distinctly physical…' He let the implication hang in the air.

'Well I can think of half a dozen men on the estate who would fit the bill,' said Edward.

The older man nodded thoughtfully as they resumed walking. 'I'm sure. It's the discretion aspect that needs consideration. This thing must remain a secret for ever. Let's reflect on that for a little while and consider the other practical difficulties that immediately spring to mind. For example, do we know exactly where the grave is in the cemetery? Is the place guarded at night? How will we move the body and above all, how will we cross the Channel with it? Once we have started to address these questions perhaps the issue of who to choose as our third will become clearer.'

'Well as we know the location of the cemetery, a simple reconnaissance will be all that's needed to find his grave. It will be marked with his name.'

'Will it though? What if the names and plot numbers are only noted on a piece of paper in a file in an office somewhere in France?'

Edward said, 'I think that's unlikely. I saw plenty of temporary cemeteries and the individual graves were marked with plain wooden crosses and the men's names were painted on those.'

'Well that's a relief and it means you're right – an innocent visit to the cemetery at Rouville should tell us exactly where he is. And in essence the exhuming will be a question of planning, nerve and luck. For now I think the biggest question is the business of getting him back over the water.'

'What are your thoughts on that?' Edward asked. The colonel's experience of command was apparent and the relief he felt at having a capable partner in crime was immense.

'To smuggle or not to smuggle?' The colonel chuckled lightly and continued. 'The fundamental decision we need to make is whether we bring him back openly but with a false declaration through normal customs, or whether we choose a clandestine route using our own boat or possibly a co-operative fisherman who knows a nice quiet spot on both sides of the Channel. If we use our own boat then maybe our third man should be a competent sailor with a suitable craft.'

In the short silence that followed these remarks they looked at each other again as the enormity of what they were discussing became clear.

'What do you think the penalty for smuggling a body is?' Edward wondered aloud, then added, 'Jocelyn, are you really sure about this? I mean you're the chief constable of Oxfordshire, for heaven's sake. If we do get caught they'll throw the book at you.'

The answer he got was an enormous grin and for a moment Edward saw the daredevil younger man that he must have been. 'I think there's enough life in me for one last hurrah, Edward. And we will not fail, and we will not get caught.'

'I wish I had your confidence, but I am committed to this so we will have to do our best.'

'The first option would involve a massive bluff of course,' said the colonel thoughtfully. 'You still have your padre's uniform I assume?'

'I do, yes.'

'What would be more natural than a regimental chaplain accompanying a coffin containing a soldier who had recently died in a road accident back to England? The Commission's rules apply to casualties during the war, not those sent over there afterwards to help sort out the peace.'

Edward hesitated. In his mind's eye he pictured a tense scene on the quay in Calais as a frowning French customs officer looked at his papers and said, 'There is a problem, monsieur, please open the coffin.'

'I'm not sure. We'll need forged papers that are good enough to pass muster. How on earth would we do that?' he said cautiously.

There was another chuckle from the chief constable. 'You forget, Edward, I know a considerable number of criminals.'

*

At half past eight that evening Edward called in unannounced at Langford Hall. He let himself in at the back door and met Dereham as he was coming out of the kitchen.

'Mr Edward, good evening, sir. May I assist you with something?'

'No thanks, Dereham, I'm just off for a word with my mother. Is she in the drawing room?'

'I believe she has gone up, sir. Her mood has slumped right back down since yesterday and if anything she seems worse than ever. Very tearful I am afraid. Lilly wondered if we ought to call the doctor, but I said wait until the morning.'

'I suspect that she will be absolutely fine by then.'

With a nod to the butler Edward made his way to the entrance hall, climbed the great staircase, and walked along the corridor to his mother's bedroom. As he stood outside he could hear voices through the door and realised that Lilly was still with her mistress.

He knocked. 'Mother, it's me, Edward. Are you decent?'

The voices stopped. Then after a long moment the door opened, and the maid's face appeared. She looked tense and gave him a look that was less than complimentary. 'Good evening, Mr Edward. Yes, Lady Langford will see you.' With a little bob she squeezed past him and slipped off down the corridor.

He entered the room and saw his mother sitting in her dressing gown in an armchair by the un-curtained window. With a shock he realised that she suddenly looked much older. Their eyes met and her drawn and painful look of reproach was more than he could bear. He crossed quickly to her and kneeling by the chair he took her hand.

'I'll do it. I'll go and get him. I can't guarantee I'll manage it, but I will have a go. A proper go.' He felt a huge sense of relief as the words tumbled out and with a gasp of joy his mother's face broke into a wonderful smile which was immediately followed by an outpouring of tears as she reached for him. Edward found his own eyes were watering as they hugged and she whispered, 'Thank you, thank you,' in his ear.

Five minutes later the tension between them had dissolved completely and she was lending her able mind to the practical difficulties that were involved. However, as the suggestions came thick and fast, he felt the need to forestall her and said, 'I think there is some virtue in you not knowing the details. If you are heavily involved then it's likely the household will become aware of the plan. Staff come to know things without ever being told and in this case that is not desirable, no matter how loyal and trustworthy they are.'

She nodded slowly, disappointed, but seeing the reason behind his words. 'Very well. I will say this though, don't forget Candover Castle, Billy Montague's place down near Rye.' Her eyes softened at a memory as she continued, 'It's where I first met your father and if memory serves they have a mile or two of coastline.' She looked at him. 'A very quiet stretch of coastline.'

'Really? Do you know them well?' Edward asked. 'Have they been here?'

'Yes I do and yes they have. Most recently while you were in France. Billy is stout and very short of stature and his wife Adelaide is tall and willowy. It's funny how often that happens,' she added reflectively. 'Anyway they are both tremendously good sports and I'm sure they'd be happy to look the other way if they thought some rag was going on.'

'Do they have a boat, do you know?'

'I imagine so, living by the sea like that.' Then she added carelessly, 'Have you thought about flying?'

'Flying?' For a split second a bizarre image appeared in Edward's mind of his dead brother sitting in the rear seat of a biplane wearing a flying helmet and a rictus grin, but he quickly realised she had a point. If it was in some way possible to get him into an aircraft in France, then with the right pilot they could fly all the way back to Great Tew and land on the estate somewhere without any difficulties with customs.

'Yes, flying. It just seems worth considering anyway,' confirmed his mother.

'I can see that. But the problem would be finding an aircraft big enough and a willing and discreet pilot. And of course a suitable place to land in France. It would be a tall order, although I can see the benefits.'

'Well you will have to work these details out but let me say again how pleased I am, Edward. I was a little cruel to you I think, and I am sorry for that. Will you forgive me?'

He looked at her. 'You know I will. We've lost father and Hugh, the rest of us have to stick together. Are they on the telephone down at Candover?'

'Yes, I'll have the number in my book.'

'Would you ask them up for the weekend? Then I can have a word on the QT.'

'Of course. I'll speak to Adelaide in the morning and let you know when they are coming.'

Shortly afterwards Edward took his leave and in a thoughtful mood called in to the Black Horse before returning to Holly Cottage. A gentle buzz of conversation filled the simply furnished room and he returned nods of greeting from three men sitting around a table below the front window. Dressed in civvies Burrows was at the bar with a half empty glass of cider in front of him, his face in gentle repose. Laura Bessing was watching him. She glanced up as Edward approached, then flicked her head in the constable's direction and rolled her eyes in frustration.

Amused at the impasse he decided he would lend a hand if he could.

'Evening, Burrows, keeping an eye on your charges?' he said easily as the girl filled a pint glass from the barrel racked up behind the bar. He knew that sadly for Miss Bessing it wasn't she who was the attraction. Constable Burrows liked to lean on the bar for a couple of hours every week and listen to the local gossip.

It had been the colonel who had advised him to do it. 'Let them see you when you're not in uniform from time to time. A pint or two with the villagers doesn't do any harm at all. It gives them a chance to mention things informally if needed, and vice versa.'

'Another one?' Edward gestured at his glass.

'Oh right, thank you.' The constable finished his drink in a couple of large gulps and placed it on the bar.

'And for you, Miss Bessing?' Edward added.

'Thank you, sir. I'll have a small one. At least you know how to treat a girl,' she replied with an arch look at Burrows, who was clearly still blissfully unaware of her interest.

With a sigh she put the two full glasses on the bar and turned away in disgust.

'Pretty girl, eh?' said Edward quietly, giving the constable a pointed nudge.

He responded with a lugubrious stare. 'Miss Bessing?'

'Yes, Miss Bessing. Attractive wouldn't you say?'

'I suppose so,' came the cautious reply.

'Is she walking out do you know, Burrows? Or spoken for?'

'Not that I'm aware of, Mr Spense.'

'Ah. Available then?'

'I imagine so.'

Edward smiled inwardly, starting to realise why Laura Bessing was having an uphill battle. Nevertheless, he pressed on. 'Do you think she might welcome a bit of company when she's not working?' he asked the tall constable.

'Well she might. It's not my place to say.'

'Would you ask her?'

'Me ask her?'

'Yes you, Burrows. I really think you should. Do it for me would you?'

The young man stared out over the room for a moment and when he answered his voice was resolute. 'Alright then, Mr Spense, I will.'

Satisfied that he had done his best, Edward steered the conversation onto other things. *Surely the man would at least ask her out for a walk now.*

And so it proved. To Laura's delight Burrows rather obviously waited until everyone else had left at closing time, then with a conspicuous clearing of his throat, he spoke.

'Miss Bessing, may I have a quiet word?'

'Of course you can, Burrows.' She gave him a smile that seemed to warm the whole room and leaned forward, her face alive with interest. 'What is it?'

He coughed and shuffled his feet. 'Well it's a little embarrassing.'

She widened her eyes. 'I'm not embarrassed. I've been hoping you'd have a little chat with me. Something on your mind, is there? I've noticed you at the bar here often enough. I mean what girl wouldn't, a nice big strong chap like you.'

'Well, it's just that…' He hesitated. 'I'm not sure I should speak out or not.'

'Oh you should. You definitely should.' Her tongue played over her lips as her smile got even sweeter. 'Don't be shy, Constable, I'm all ears.'

'Well to be honest, I reckon Mr Edward fancies you.'

# Chapter Eleven

The following afternoon Lilly arrived at Holly Cottage with a note for Edward from his mother.

I've spoken to Adelaide Montague. They are busy until early September but are coming on the weekend of the 14th. Perhaps a reconnaissance over the water in the meantime? X

Edward reflected on his mother's suggestion. He had reached the conclusion that using Candover Castle made sense – being able to bring the body ashore without fear of interruption would make a huge difference. The colonel's idea of a bluff had its attractions, but they would need forged French documents to get through Calais and he wasn't confident that they could produce anything that would pass muster, no matter how skilled the forger.

There was also the danger of a person of questionable morality being aware of what was happening. The same was true of flying. So even though it meant a delay, probably until October, he instinctively felt that the Montague's estate was the way to go. And a visit to France in the meantime was a good idea. It would mean they could find out exactly where the grave was and check if the cemetery was guarded.

He called round to Marston House, but the colonel was in Oxford on police business all day, so he left a message asking him to come to Holly Cottage after supper, when Innes and Burrows were meeting him to discuss the Freeling case.

In the event all three arrived at the same time so they took the opportunity to bring the colonel up to date with their progress.

Innes took the lead with the other two interrupting when they felt the need. She told him about Edward's conversation with Jane Freeling and their puzzlement over her husband's departure on the fateful morning carrying a rope, especially as Mr Atkins had confirmed that he wasn't undertaking a task at his request.

'The thing is, Colonel, why did he have the rope with him? In fact why did he go at all? The conclusion we've reached is that someone asked Christian Freeling to meet them at the Langford Yew for some invented task that required a rope. But in reality there was no task, their intention was to kill him at the tree and then fake the suicide.'

She paused and then remarked, 'When you think about it, it's quite brilliant. The murderer contrived a situation where Mr Freeling left home with a rope and was found hanging in the tree. And they must have known it was likely that Jane Freeling would see him leaving with it and that she would make a statement to that effect.'

'It's clever, for sure. Which implies a lot of planning, so the question of motive raises its head, as it always does,' the colonel replied with a glance at Burrows.

'It's worth saying that we think one man working alone could not have strung him up after death. Not with so little damage to his neck. It just wouldn't be possible. You'd need one to lift him and another to tie the rope off,' said Edward.

The older man raised his eyebrows in surprise at this. 'So two people are involved, you think? Both present at the scene?'

Edward nodded. 'It looks like it.'

Innes said, 'Mr Freeling's brother over in Gloucester doesn't believe his brother killed himself. "Happy to be back unscathed and looking forward to settling down," was how he phrased it. But he also said Mrs Freeling saw no harm in playing both sides against the middle and had made eyes at a labourer over at West Lea Farm by the name of Jack Wright. In the end she chose Mr Freeling and Jack Wright wasn't happy by all accounts.'

The chief constable stirred in his seat. 'Right, well that's interesting. An aggrieved and rejected suitor would fit the bill, I'd have thought. Did you go and speak to him?'

'Yes I did, sir,' said Burrows.

'I was wondering when you might stir yourself to action,' the colonel observed.

Unperturbed by the implied slight, the constable withdrew his notebook from his pocket and cleared his throat. 'Acting on information received I attended West Lea Farm on the twenty-fifth of July, with the intention of interviewing Mr Jack Wright, aged thirty-seven and an agricultural labourer…'

He spoke for ten minutes and when he had finished his report, there was a brief silence.

'And that is as far as we've got to date, Colonel,' said Innes.

'I think you've done well. The information this Jack Wright gave you seems to offer a real line of enquiry. Brawls in pubs are not a motive for murder but affairs and illegitimate children are. If what he says is true and Freeling was in the habit of pursuing women who were already spoken for – well that sort of thing can lead to violence.'

'It might also help to explain the timing, sir. If a fellow discovered his wife had had an affair with Freeling, he would have had to wait until he was back from the war before he could do anything about it,' Burrows remarked.

The older man nodded thoughtfully. 'How long had he been back?'

'Three weeks,' Edward answered. 'Long enough to put a plan into action. Especially if you'd been brooding about it for two years.'

'I agree. So tell me who these women are.'

Burrows said, 'Wright mentioned two people. Mrs Virginia Bilson, and Mrs Annie Trotter. Mrs Bilson lives in Little Tew where her husband George is a carpenter. He does a lot of estate work. Mrs Trotter's husband is Ronald Trotter the pig farmer. Their place is a mile or so down Rivermead on the far side of the valley.'

'Yes, I know them both,' the colonel remarked. 'They're not the same age though. Mrs Trotter must be well into her forties now, but Virginia Bilson can't be more than twenty-five. I remember her getting married at St Mary's. She was obviously pregnant, but as she was walking down the aisle with a big grin on her face no one turned a hair. She'd hardly be the first girl to make sure things would be alright between her and her husband before the happy day,' the colonel said.

'Well that's true enough,' Edward agreed.

'So Wright's belief is that both these women had affairs with Christian Freeling before he settled down with his wife to be? And that it's possible he fathered Virginia Bilson's child? That's your current working hypothesis?'

'That is where the trail seems to be leading, yes,' Innes answered.

The colonel sighed. 'You know it's a devilishly tricky thing to investigate. Short of asking the ladies directly and hoping you get an honest answer, which seems unlikely, nothing springs to mind. And even if you do find one or both of them transgressed, there's still the business of proving one of their husbands is a murderer.'

'Or both,' said Burrows reflectively. There was a moment's silence as they all looked at him. 'Well we are looking for two men, aren't we. What if they discovered they were both cuckolded and planned the thing together?'

'A fair point. Well you've got your work cut out. Keep me informed. I will say this though, it feels as though there might be a case to answer in this somewhere. I meant what I said, Innes, if you can provide me with a strong suspect we will openly examine it.'

He nodded at Burrows and continued, 'And if your instincts are that Jack Wright is a wrong 'un too, then keep him on the table. He might have invented the whole philanderer line to take the pressure off himself. Beyond that I'll leave you to carry on and will await developments with interest. Edward, did you want a word about that other matter?'

'I did, yes.' With that the meeting broke up and shortly afterwards Edward and Jocelyn were alone in the parlour.

'I've told my mother that I am going to get Hugh and that you will be helping,' Edward said without preamble.

'Ah, how did she react?'

The broad-shouldered sandy-haired man smiled. 'It would be fair to say she was delighted. And I must confess I am relieved. If I had continued to refuse it would have hung over us for the rest of our lives and that would have been intolerable.'

The colonel nodded. 'True. Well the die is cast then. Will she tell Piers, do you think?'

Edward shook his head. 'No. We have agreed between us that it is better to present him with a fait accompli, assuming we are successful. My brother is not a risk taker and there's no telling what he might do if he knew.'

'Fair enough. Any further thoughts following our conversation the other day?'

'Well yes. It turns out mother is friends with a family called Montague who live in a place called Candover Castle near Rye. They own a nice quiet stretch of coast, and she thinks they would not be averse to turning a blind eye if we wanted to bring Hugh ashore there. Although we wouldn't be specific about the cargo of course.'

'Really?' the older man responded. 'Well that might be handy.'

'Quite. They're coming up for the weekend in September, so I'll have a word then. It means a delay but that's no bad thing because I increasingly feel that the scheme would benefit from a scouting trip over to France before we go in earnest. Assuming the Montagues agree then, rather than the false papers idea I think I'd prefer a discreet boat ride across the Channel, and that will necessitate some planning on the French side. We'll need to see the lie of the land.'

The colonel scratched his forehead before replying. 'Yes, I see your point. Very well, let's organise a trip. Three or four days should be enough. We'll need to reconnoitre the cemetery first and foremost of course, but we also need to put some transport arrangements in place in advance. We'll need to hire a large car or small lorry over there.'

He hesitated at this point and the young man saw a rare indecision in his eyes. 'What is it?' he asked.

'Edward, I'm going to suggest something difficult but it's my belief that it is necessary. When we recover Hugh I think we will need to leave the coffin where it is and transfer his body into a crate of some sort.'

'That really is getting down to the nitty gritty, isn't it.' Edward grimaced. 'You're thinking that a coffin would be too easily identified if we get stopped for any reason?'

'Correct. Especially if it looks as though it has been in the ground for a year or so. There is also the question of leaving the cemetery looking normal. If we remove the coffin there won't be enough earth to fully refill the grave. Someone might notice. He shrugged and looked at his friend.

Edward nodded slowly, turning the images over in his mind. 'Yes, I see what you mean. A nice nondescript crate. Something we can fold him into, in a blanket. Maybe a yard or so cube.'

'That's right. Lined with thick oilskin so we can seal it tight. And with carrying handles. So we can slip a couple of lengths of wood along the sides and lift. I'm assuming we won't be able to get the vehicle right next to the grave.'

Edward stood up. 'I'll find a notebook. We need to start writing these things down.'

*

A week later the pair of them caught the train to London and travelled on down to Newhaven for the ferry to Boulogne. The colonel had told his wife and received whole-hearted support and Eve had told Lady Langford that she was in on the secret. So in that second week of August 1919 four people knew of the plan to illegally exhume Hugh Spense.

After staying overnight at a hotel on the seafront in Newhaven the two men boarded the elderly SS *Caledonian Star* for the crossing. It was a miserable passage. The weather was poor and the vessel vibrated and laboured in steep short-pitched waves, while heavy squalls meant the passengers were confined in the crowded and increasingly malodorous saloon. However, as they came alongside the French quay the clouds started to break and a watery sun appeared.

By half past twelve they were perusing the menu in a restaurant on the edge of the main square. Edward's French was reasonable, the older man's less so, although he did lay claim to 'being quite useful in Cantonese', to his companion's surprise. In any event they ordered without difficulty and enjoyed sole and an excellent bottle of Muscadet.

After they had finished eating Edward asked the waiter where they might hire a vehicle for a few days and received directions to a place a ten minute walk from the square. Shortly afterwards they found themselves outside a cavernous working garage with several cars parked on the forecourt. The proprietor proved to be a jovial and expressive man by the name of Benedet and after inspecting various vehicles, they decided on a large new Citroën with a folding roof.

'You are taking a touring holiday?' Benedet asked as they completed the paperwork and laid down a considerable deposit in cash.

'We are going to see a member of my family near Cambrai,' Edward replied, on the basis that the best lies are closest to the truth. 'We will bring the car back in two or three days. We intend to repeat the trip in October and on that occasion we will need a small lorry. Can you assist us with that also?'

'Of course, monsieur. I have such a vehicle available at a few days' notice, so if you send me a telegram advising of your requirements I will ensure everything is in order.' He handed over a card with the necessary details embossed on the face.

'Excellent. I would also appreciate a road map if you have one. The last time I was here the army did the driving.'

The Frenchman laughed. 'I'm sure we can find something in the office. You fought in the war, monsieur?'

'I was here for three years. I must say it will be nice to enjoy your country without being shot at.'

The Frenchman extended his hand, his expression suddenly serious. 'Welcome back, monsieur and thank you. We know what you British did and how you suffered alongside us. It will not be forgotten.'

Twenty minutes later with the weather improving by the minute the men drove through the outskirts of Boulogne and headed south on the main road, as suggested by the obliging Monsieur Benedet.

'Along here as far as Montreuil in about twenty miles,' said the colonel, peering at the road map, 'and then we strike east for Arras. I suggest we plan to put up there for the night and push on to Cambrai in the morning. If there's time we can call in to the War Graves Directorate regional office in Arras tonight and find out the location of the cemetery where Hugh is buried. If not first thing in the morning.'

Edward nodded silently, his eyes on the road. The Citroën was a fine vehicle, and he was enjoying driving it, but the business of being on the other side of the road was a complication he had forgotten about, although thankfully traffic was light.

They reached Montreuil without incident and then had an enjoyable run through the attractive countryside of Pas-de-Calais in the afternoon sunshine. Many of the roads were tree-lined and the colonel noticed that there was surprisingly little to show that they were driving through the hinterland of the war to end all wars. In fact it was only when they approached the western side of Arras and the battlefields that marked the furthermost point of the German advance that craters began to appear in the fields next to the road.

As they continued east the destruction steadily increased and they saw farmhouses that had been reduced to rubble, woodlands shelled to destruction, and finally whole villages with barely a wall standing. The quality of the road surface deteriorated greatly, and they were regularly diverted onto temporary bridges to cross a canal or river. The rich farmland they had passed through on their journey disappeared and by the time the skeletal outline of Arras appeared in the distance they were surrounded by broken bare earth.

Barbed wire, shattered tree stumps, redundant trenches and dark pools of water stretched away in every direction. It was a hellish prospect and as the mood in the car darkened Edward pulled into the side of the road and turned the engine off.

A silence fell. There were no birds singing and no movement in the landscape.

'The French call this the Red Zone,' he said quietly. 'The area of complete devastation. In many places it's over twenty miles wide and it stretches all the way down to Verdun – over two hundred miles.'

He sighed before continuing. 'Look here, Jocelyn, I think we've miscalculated. I suggest the best thing is to turn around and head back the way we've come until we get out of this area. Then we've a chance of finding a hotel. I can't see a single building up ahead that's got a roof on it. In the morning we'll see what we can find out regarding the War Graves Directorate. What do you think?'

The older man was staring out across the wasteland, his expression grim. 'I fought in conflicts abroad, Edward, small colonial wars mainly, out in the Far East, but nothing like this. One read about it of course, even saw photographs, but to see it here and now, the reality. Well, I must admit it is sobering.'

'Imagine it on a freezing night with gas drifting over from no man's land and the Germans following it in behind a bombardment,' Edward said. 'Hell on earth doesn't do it justice.'

Something in his tone alarmed his travelling companion, who turned and looked at him, his face concerned. 'Are you alright?' he asked.

'It's seeing it all again. This is the place where I lost my mind, Jocelyn. And with good reason. Look in any direction and I guarantee there will be bodies buried under the mud. British, French and German. The ones who simply disappeared, shot, blown up or drowned. I should have thought about it before and prepared myself.' He shook his head then wordlessly restarted the car, turned around, and they retraced their steps.

Within twenty minutes they were back in untouched countryside where verdant green pasture was scattered with cattle, and woods and canals stretched across the sunlit farmland. The contrast with the monochrome brown of the Red Zone was jarring and they were both silent and thoughtful as they entered a small town they had passed through earlier and parked in the main square. A hotel faced the town hall and they entered and took two rooms without difficulty.

They dined in the hotel and struck up a conversation with a middle-aged balding Englishman who was eating alone at the next table. They invited him to join them for a brandy in the lounge. His name was James Knighton, and he was a construction engineer on secondment from a British firm.

'I'm over here helping to plan the rebuilding of Arras. The destruction is appalling, ninety-five per cent of the houses have been destroyed and most of the public buildings too. It's the same all the way along the Red Zone. Imagine a wasteland twenty miles wide being blasted through the midlands of England from coast to coast. Our entire industrial heartland destroyed, Birmingham, Coventry, Wolverhampton, all gone – all the iron and steel plants, the heavy manufacturing, entire towns and cities laid to waste, and all the farmland that surrounded them. That's what they're dealing with over here.'

He paused and looked at them. 'There are millions of displaced refugees in temporary accommodation. Even getting reliable supplies of drinking water re-established has been a huge challenge. The shelling destroyed all the wells and springs, you see.'

'How long have you been over here, Knighton?' asked the colonel.

'Three months. There is a plan in place for Arras now and there will be work for British firms, but even clearing the rubble will take years. And the cost of it all is frightening of course. The French government is footing the bill and has undertaken to pay reparations to those who lost everything. You wonder how they will afford it.'

As he continued to talk, the sheer scale of the task facing the French became clear to the two listening men. In Britain the main emphasis had been on the casualties they had suffered and to some extent the cost of the war, but in France and Belgium the scars ran much deeper. The very fabric of the country had been torn apart.

Edward fobbed off Knighton's enquiry about their reason for being there with vague references to family connections near Cambrai.

'I'm afraid that copped it like Arras, so I hope you find what you're looking for. People back in Blighty think the war's over and that's an end to it. But here in France in some ways the battle is only just beginning.'

The following morning Edward and the colonel drove into Arras. They were mentally prepared for the destruction but even so the scale of the rebuilding task was shocking. The entire city had been reduced to rubble and in many places no walls were left standing. Narrow-gauge railway lines had been laid in some roads and gangs of labourers were slowly loading the shattered stonework into light wagons pulled by horses.

After stopping and enquiring twice they found their way to a British military encampment on the eastern side of the town. At the gate they were directed to the offices of the War Graves Directorate and found the place after five minutes' walk.

In the car they had discussed the best approach to take and had decided that there was little risk in simply declaring themselves and asking for the location of Hugh's grave in order that they might visit and pay their respects. Edward felt it was a reasonable enough enquiry and assumed they were unlikely to be the only ones making such a pilgrimage.

And so it proved. The army clerk who attended to them did not bat an eyelid at their request. With a respectful nod and a suggestion that they, 'Please take a seat for a moment, gentlemen,' he walked over to another part of the marquee where a long row of filing cabinets stood. They watched as he peered at the labels on the drawers before opening one and having flicked through a number of files, pulled one out and returned with it.

Both men stood up again at his approach.

'Here we are, sirs. Spense, Hugh George, Lieutenant 2nd Battalion Coldstream Guards. Is that the gentleman?'

To Edward's horror emotion suddenly overwhelmed him and he felt his eyes starting to prick as tears welled. 'Yes,' he managed to say, 'that's him.'

The colonel glanced quickly at him and took over. 'Indeed it is, Private. Where is he?'

'He's temporarily interred at Rouville military cemetery three miles south-west of Cambrai, sir. Rouville is the name of the village. The precise grave location is number twenty-four on row sixteen. It will be marked with a named cross.'

'Thank you, would you write that down for us?'

'Of course.' The private looked sympathetically at Edward. 'A glass of water, sir? Or a mug of sweet tea before you set off? I'm sure we can rustle something up.'

'That's kind but we'll press on,' the older man replied firmly. The less the man remembered the better, he thought.

They headed out of Arras on the Cambrai road and slowly signs of normality started to appear in the landscape. Some farm buildings were still standing, hedges, woods and individual trees were undamaged and the condition of the road improved. As they approached the town it was clear that the damage across that part of the countryside was relatively light, although Cambrai itself had been heavily bombarded.

Aided by the colonel's efficient map reading and some shouted instructions from a beret-wearing local they finally drove into Rouville at lunchtime and stopped to ask for directions to the British cemetery. On hearing that it was only a ten minute drive away they decided to eat before proceeding.

It was the colonel's idea. He could see his companion was in an emotional state and the older man felt that a plate of food and a brandy or two would stand them both in good stead for the trauma to come. They sat outside a homely bistro on the square and looked at the church as they ate roast chicken.

'Hit you hard has it, coming back?' he ventured as they drank their coffee.

'More than expected. Hearing the clerk say his name was like a hammer blow, Jocelyn. The reality of knowing I'll be standing three feet from him.' He shivered. 'In Great Tew his death was appalling but remote somehow. Now I feel I'm having to confront it all over again. I hope that I don't let you down.'

*And I hope you don't see anything. That might be the last straw, especially as we've got to dig him up*, thought the colonel, but his face gave nothing away as he answered.

'You won't, I'm sure of it. This reconnaissance was a good idea for both of us. It will be a huge help knowing what to expect when we come back so we can concentrate on the task in hand.' He gave his companion an encouraging smile. 'We're doing well, Edward, and we're making progress.'

# Chapter Twelve

Even though there was little sign of war damage, the temporary British military cemetery at Rouville was a grim place. The colonel guessed that there were about a thousand men buried there, concentrated from hastily dug field graves or recovered from where they had fallen on the battlefield.

The two men walked silently along the end of the numbered rows. At twenty-four they turned and slowly progressed between the graves, counting in their heads. Each one was marked with a pile of earth rising six inches out of the grassy field and a white cross that had a name and regiment painted onto it. There were no other details, and the colonel assumed the rest was held in filing cabinets in Arras.

Edward stopped and said quietly, 'Here he is.'

They looked down. It was just the same as the others. Apart from the uneven black letters – Hugh George Spense, Coldstream Guards.

'We've found him. That's a good thing. A very good thing indeed.' The colonel looked at his friend whose cheeks were wet with tears. 'I'll give you a minute.' He squeezed his upper arm and walked on down the row, listening to the raw sobs that followed him.

The dismal white crosses stretched away in every direction, each one representing misery and grief for a family in Britain. *The best and bravest, cut down in their prime.* Feeling heavy with emotion himself he walked gloomily on, trying to think tactically about how they would get Hugh out.

The cemetery lay on its own, half a mile from the outskirts of the village. The road ran along one side for its entire length and the entrance was halfway down. The gate crossed a water-filled ditch that ran parallel to the road, which he assumed was why there was no hedge on that side. Anyone driving along would have a clear view of the graves, he realised.

The other three sides were enclosed by a head-high hedge with trees at intervals and he realised that it was simply a farmer's field that had been commandeered. The land was flat and as he slowly rotated his gaze he saw that there were very few buildings in sight. Ahead of him a wood bordered the far side of the cemetery and he walked on towards it before stopping and looking at the last of the crosses in the row.

The end man was Albert Arthur Bacon, Royal Artillery. The paint had dribbled down from the capital B in Bacon. It looked uncaring and he hoped that Albert's parents wouldn't see it.

*These are men who almost made it. Another two or three months and the war had been over.*

It was a depressing thought and, sighing, he looked back along the row. Edward was kneeling by his brother's grave and seemed to be speaking to him. In the distance the Citroën was visible, parked on the road. It wasn't a long way from Hugh's grave back to the gate. If they had a crate with carrying arms they could do it, he was sure. But to be caught would be appalling – beyond disgrace, so they dare not risk a torch or lantern. The thing would have to be done on a night when there was a little moonlight but not too much. In the small hours. An approach in the lorry with the lights off. Into the graveyard with the empty crate. One man left at the gate to keep watch on the road, two do the deed.

*Yes, it all begins to fall into place now I've seen it.*

He saw his friend stand up and raise his arm. Signalling in return he walked back along the row. 'How are you?' he asked when he reached him.

'I'm alright,' Edward said sadly. 'It's just the reality of knowing he's here. So close.' He looked out across the graves and visibly shivered. 'This place is full of bitter anger and regret. It's drifting around the crosses like smoke from a fire. I had a sudden strong feeling that we shouldn't disturb him, but these men will all be moved again anyway once Mr Lutyens and the builders have finished their work. That'll be twice, in many cases, no wonder people at home are upset.'

The colonel frowned sympathetically. 'True.' He briefly outlined his thoughts on the tactics they should employ when they returned, and Edward nodded his agreement.

'That sounds sensible.' He stood and looked around for a moment. 'This will do for now, won't it? We've seen the set-up and can find him again easily enough.'

'Agreed. Let's head back to the coast and continue our recce there.'

The two men turned and walked slowly back along the line of graves, then out through the gate. Shortly afterwards the big Citroën started up and set off in the direction of Rouville.

*

In Great Tew, Eve found herself at something of a loose end. Not that she needed her beloved husband around, he was often away on police business anyway, it was simply that for the next couple of days there was nothing in her diary. Normally she would have called in at the hall, but Lady Claire had disappeared off to London to 'refurbish her wardrobe', taking Lilly with her.

With the afternoon drifting on, she decided to take a stroll along the high street and see whom she met. This turned out to be Bert Williams, who was making his way down the gentle slope from the church. She smiled at his approach. Somehow he always looked as though he was returning from some errand that had been just a little on the wrong side of the law.

'Good afternoon, Bert. How are you?' she enquired, stopping.

'Very well thank you, Mrs Dance, and you too I hope. I'm just heading over to Holly Cottage to pick up my wife. We're going into Banbury to see her mother.' His even tone gave nothing away, but his eyes suggested there were many things he considered preferable to this excursion.

'Family duties, we all have them. Tell me, any local gossip, Bert? Anything I need to know?' She said it jokingly and with a smile but to her surprise a guilty shadow crossed his face.

'What makes you say that?' he enquired.

Curious, she smiled disarmingly and said, 'Oh just that you seem to be a chap with his ear to the ground. Don't worry, you can ignore the fact that I'm married to the chief constable, Bert. Have you been out with your fishing rod again? Nocturnally, I mean?'

This sally produced a blank look for a moment. *He's thinking what to say*, Eve thought. *There is something.* Then a grin appeared on his face. 'As it happens I have been out once or twice…'

He told her about Constable Burrows, Mrs Sutton, and the three fat trout from Dipper Pool. She laughed, amused at the way he had wriggled off the hook. Not for the first time she reflected that there were many people like Bert Williams in Great Tew. It was a great mistake to assume because they led simple lives they were stupid.

'Anything else, Bert?' she asked him in a conspiratorial tone as he concluded his tale. She was certain that there was, and now she had him talking she was intent on extracting it.

His eyes shifted from her, and he stared down the road towards the market cross. 'Did I hear right? There's a question about whether Christian Freeling killed himself?'

She looked at him and then waited as Ada Dale the greengrocer's daughter passed them with a nod of greeting, before replying. 'In confidence, Bert, and this time you must remember that I am married to the chief constable. Yes, I believe some quiet enquiries are being made. Why do you ask?'

His next question was a genuine surprise. 'When a woman is pregnant, how long is it before she shows?'

Eve was startled. 'What on earth has prompted that?' she asked.

'Just wondering. For a friend, like.' The lie was so obvious that she ignored it.

'Don't tell me you and Edna are expecting another happy event,' she teased him.

Instead of smiling back he looked at her directly. 'Seriously, when would you know by looking? If she was dressed.'

Eve thought for a moment. 'Well it depends on the woman in question and what she's wearing of course, but anything between three and five months I'd say.'

He nodded. 'Yes, thought so.' And with that he nimbly sidestepped around her and set off at a brisk pace for the corner of Stream Cross. Within ten seconds he was out of sight.

Eve stared after him, turning over the exchange in her mind. Bert and his wife were in their fifties, so she assumed he had not been referring to their intimate domestic arrangements.

*But without doubt something had prompted his question.*

She continued thoughtfully up the street and bought some currant buns from the bakers. The wean was an enthusiastic consumer of these delights, especially when piled high with the cook's blackberry jam. With her package in hand she wandered on up to the churchyard and walked round to the wall where Innes and Edward had made peace after their first meeting at Marston House.

She sat down and looked out across the valley, still absorbed by Bert's cryptic questions. She knew of two young women in Great Tew that were pregnant, and both were happily married. Jocelyn had also mentioned that Nell Atkins at Beech Farm was finally with child after a long wait. These things were hardly an uncommon event. Was someone else in the village pregnant but not happy about it? Perhaps even concealing the fact? Was that what he meant?

She removed one of the buns from the bag and ate it slowly, relishing the moist sweet taste and little bursts of flavour as she chewed the currants. Then a thought struck her. The occasional attentions Bert paid to Mrs Sutton his wife's younger sister were an open secret in the village. She would be in her early forties, Eve imagined. Not too late to make a mistake. Certainly it wasn't out of the question to fall pregnant at that age.

Satisfied that she may well have hit upon the solution she resolved to have a good look at the woman next time she saw her, even if it meant inventing some pretext to pop round.

When she got back to Marston House she deposited the buns in the kitchen, where they were received with a smile of approval by Mrs Franks. Making her way into the drawing room she saw the French windows were open and Ellie and the wean were playing with a ball on the lawn. Deciding to change her dress she climbed the elegant staircase and made her way along the landing towards their bedroom.

Splashing noises were coming from the bathroom and she realised that Innes had decided to bathe before supper. For reasons that were not entirely clear to her, she walked down the corridor to their guest's bedroom. The door was ajar, and swung open at her gentle touch.

It was a pleasant airy room, with a wide sash window that looked down into the back garden. A small dressing table stood in the bay and a walnut chest of drawers was placed against the wall to her right. She noticed Innes's spectacles were sitting on top of it, next to her handbag.

Noting the continued splashing coming from the door behind her, she entered the room and picked the glasses up. She turned them over in her hand. They were surprisingly heavy. On impulse she put them on and stared out through the window. To her surprise she could see perfectly clearly. The faint shading in the lenses turned everything a little darker but there was no distortion in the focus. They were clearly made of plain glass.

*A girl who hides her face behind spectacles she doesn't need. Why would she do that?*

These intriguing deliberations were interrupted by the sound of the plug being pulled and a gurgle of draining water. Quickly she removed the spectacles and replaced them, and by the time the bathroom door opened she was safely ensconced in her own room, considering what dress to wear for the evening.

However her discovery would not go quietly to the back of her mind. In conjunction with what she had realised about Innes at the Beltane stone some weeks earlier, she increasingly felt it might be time for some plain speaking. And as Jocelyn was away for another couple of days, now was as good a moment as any. So, after dinner, and with the wean tucked up and lovingly kissed goodnight by Innes, Ellie, Mrs Franks and Eve in turn, as he clearly considered his right, she broached the subject.

'It's wonderful that you have developed such warm feelings for Jaikie. I'm sure if your sister is looking down from on high she will be relieved that he has such a loving and trustworthy guardian.'

Innes looked at her through her spectacles. They were sitting in the drawing room and the French windows were now closed to keep the chill of the night air at bay. 'Yes, let's hope so,' she replied.

Eve tiptoed forward. 'I mean, she will be looking down won't she, Innes?'

The younger woman raised her head and smiled. 'Are you suggesting she'll be looking up? From the other place?'

'I suppose what I'm really asking is this. Will she be looking at all?' Eve responded gently.

Innes stirred uneasily in her seat. 'Meaning what exactly?'

'Meaning, dear Innes, and please understand I make no judgement here, do you have a sister at all?' The young woman looked at her but said nothing, so Eve carried on as though walking on eggshells.

'Nothing of this conversation will go further, I can assure you of that. It's just that I've watched you with the boy. You don't just show a fondness for him, you show a mother's love. I think that the delightful fellow is your son and that your sister is perhaps an understandable invention to protect you both. Would that be a fair thing to say?'

Innes looked out of the French windows for a long moment.

*At last. It had to come. You always knew that.*

She turned and looked at the older woman. 'Yes, that would be a fair thing to say. The wean is mine, conceived out of wedlock.'

'And the father?' Eve asked quietly.

'A travelling salesman. From Arbroath. Or so he said,' she added.

'You are not in touch I take it?'

'Correct. It was a one-night stand while I was on holiday in Oban. My foolish, foolish, highland fling,' she said bitterly. Eve moved to her side and took her hand.

'Innes, I say again, I will not judge you and our conversation is utterly confidential, but please tell me what happened. Get it off your chest.'

And with her friend's hand held tightly in her grip Innes started to talk.

'I was twenty-two years old and had just finished my third year at medical school. A mixed group of us were on a walking holiday and as the days passed a couple of the fellows let me know they were keen to get to know me better. Since my teens I have always attracted the attention of the opposite sex, Eve, but I didn't welcome it. My focus was on my studies. I wanted to qualify and get on. I didn't dislike men, just didn't have time for them. I had other priorities.'

'How very sensible, my dear,' Eve murmured. 'So what happened?'

'One night when we were in Oban we all went to the public house and one of the men in our party got a little too pushy. I was angry with him and ended up leaving our group and talking to this other fellow who was drinking at the bar. It was just to teach my admirer a lesson really. I had a dram or two, which was unusual for me, and somehow when the others went back to our digs I stayed behind. Then I had another dram or two and, well,' she hesitated, and her voice tightened, 'I ended up in his room. Oh, make no mistake he didn't force himself on me, I was more than willing.'

Eve could feel the bitter self-recrimination that still burned in the girl and squeezed her hand. 'If it's any consolation you're not the first and you won't be the last. So you discovered you were pregnant?'

'Yes, a few weeks later, but I was back in Glasgow by then and of course the fellow was long gone. I simply had no idea how to contact him. To this day he doesn't know that he's fathered my child.'

'And what happened about your studies?'

'I told them my mother was ill and requested a sabbatical, which they granted. Then I confessed to my parents and thankfully they were understanding enough to have me back. We decided I should leave Glasgow until the thing was done and they rented a house in Dumfries. My father couldn't come because of his job, but mother and I lived there pretty much incognito until Jaikie arrived. Once the wean was feeding on solids I went back to the city and left him there.'

'That must have been very difficult for you.' Eve was starting to understand just how single-minded this young woman was. 'Leaving your boy like that.'

She nodded wistfully. 'I went back every weekend. Fridays were joyful but leaving him on Sunday nights was horrible. Every single time. It never got any better. He'd go to bed and I'd catch the late bus back to Glasgow ready for lectures on Monday. My parents were marvellous, they never blamed me just accepted what had happened. In time my mother moved back to Glasgow, and we settled down in the house. The story was that a cousin had succumbed to the flu and my mother had taken the wean on.'

She shrugged, and added, 'When I came down here I just amended the lie a little.'

'They must miss him terribly now, with you being down here.'

She nodded. 'I write every week of course, and I tell them all about how kind you have been and how well we've both settled, but yes, I'm sure they must.'

There was a brief silence then Eve said, 'Anyway the scheme worked, and you qualified two years later?'

'I did. And it wasn't easy. I was so angry, with myself mainly, but with all men too. Which is rather unfair of course but the thing was very raw.' She pointed to her glasses. 'I got these made by an optician. I told them they were for a stage play and that I needed the biggest, ugliest spectacles he could come up with. The lenses are just plain tinted glass. For the rest of my course I wore them every day, to keep the men at bay and to remind myself of my own stupidity. A hair shirt of a kind.' She shrugged rather hopelessly. 'Now they're just a habit. My protective shield against the world.'

'Take them off,' Eve said with a warm smile. 'Let me have a look at you.'

'If you like.' As she removed them Eve found herself looking into a pair of the most luminous blue-grey eyes she had ever seen. With her full face in view Innes Knox was a strikingly beautiful young woman. *No wonder she attracted men.*

'Oh, my dear, I can see why you were pursued.' She squeezed her hand again. 'Can I just say thank you for telling me your secrets. I feel it is incumbent on me to tell you mine, and perhaps I will, but we've had enough confidences for one day. Rest assured you and the wean are welcome here for as long as you wish to stay, and if you wish to continue sporting your man-repellers for the moment, then I will not stand in your way.'

She smiled as she said this and thought, *But we're going to have to make sure Edward Spense sees you without them, Innes.*

'Thank you. You have all made us both so welcome, we really are truly grateful.'

'I do think you should invite your parents down. I'd like to meet them if nothing else. Now then, perhaps we'll have a little whisky to celebrate a Rubicon crossed.'

# Chapter Thirteen

August drifted into early September and in Great Tew the familiar routines of rural life were observed with relief by a population hungry for normality after the horrors of the past four years.

For parents whose sons had gone to war the waiting had been the worst thing – the dread sense that at any minute of any day they might hear the knock of the post boy bearing a telegram with OHMS printed on the envelope. If the son was an officer the telegram would be handwritten. The parents of enlisted men received form B.104-82 with the blanks filled in by the postmaster.

*It is my painful duty to inform you…*

Over the four years of war twenty-seven such telegrams had been received in Great Tew and its environs. The first had been greeted with profound shock, the last with familiar and sympathetic acceptance, and feelings of grief and loss still resonated through many homes and families across the estate.

Nevertheless, slowly the timeless rhythms of an English village summer wove a healing magic. Cottage gardens were in full flower and alive with bees, and neat rows of vegetables ripened in carefully tended plots. A sign on the pub door announced that the giant marrow competition had been re-established and the village cricket team played some matches. And to the relief of the Reverend Tukes church fetes were no longer solely dedicated to fundraising for the war.

To general celebration a second hay crop was grown and cut – it was a good year for it after the storms had passed – and the lambs and calves were finally weaned off their mothers and grew fat and strong in the lush pastures by the river Cherwell. Cornfields were cropped and the land ploughed and, as mid-September approached and tones of russet and brown appeared in the landscape, one of the high points of the year arrived; the Great Tew ploughing match and Ball.

The whole day was personally sponsored by Lady Langford in memory of her husband who had been a popular and enthusiastic patron. A great marquee was erected on the lawns of Langford Hall and in the afternoon the high street echoed to the sound of hooves as six grinning and waving ploughmen rode their magnificent heavy horses up towards the field beside St Mary's. The village emptied to follow them.

Each man ploughed a fifty yard furrow down to a peg in the field, turned and came back and then went down and back again. Four furrows in parallel. Marks were awarded for straightness and evenness of depth and width, and the neatness of the turn. A man leaving the slightest gap between furrows would not expect to win.

It was an exacting test of man and horse working together and a respectful silence settled across the large crowd as each team took their turn, punctuated only by the jingle of the harness and instructions given to the horse by each ploughman. The three judges with the onerous task of choosing the winner were Lord Langford, Giles Stafford the estate manager and Thomas Watkin the senior arable farmer on the estate. All three men wore tweed suits, brown boots and trilby hats and approached their task with due gravity. Stafford carried a clipboard and the ploughmen stood as impassive as their horses as their work was assessed.

Finally a decision was reached, and Lord Langford walked forward and shook the hand of a young man called Dane Calthorpe. 'Congratulations, Mr Calthorpe, you set a very high standard of ploughing and are a worthy winner. As normal, you will be presented with your trophy later in the evening in the marquee by Lady Langford. Well done again.'

Then as five chimes from the bell of St Mary's rang clear over the field he called out the traditional invitation to the expectant crowd. 'Ladies and gentlemen, the dowager Lady Langford invites you to join her for refreshments and later on a dance, in the grounds of Langford Hall. I'm sure you all know the way, but just in case you don't, follow me.'

He raised his trilby and carrying it high in the air, strode towards the gate. With a great cheer the grinning villagers, estate tenants and farm workers, all dressed in their best clothes, followed him.

*

Later in the evening after everyone had eaten their fill from a beef steer that had been slaughtered and spit-roasted especially for the occasion, Lilly and Ellie the maid from Marston House managed to find a seat at an empty table in a corner of the noisy marquee. They each had a glass of cider and were waiting for the music to start, while keeping an eye on three grinning, nudging, farm lads who kept looking over at them.

'Look there's Laura Bessing from the pub. Let's get her over here to even the numbers up,' whispered Lilly, who saw no reason not to move things along a bit. When the girl saw her beckoning she came over.

'Sit down for a while won't you, Laura?' said Ellie. 'The band will be starting soon and we're hoping those fellows might offer us a dance.'

The latest arrival gave them a long cool look. 'They're from Little Tew, aren't they?'

'Yes. Mine's the tall one, in case you're asking,' giggled Lady Langford's maid, emboldened by the cider.

'Lilly White, don't you be too forward now,' Ellie said in a shocked tone. 'They might get expectations.'

'Lilly White by name but not by nature, is that it?' Laura smiled. 'Well I hope you have better luck than me.'

'The long arm of the law still evading you, is he?' Lilly grinned back. The barmaid's unrequited pursuit of Constable Burrows was common knowledge in the village, although the object of her affections remained sublimely unaware.

'I sometimes wonder if he's set up to be a policeman at all, he's not one to take a hint, that's for sure.' She told the girls about his erroneous interpretation of Edward Spense's attempts to smooth the path for her, and the story was greeted with hilarity.

As the laughter died down Lilly noticed that a fourth man had joined their quarry, meaning the numbers were unequal again. 'Darn,' she said. 'We need another. They'll only come over if there's a match.'

'You're an expert then?' enquired Laura.

'I wouldn't say that,' she replied primly, then as her eyes scanned the room she stood up and called, 'Winnie, Winnie, over here.' A moment later the maid from Beech Farm joined them.

'Hello, ladies,' she said, her cheeks clearly flushed. She sat down at the last available seat around the table and gave a little hiccup. 'Whoops.'

They watched and applauded as a bashfully grinning Dane Calthorpe received the Ploughman's Cup from Lady Langford, then Giles Stafford announced, 'Ladies and gentlemen, dancing will begin in five minutes, so please take your partners!'

'Anyone else here from Beech Farm, Winnie?' asked Lilly, her eyes on the men from Little Tew.

After a pause for another hiccup she replied, 'No, just me. I borrowed a bike to cycle over. Nell's seven months gone now, and Isaac's stayed in with her. I'm not sure why Mr Atkins hasn't come, to be honest.'

'Perhaps he still misses his wife?' Lilly pointed out. 'It's only been a couple of years.'

'Maybe, maybe not,' she replied, then took another long gulp of cider.

'Meaning what, Winnie?' asked Laura. She didn't really know the girl but something in her tone stirred her curiosity.

Winnie looked at her. 'Some mornings Mr Atkins's bed hasn't been slept in much when I go up to do him. Like he's just had a quick snooze in it. One day he said to me, "Winnie, I'm still that grief-stricken I can't sleep at night, so I go out and wander the estate." It was like he was giving me an excuse, you know?'

She paused, her face suddenly troubled.

'Is everything all right, Winnie?' asked Lilly.

A look of indecision appeared on her face for a moment and then she blurted, 'It isn't my place to say, but I think there's something else. A thing that no one knows…' The girls leaned forward, realising that a tasty piece of gossip was about to be revealed.

But before she could say any more Laura saw Lilly's eyes look over her shoulder and her face widen in a welcoming smile, rich in promise, as a voice behind her said, 'Evening, ladies, we were wondering if you'd like to have a dance with us?'

'We certainly would,' said Lilly gleefully and before Laura had turned to face the men, the lady's maid was round the table and right in front of the tallest of them. 'That would be lovely,' she said, standing close with her face turned up to his. Then taking his hand she led him off through the crowd towards the far end of the marquee where a wooden floor had been laid.

'Blimey, she's quick off the mark,' one of the remaining men remarked, slightly bemused, but within moments the other young women had organised themselves and paired up. The Ploughman's Ball was one of the matchmaking events of the year and, for tragic reasons, young men were in short supply. A girl had to be ready to take her chance.

And whatever telling remark Winnie was about to make about life at Beech Farm was forgotten.

At the only reserved table in the marquee Lady Spense sat with Eve and Innes and watched the throng. She saw the four men cross the floor to the maids' table, the tall one in the vanguard, two close behind and a nervous tail-end Charlie at the back, and gave a little laugh as her maid jumped to her feet and captured the leader. *He is definitely the best looking*, she mused, and Lilly had clearly been ready.

She hoped she would be careful. The occasional rumour had reached her about the girl, and she thought the sooner she was safely married off the better. The last thing they needed to be dealing with was an unwelcome surprise arrival in the household.

She looked over to the bar where Edward was standing chatting and laughing with Burrows and Stanley Tirrold, a pint glass in his hand. She was glad he was enjoying himself. She shivered momentarily as she remembered the state he had been in when he'd arrived back from the war in 1917. For week after week he had taken refuge in drink, trying to numb the effects of what he'd seen in France. Thank heavens he was on the mend at last.

*And what of Innes Knox?* The girl was sitting opposite her but had turned to watch the first dance, so she was able to observe her profile at leisure. She was wearing a well-chosen knee-length dress that fitted her beautifully. The pale blue colour was very complementary, and she sensed Eve's skilful hand behind it. If only she'd take those spectacles off. The girl was clearly a beauty underneath and the more she got to know her character the more amenable she was to the idea of an association with her youngest son.

She felt Eve's gaze on her and glanced over. Their eyes met and they smiled in mutual recognition. Her best friend had relayed the confidential conversation she had had with the young Scottish woman. It was a blatant betrayal as Eve had acknowledged, but the information was too important not to share and she knew it would go no further. After her initial surprise Lady Langford had reflected that the girl was clearly very determined, quite capable of managing a crisis and also quite capable of bearing children.

As she well knew, when it came to being a wife in the Spense family these qualities were significant beyond all others. And provided the secret was maintained, the girl's gracious act in taking on her sister's child would be seen to be to her credit.

But difficulties remained. Her son had witnessed the grief of the bereaved on the estate and seemed disinclined to romance, and Innes was wounded by her experiences and not in any hurry to get involved with a man. She sighed inwardly. Time would tell, but both she and Eve were now resolved to work together to ensure the path was as smooth as possible.

*And for now it would help a great deal if her son would only leave the bar for a moment and come and ask Innes for a dance.*

She glared over at him, trying to catch his eye, but he put his head back and roared with laughter at some remark by the publican. She looked at Eve again. The other woman understood only too well and rolled her eyes with a rueful smile.

*

At the interval Laura had a quiet word with the bandmaster so when he announced the opening dance of the second session with the words, 'Ladies, please take your partners for the ladies' choice,' by a curious coincidence she found herself standing next to Burrows, her lipstick refreshed, a dab of scent on her neck and her hair newly brushed.

She gave him a gentle nudge and said in a firm voice, 'Hello, Burrows. Hear that? It's the ladies' choice. And guess who I'm choosing. Put your glass down and brace yourself, McDuff. Come on.'

With that she took him by the hand and led him onto the dance floor. They came to a halt next to Lilly and her tall farmhand. The maid was standing on tiptoes, holding both his hands and talking nineteen to the dozen, her face still upturned.

'I suppose you can dance, Burrows?' Laura enquired as she saw the look of alarm on the constable's face.

'Err, well…'

'Good. That's fine, whatever they play we will do a waltz. Slow and steady wins the race. Just do what I do.' She pressed gently against him, put her hand on his shoulder and said quietly into his ear, 'You'd better take hold then.'

And as the band struck up a foxtrot, off they went. Although most of her attention was focussed on ensuring her partner understood certain matters, as she looked over his shoulder she was amused to note the variety of dancing being exercised within the marquee. Giles Stafford and Lady Langford eased past them, moving smoothly and expertly into gaps, Eve and Jocelyn Dance, as their name belied, were also very good, she thought, but there were also many couples from the farms for whom formal dancing was a closed book. Plenty just got up and jigged away to their own composition, simply happy to be together.

In later life Laura would remember that moment often – the first Ploughman's Ball after the war. Yes, there was relief and joy, but she also sensed an undercurrent of wildness in the marquee, as if a vital spirit had been rekindled. The hostilities were over and the ones who were left were coming alive again. As she leaned in to the tall, strong policeman and put her head on his shoulder for the first time, she felt him squeeze her waist.

'That's the ticket, Burrows,' she whispered. 'Just like that.'

Much later he walked her home. They were some of the last to leave and made their way slowly across the lawn towards the drive and the hall gates. Outside it was a mild still evening and the great fire from the roasting still smouldered and glowed. A couple were standing hand in hand watching it. Lilly and her man, Laura realised.

'Where were you brought up?' she asked.

'Cowley. It's a part of Oxford.'

'Yes, I've heard of it. Have you any brothers or sisters?' she continued.

'No, it's just me and my dad.' He didn't volunteer anything else, so Laura moved gently forward.

'What happened to your mother, did she pass away?'

'In a way. She caught the train to London and never came back. I was twelve. After that my pa always said she was dead to us. He didn't remarry or anything. He told me women aren't to be trusted.'

The scales fell from Laura's eyes. The problem was out in the open at last. She was both relieved and distressed in equal measure. 'You poor thing. That's a terrible age to lose your mother.'

'We managed,' he said shortly and increased his pace.

They walked on in silence, out through the gate and down the high street. It wasn't long before they arrived outside the Black Horse where she had her room. *Not nearly long enough*, thought Laura, who felt the evening's progress was slipping away. Eyeing the bench below the saloon bar window she said, 'Sit with me for a minute.'

Without waiting for his reply she moved over to it and sat down, looking up at him expectantly. With a slight shrug he sat next to her.

'I enjoyed dancing with you. Did you enjoy it?' she asked.

'Yes I did. I was nervous at first but once you get going it's alright, isn't it?'

*So true of many things, Burrows*, she thought.

'I liked you holding me. You shouldn't think all women are not to be trusted, you know.'

'Are you saying my dad's wrong?' he replied, a slight note of truculence in his tone.

'I'm saying that both of you had a bad experience with a woman who couldn't be trusted, but that doesn't mean we're all bad. Some of us are very trustworthy and loyal. We just need a chance to show it. I like you very much and it's a lonely life all on your own. I'm lonely sometimes, aren't you? Wouldn't it be nice to have a special girl on your arm?'

As the words came tumbling out the policeman said nothing, just stared across the street.

She felt for his hand and took it. 'I mean it, Burrows, you can trust me. I won't let you down.' Then she sighed and said, 'For heaven's sake, what's your first name? I can't keep calling you Burrows.'

He told her. A single word.

'Good lord, really? Perhaps I will then. When we're walking out.' She squeezed his hand and felt it tighten on hers. 'We will be walking out, won't we? You'll give it a try?'

He turned and looked at her in the moonlight. 'Alright then,' he said. 'No funny business though.'

Laura felt a surge of joy and smiled at him with warm eyes. Then she reached up and gave him a lingering soft kiss on the cheek and whispered, 'Oh no, Burrows, absolutely no funny business… not unless you want to.'

\*

The investigation into Christian Freeling's death was in danger of petering out. Although the trail pointed towards the two women whom Jack Wright had named as having had an illicit affair with Freeling, Edward, Innes and Burrows could not think of a way to establish if the allegations were true.

'I mean, we can hardly sidle up to them after church and ask them if they misbehaved, can we?' Edward remarked in frustration as they sat in the front room at Holly Cottage.

'Quite,' Innes agreed. 'Any kind of direct approach would certainly be met with a denial. Any advice from the manual, Burrows?'

He responded with a lugubrious stare then said, 'If this was a formal police investigation, the ladies could be interviewed in private and under caution. As things are, enquiries in the village could be seen as spreading malicious rumours. For now I suggest we assume that Jack Wright was telling the truth and try to find out what their husbands were doing the morning Mr Freeling died. If they both have alibis then we need not take things any further.'

'And if that's the case, I'm not sure where it leaves us,' Innes replied with a frown, 'but it's a good suggestion, Burrows, thank you. Will you do that then?'

'Yes, Miss.'

Edward glanced at his wrist watch. 'Good. Well that's settled then. Now if you'll excuse me my mother has guests at the hall this evening and I promised to dine with them.'

*

Billy and Adelaide Montague, the owners of Candover Castle, were, as Lady Langford had suggested, completely different in stature but united by a sense of *joie de vivre* that made them tremendous company.

After a merry evening Edward invited Billy Montague for a morning's fishing at Dipper Pool. He readily agreed and they set off after breakfast carrying a couple of trout rods, a landing net and a bag. As they cast out from the little beach Edward broached the subject on his mind. He didn't like to lie, but it was an unavoidable necessity in this case.

'My mother mentioned you have a run of coastline with the estate at Candover, is that correct, sir?'

'It is. The place sits near the mouth of the river Rother, and we've got a mile or so of sea coast and nearly all the left bank of the river leading up to Rye. You should come down, you know. Your mother met your father there, if I recall correctly.'

'So I understand, and I would love to come down and stay, but I must confess to having an ulterior motive in making my enquiry.'

'Oh really, what's that?'

'I'm involved in a bit of a rag to tell the truth. Some friends have challenged me to bring an item of cargo back from France. It'll be a crate about four feet cube. The thing is, it's not something that we want to bother the customs and excise people with.'

His companion cast economically into the wash running into the pool from the rapids upstream and watched his fly drift towards the deeper water under the far bank. Had he but known it, he was standing exactly where Bert Williams's pregnant dryad had slipped naked into the water some weeks earlier.

Slightly anxious at the ensuing silence Edward looked over at him and was relieved to see a grin fixed on his face. 'The prospect doesn't alarm you?' he asked.

'Certainly not. I won't ask you what is in the crate, but I will take your assurance that no harm is intended as a consequence. Does that sound reasonable?' he said, his eyes fixed on his fly.

'It does and I can absolutely give you that assurance.'

'Yes!' The older man struck and grunted in satisfaction as a swirl in the water indicated that he had a trout on the line. 'Wind in, Edward, while I try and land this beauty, will you?' With his companion speedily retracting his own line Montague walked up the little beach playing the fish, and all conversation stopped as he frowned in concentration. As it tired Edward approached with the net and moments later they had it on the shingle where it was quickly despatched.

'A nice fish, well done, sir,' Edward said.

'I am pleased I will admit it, it's a light line and he was quite a fighter.' Then he looked at Edward and his face grew serious. 'If you get caught I'll deny any knowledge. I have to protect Candover's reputation. Is that understood?'

'Yes,' said Edward unequivocally.

'Very well.' Montague put out his hand and they shook. 'Do you have a vessel in mind?' he asked.

'Not yet,' Edward admitted.

'Hmm. Well running has been a pretty regular activity in and around Rye for hundreds of years. Many a fishing boat has come back with more than mackerel in its hold, and it still goes on. My gamekeeper is well connected in the town and it's not inconceivable that he could find someone to run a cargo for you. There's a quiet little jetty about a quarter of a mile up river from the sea, on our land. That would be the place to come ashore, I'd imagine. It's got water at all stages of the tide.'

'Could we get a vehicle to it?'

'Yes. There's a track that leads off from the drive before the park gates.'

'That would be marvellous.'

Montague nodded. 'Very well. I will raise the matter discreetly with my man when we get home on Tuesday. I'd imagine that by the end of the week I could write to you with the name of a boat, and it will then be up to you to pursue the matter directly with the master.'

'I am most grateful to you. That will be a huge help.'

'Well I'll ask no more questions, just let me know when the thing is done, will you? And not a word to Adelaide, there's no need to involve her in this.'

'Of course. Thank you, sir.' They both eyed the pool as another swirl stirred the surface.

'Back to work then, Edward. Let's see if we can catch a brace before lunch.'

*

True to his word a brief note arrived at Langford Hall in the post some days later. Edward was both amused and interested to see that it was written on un-headed paper and was unsigned. Clearly Billy Montague was a careful man and not inexperienced in subterfuge.

*Apropos of our conversation, I am advised that the steam trawler* Mary Ellen *(green hull, brown funnel) would be a suitable craft for the charter you envisage. Good fishing!*

After discussing it with the colonel, Edward borrowed the Alvis from an anxious Fenn and, ignoring his plaintive request to, 'Please let me drive you, sir,' drove down to Rye one fine morning in late September.

He arrived in the picturesque old town in the afternoon and secured a hotel room with no difficulty. The reception desk gave him directions to the harbour, and he worked his way through the characterful streets until he arrived at an attractive stone balcony, clearly designed as a viewpoint, which overlooked the confluence of the rivers Rother and Brede.

He lingered for a moment, taking in the fine prospect. The river Rother snaked away from him across fields to the distant coastline.

To the left flat land reached into the blue haze of Romney Marsh, an area notorious for smuggling activities over the years. On the right bank the land was more undulating and wooded and he could just make out the turrets of a great house which he guessed was Candover Castle.

Below the balcony he could see a quay with three fishing boats tied up, although none had a green hull. Nevertheless he descended, and five minutes later he found himself amid a jumble of nets, lobster pots and other marine equipment. As a salty, fishy, breeze caught in his nostrils he noticed a black-painted wooden office with a window facing the river.

He walked over and saw a sign saying Harbour Master but, as he reached for the door, he hesitated. A casual conversation with one of the crew on another boat would be less memorable than a direct question to the man in charge of the port, he reasoned, so he turned away and strolled across the quay to the nearest vessel. She was called the *Fair Venture* and a grey-haired middle-aged man with a weather-beaten face was leaning on the stern rail smoking a cigarette. He gave a nod of greeting as Edward approached.

'Good afternoon, I was just wondering if you happened to know if the *Mary Ellen* is due back this evening?' he asked.

The man took a last pull on his cigarette and flicked the dog-end into the river with casual ease. 'Depends on the fishing. If her holds are full she'll be back. If not, it may be tomorrow. You looking for her then?'

Edward could see a note of caution in the man's face but was not unduly disturbed by it. If the boat was involved in the occasional smuggling run to France then he imagined others would be too. They would be wary of strangers.

'I've a message for one of the crew is all,' he answered easily. As the fisherman eyed him, Edward realised he'd made a foolish mistake. The man's next question was all too obvious.

'Oh yes? Who's that then?'

'The mate,' he answered, heart suddenly beating hard in his chest.

'Jim Mason?'

'Yes, that's right.'

'That's odd, because the *Mary Ellen*'s mate is Robby Hawk. My name is Jim Mason as it happens, maybe you've got a message for me?'

A seagull swooped over the water, its harsh call loud in the silence that followed this question. Then he smiled across the gap between the fishing boat and the quay, withdrew a packet of tobacco from his pocket and expertly rolled another cigarette one-handed. Glancing back at Edward he remarked, 'You need one hand for the ship when she's pitching and you fancy a smoke.'

'Yes, I can imagine,' he replied, wishing he was somewhere else.

The man lighted his cigarette and flicked the match the same way as the previous butt. He inhaled with pleasure and blew the smoke out again before giving Edward a direct look.

'I noticed you heading for the harbour master's office and then changing your mind. *Now that's curious, Jim,* I thought, especially when you came over and asked about the *Mary Ellen*. Because anyone with a legitimate enquiry would ask in there. But if you didn't want it known too publicly that you were interested in the *Mary Ellen*, you might conclude a quiet word with another fisherman would be a better way to do it.'

Edward noticed the slight emphasis on the word 'legitimate' in Mason's sentence and replied carefully, 'Yes, I suppose one might.'

'I'm the captain of the *Fair Venture* and she is a fishing boat by and large. But she's a general working boat too, and available for charter to discerning gents who like to test their mettle on the briny. If your enquiry regarding the *Mary Ellen* was along those lines, then perhaps we should talk some more?'

Edward smiled with relief. 'A special charter is what I had in mind as it happens.'

Mason gave him a knowing smile. 'Then come aboard, my friend, and let's discuss terms over a drink, like gentlemen.'

Five minutes later the two of them were ensconced in a stuffy little saloon below the wheelhouse. A narrow stained table ran down the middle and they sat opposite each other on settles that Edward assumed doubled up as bunks when they were at sea. There was a strong smell of pipe smoke and tar and the weak daylight that reached down the steps was boosted by a porthole on either side.

Mason put a bottle of rum and two glasses on the table. 'Were you in France for the war, sir?' he enquired.

Edward nodded. 'Yes, I joined up in '14 and was invalided out three years later.'

The captain looked at him approvingly. 'You did your bit then, like us. The *Fair Venture* was taken up by the navy. They gave us a little gun on the bow and a couple of gunners and sent us off to look for German submarines. We got to know the French coast very well. All the places where they used to hide. Yes,' he added reflectively as he poured the rum, 'it's fair to say we know plenty of quiet spots over there.' He pushed a half full glass across the table and raised his own. 'Cheers.'

'Cheers.' Edward took a sip. It was strong but good.

The two men talked for another ten minutes, mainly about the war and Edward felt that the captain was getting his measure, which was only to be expected under the circumstances. It was noticeable that he didn't ask him his name, and whatever impression he gave must have proved satisfactory because once their glasses had been refilled Mason caught his eye and smiled.

'Now then, sir, why don't you just lay out what it is you've got in mind, and we'll see what can be done. No names no pack drill for the moment, just the charter in outline. You can trust me to keep cavey.'

Edward took a deep breath and crossed the point of no return. 'Very well. I want a crate about four feet cube picked up from France and landed on a jetty down the river. It's on Candover land I believe. No customs involvement. Just a nice quiet night-time job. Is that the sort of thing you can do?'

The man opposite nodded slowly. 'Yes, that's the sort of thing that can be done I'd say. Where in France?'

'I don't know yet. If we come to terms I think we could deliver it to any location you suggest within reason. Certainly anywhere along the Boulogne coastal area, but there must be a road all the way to it as we'll be using a small lorry.'

'How heavy is the crate?'

Edward paused. *Good question.* 'It will be liftable by two men and will have carrying handles,' he said after a moment.

'And when do you have in mind?'

'Not long, I think mid to late October. I'll be able to confirm the date exactly in a week or two.'

A silence descended on the saloon as Mason considered the matter. Edward sipped his rum and waited. Then the man opposite spoke again. 'Begging your pardon, but how come you're mixed up in a lark like this? You don't seem the type, if you get my meaning.'

'It's a family matter, to do with the war. Something needs to be brought back and I have been charged with the task.'

'So it isn't guns? Because we don't touch those.'

'No, I can give you a categoric assurance that it isn't anything that might cause harm to anyone else. It's personal property and we just wish for the matter to be done privately and discreetly.' Their eyes met and for a moment Edward felt the older man was staring directly into his head.

*He thinks we're avoiding duty on family heirlooms, probably pictures*, he thought.

'Alright then,' Mason said. 'I think we can do a deal here. What shall I call you?'

'I'd suggest Mr Oxford, although I warn you that's not my real name.'

'No problem, sir, Jim Mason isn't mine either,' the captain said with a smile. 'Now then, I'd say a fair price for this charter is two hundred pounds. And I do have one condition that I will exercise if needed. If we get caught by a revenue cutter before we get back to Rye, the crate goes over the side. No ifs no buts. Apart from that, we'll undertake to be on the French coast at an agreed time and place, take the merchandise on board and bring it back to Candover jetty and put it ashore. You must travel back with us though. Those are my terms.' He spat on his hand and reached across the table.

Edward held back for a moment. 'You charge a hefty price, Captain Mason. I prefer the sound of a hundred pounds to be honest.'

The man chuckled and did not remove his hand. 'Maybe so, but we're not being honest, are we? We're taking a big risk and breaking the law and there is a cost to that. We'll keep our side of the bargain. You'll have your crate ashore in Blighty and we'll keep our mouths shut about it for ever. Two hundred is the fee.'

'Alright then, your terms are agreed.' Edward shook his hand and they clinked glasses.

'Thank you, sir. Now then, let's have a look at a map.' He opened a locker and removed the topmost chart, then spread it out on the table. 'This is the English Channel from Dunkirk to Dieppe and here is the Bay de L'Authie where the river of the same name reaches the sea. About a mile up river, below a village called Groffliers, there's a little quay called Port de la Madelon. Very nice and quiet it is. You might say the *Fair Venture* knows her way in there, if you understand me.'

Edward nodded. 'Is there a road to it?'

'I've seen a car at the back of the quay so there must be. You'll have to find it though. The landward bit is your job.'

'Yes, fair enough. A decent map should do it.'

'That's right. Now it's tidal there so we need to time things carefully.' He reached over and pulled a book onto the table. Flicking through the pages he found what he was looking for. 'Here we are, high tide in Le Touquet is in the small hours between the twentieth and twenty-third of October. How would that suit you?'

Edward noticed something as he peered upside down at the book of tables. 'Does that show the moon's phases too?'

'It does. The moon will be waxing through a half-moon during that time.'

He thought about the graveyard at Rouville. A half-moon would be ideal – enough light to see but not the glare of a full moon. 'Yes,' he said simply. 'That would suit me.'

'Well you'll need to tell me the exact day. We have two hours on either side of high tide, so a four-hour window in total at the quay.'

'How can I reach you?'

'A telegram to the *Fair Venture* care of the Harbour Master. Send "*Don't forget David's birthday 22nd*" and I'll know it's the 22nd. Alright?'

'Yes, I understand. I'd better write these French names down, and the tide times.' He pulled out his notebook and jotted down the details. 'How many will be on the boat?' asked Edward.

'Three, myself, the mate and the engineer. We've done this sort of thing a time or two. They know the score and are glad of the money. At the Candover end, we'll put the crate on the jetty and steam off. And that'll be it, you understand?' he said firmly.

'Yes. When do I pay you?'

'Fifty pounds now and the rest when we pass Camber Beach Buoy as we head in.'

Edward had removed sufficient funds from the safe at Langford Hall. He handed over the cash and they shook hands again.

'Our lights will be off when we come up the L'Authie river but as we approach the quay we'll show a single blue light at the masthead. That way you'll know it's us. Make sure you have a torch that works. When you see the blue light give us three flashes, then another three. Unless we see that we'll turn round. You clear on that, Mr Oxford? Three flashes then another three.'

'Yes, quite clear.' He made another note in his pocket book. *These people know their business*, he thought, quietly impressed. He also felt a surge of excitement. Sitting here with Captain Mason the thing seemed entirely possible.

It was dark on deck and the tide had dropped during their conversation. He climbed up the quayside ladder and at the top he turned and looked down. 'Well, cheerio then.'

The older man looked up and raised his arm. 'See you in France, Mr Oxford,' he said quietly, his face serious. Then he descended the ladder and disappeared.

Edward made his way back to the hotel. He was elated. *They had their smuggler.*

# Chapter Fourteen

When he arrived back in the village he called in to Marston House, where the maid showed him into the colonel's study. The chief constable joined him shortly afterwards. 'Any luck?' he asked without preamble.

Edward smiled. 'Oh yes, we're in business, Jocelyn. Let me bring you up to date.'

Once he had done so and the colonel had congratulated him on his success, they poured over the calendar and made some decisions. They would drive down to Newhaven on the morning of the twentieth of October, overnight there, and get the ferry to Boulogne early on the 21st. After collecting the lorry from Monsieur Benedet, they would carry straight on to Rouville and lift the body once darkness fell.

Then during the day on the 22nd they would drive to Groffliers and meet the *Fair Venture* and load the crate that same night.

'I'm glad we had the foresight to order that crate in Boulogne when we went back through,' observed the colonel as they checked the schedule again. 'If the ferry is on time we can be on our way to Rouville with the lorry and empty crate before lunchtime.'

'Exactly, although we'll need to buy a couple of spades remember,' his friend replied. 'And a length of rope and ground sheets. Then when I'm on board the *Fair Venture* with the crate, you drive the lorry to Boulogne, collect the deposit and take the ferry back to Newhaven. The Alvis will still be in the hotel car park.'

The colonel nodded. 'Which brings us to the business of getting the crate from Candover to Langford. Because the *Fair Venture* will disappear, leaving you and Hugh alone and palely loitering in the middle of the night on the river Rother. I'll still be in transit somewhere and once daylight comes you'll stand out like a sore thumb.'

Edward looked thoughtful. 'Look, this is where the third person really comes in. Having seen the set-up over there I think the two of us can cope with the French end on our own, you know. There's no doubt that's the risky element and I'd rather keep it in the family, as it were. What do you think?'

'I think we can probably manage. We'd better both take a pair of dungarees though, if it's been raining and the soil is wet we'll be damnably dirty by the time the thing is done.'

'Good point. So that leaves me needing a lorry at Candover quay during the night of the 23rd. I'll give Mason an arrival time and he can work to that. Let's say two o'clock in the morning.'

'Well we can hire something suitable in Oxford easily enough. It's just a question of who drives it.'

'What about Bert Williams?' Edward asked. 'He drove a lorry during the war so he can cope with that side of things. And he's not going to be phased by a bit of night-time skulduggery.'

'No, we can be sure about that,' observed the colonel with a wry smile. 'Is he trustworthy though? If the chips are down, I mean.'

'He's very loyal to the estate. Our family and his have been intertwined for centuries, you know, and if I cross his palm with silver as well, I think he'd be fine. And of course there's no need for him to know what's inside the crate.'

The colonel shivered. 'Ye gods no, that's absolutely certain.'

Edward looked at him. 'Are we agreed then? We approach Bert Williams?'

'Yes. I'll do it, Edward, you've done your bit for the moment.'

'Very well. I will send the telegrams to France and Rye in the morning. The main post office in Oxford would be best for that.'

After work the following evening the colonel called round to the Williams' cottage on Rivermead. Edna answered the door and in response to his enquiry she turned and called back down the narrow hall.

'Bert, here's the colonel to see you.'

Moments later the man himself appeared. 'Evening, Colonel,' he said. 'What can I do for you?'

As his wife muttered something about 'getting the tea on' and squeezed past her husband, the chief constable had a long look at the man in front of him. He was in his early fifties, he guessed, and of medium height with a swarthy stubbly skin and dark eyes. *There is a capable leanness to the fellow*, he mused, and his normally humorous expression was overlaid with a wariness that suggested visits by policemen were rarely good news at the Williams' residence.

'Sorry to disturb you at this hour, Bert, but I'd appreciate a word if I may. A quiet word as it happens,' he remarked evenly. 'Nothing to worry about, I'm not here officially.'

'Ah,' said Bert and his guarded expression eased a little but not completely. He thought for a moment and then said, 'If it's a private conversation we're probably best having a walk.'

'Good idea.'

He turned and called back down the hall, 'I'm just taking a turn along the lane with the colonel, won't be long.' A cry of acknowledgement floated back and with that he left the cottage and pulled the door closed. Moments later they were walking slowly along Rivermead away from Great Tew.

'What's on your mind then, Colonel?'

'To speak plainly, I have a confidential task that needs undertaking. It must be done at night and very quietly and the fellow that does it must be able to drive a lorry. It involves the collection of a certain item and its transportation to Great Tew.'

'Right. Is it for the police?'

'No, as I mentioned I am not here officially. It is a private matter involving myself and Mr Edward.'

'Oh. Family business then?'

'I'd ask you not to speculate too much. A focus on the practical aspects would be a more advisable course, I'd suggest.'

'And those are what exactly?'

They passed the last cottage, nodding to a woman working in the front garden and walked on into the countryside. As the hedgerows climbed higher on either side, there was a silence as the colonel mentally double-checked that he could trust Bert.

'Before I explain further I need your assurance that you will go to the grave with this information. I mean it, Bert. This is an intensely private matter. I have become involved as a close family friend because Edward needs assistance and we have chosen you as the third and only other conspirator. You can consider that as being to your great credit. We believe you can be trusted but I need your solemn vow that you will never speak of it.'

Bert stopped and turned to look at the older man. For once his face was serious. 'If it's for the family I'll agree to keep my mouth shut. We go back a long way, the Williamses and the Spenses, and I reckon we've known each other's secrets a time or two.'

'I have your word on that?' The colonel held out his hand.

'You do.' Bert reached out and shook it.

The atmosphere eased as they resumed their walk and the colonel said, 'Right then, this is what you need to do…'

Twenty minutes later the two men were back outside the Williams' cottage. 'I forgot to mention that Edward feels some compensation for the risk you are taking would be appropriate,' the colonel said.

'Money, you mean?'

'Yes. A fee as it were.'

The colonel saw Bert's face tighten as he shook his head. 'No, this is a favour for the family and to the memory of Lord Colin. As fine a gent as ever walked the earth. There's no fee.'

The colonel nodded. He wasn't surprised. 'Very well. I'm sure that sentiment will be appreciated, and favours are rarely forgotten, Bert.'

A curious expression came over the man's face as they stood there. 'Well thinking about it, there is one thing perhaps…' And he told him.

Colonel Dance was still chuckling to himself as he strolled back along Rivermead and turned towards Marston House. The fellow was incorrigible, but he was well satisfied with their conversation.

Everything was now in place.

*

Later that week Burrows asked to see Innes and Edward and they convened in the garden of the Black Horse.

'What news of Messrs Trotter and Bilson, Burrows?' asked Innes.

'I am pretty sure that Mr Trotter is in the clear, but I don't have definitive information regarding Mr Bilson yet,' he replied, 'but by chance I met Jack Wright yesterday and he mentioned something which throws the cat in amongst the pigeons a bit, to my mind.'

'Really?' Edward frowned.

'Wright had a drink with a fellow who was working below Creech Hill Ring the morning of the murder. He was hedging along the path Mr Freeling would have taken, but he didn't see him. And he was there at seven o'clock. That got me thinking. Why did no one at all see Christian Freeling walking from Beech Farm to Creech Hill that morning? We know he left the farm at seven in the morning because his wife and all three Atkins saw him, and he was dead at the yew by eight thirty at the latest. There are plenty of people about on the estate at that time.'

'And knowing the propensity for gossip in the village, if he had been spotted it would have been mentioned,' Edward added thoughtfully.

'Exactly,' Burrows replied.

'So what are we to make of that then?' There was a long silence, then Edward spoke again. 'What if he believed he was getting mixed up in something that was dodgy?'

Innes nodded keenly, making the light catch her spectacles. 'Deliberately concealed himself to avoid witnesses, you mean. Yes of course. If he thought he'd been roped into something criminal then he wouldn't want anyone to see him.'

'Especially if there was money involved,' said Edward, rather pleased with himself. 'What do you think?' He looked over at the constable.

Burrows was wrestling with an annoying mental itch that was buzzing away like a fly at a window, but he nodded distractedly. 'Yes, that sounds likely to me.'

'Good,' said Innes briskly. 'So Christian Freeling thought he was getting mixed up with something illegal that required a rope and meant he used stealth to get from Beech Farm to Creech Hill. He didn't want to be seen if he could help it. But in reality there wasn't any task, it was just a ruse to lure him to the yew so he could be killed.' The men nodded their agreement. 'And you'll continue with your enquires regarding Mr Bilson?' she finished, looking at Burrows. He nodded again.

Edward looked at the constable and smiled. 'I don't wish to pry, but did I see you walking out with Miss Bessing the other day?'

The constable met his eye. 'You did, Mr Edward,' he said rather woodenly. 'We have agreed to spend some time together to see if we might be suited.'

Edward couldn't resist it. 'Well in that case, even though I thought I'd made my feelings for Laura very clear, I will stand aside. The field is yours.' Concentrating on the policeman as he was, he failed to notice Innes raise her head and look at him as he spoke.

The young constable blinked owl-like and reddened. 'Miss Bessing has explained my mistake in that regard. She found it extremely amusing. Still does in fact,' he added in a mutter.

'What's this, Constable? Is romance on the cards?' Innes asked, her glorious mouth splitting into a wide grin, in which a neutral observer might have noticed some relief.

'As I say, Miss Knox, it is early days, but Miss Bessing would like to explore the possibility.'

'And are you keen?' she pursued.

'I am not alarmed at the prospect.'

'My word, high praise indeed.' Her smile became wider. 'Don't let the girl go dizzy with compliments, will you.'

'No, Miss. I will not.'

As Innes leaned forward, spectacles gleaming, and prepared to investigate further Edward decided to rescue the young constable. 'Well I hope it works out well for you. She is a lovely girl. Also just to let you both know that I'm going away for a few days. Down to the coast. The colonel's coming too, so I'll see you when I'm back.'

'A holiday, Edward?' Innes asked.

'A bit of sea fishing at some friends of my mother's. A place called Candover Castle in Sussex.'

*

The sea fishermen drove down to Newhaven as planned. They travelled light – everything they needed would be obtained in France once they had collected the lorry.

Edward carried the money for Mason plus other necessary disbursements in his inner pocket. He had discussed the fee with his mother who had made it up out of her personal funds, necessitating a visit to the bank in Oxford, and some dissembling with the bank manager who was clearly curious as to the purpose of such a large amount of cash.

As they emerged from the handsome building she said, 'I haven't asked any questions, but can I assume you are doing it soon?'

'Within the week,' had been his short reply.

The two men had a slightly tense dinner before retiring early, each busy with their own thoughts. As the colonel prepared for bed he wondered how his partner would hold up if things went wrong and they had to bluff their way out of trouble, or even run for it.

As he had said to Eve the night before, 'I'm going to keep an eye on him as much as anything. There's no getting away from the fact that he's going back to the scene of his breakdown, and he clearly sensed something in the cemetery and was very unsettled. If he starts seeing dead soldiers again then I'm not sure he'll cope.'

Next door the man in question also had things on his mind. His mother's confident assertion that, 'You can't steal something that belongs to you,' might have been intended to provide some reassurance but the simple fact was that they were going to rob a grave in a foreign country, like a latter-day Burke and Hare. Now it was imminent the stark enormity of what they were planning sent shivers down his spine, and he knew if they were caught there would be hell to pay.

In the preceding weeks he had repeatedly imagined the moment when they prised the lid off the coffin, and he looked upon his brother again. *After a year in the ground what would he look like? Would he be decomposed? Or still in his uniform? Would there be a visible injury?* The images in his head had been relentless and disturbing.

He shivered again. He'd know soon enough. The colonel slept soundly, but Edward's fitful slumber was plagued with nightmares.

They crossed the Channel the following morning and having changed some pounds for francs, walked to Monsieur Benedet's garage where a small flatbed lorry was parked on the forecourt. He was charm personified and, 'Delighted to welcome back my esteemed English clients.'

As before Edward filled the paperwork in using a false name and address. In the unlikely event police in England attempted to trace the hirer they would search in vain for Mr Arthur Geoffrey of 42 Brean Villas, Southampton.

Instead of leaving town immediately they drove to a furniture maker's workshop close to the docks where they inspected and paid for the crate that they had ordered on their previous visit. It was built to the rough sketch that Edward had made in the owner's office, namely four feet cube with a hinged lid and lined with two layers of thick oilskin. A stout bar was bolted on either side and extended for six inches beyond the edges. Two carrying handles were also supplied, meaning the crate could be moved by two men if they slipped the handles under the bars and lifted.

'It is to your specification, Monsieur Geoffrey?' enquired the exuberantly moustached proprietor.

'It is, thank you. We are most satisfied,' Edward replied and without further ado it was lifted onto the back of the lorry and tied down.

Their final call was to a general store where they bought a pair of groundsheets, a tarpaulin, two spades, a jemmy and length of rope. A hammer and nails, dungarees and working boots completed the list.

'In England a magistrate would consider this "going equipped to commit a grave robbing",' observed the chief constable with a small smile as they drove through the outskirts of Boulogne and picked up the road south to Montreuil.

The journey to Rouville took them the rest of the day and was uneventful. At the colonel's suggestion they stopped and bought some cheese, ham and bread, and bottles of water and beer. 'Best to be able to manage our own rations,' he observed. 'We'll be travelling from now on and people might remember two Englishmen with a lorry if we stop somewhere to eat. The less of a trail we leave the better.'

They drove through Rouville at seven in the evening and carried on towards the cemetery. The weather which had been slowly deteriorating as they drove east now looked threatening, with low dark clouds on the horizon, driven westwards by a rising wind.

'We might be in for a stormy night,' the colonel said, 'but there's less likelihood of a chance passer-by if it's raining and blowing a gale.'

As darkness fell they drove slowly past the long lines of white crosses and continued until they found a narrow track that led into a wood. Guided by the colonel, Edward reversed into the gap and backed up for thirty feet so that the body of the vehicle was concealed to all but a very persistent observer.

'Perfect,' the colonel observed as he climbed back into the cab. 'We haven't met a single car so it's obviously a quiet lane. Break out the rations. We'll eat and have a snooze until it's time to go over the top.'

*

Edward's watch slowly edged towards one o'clock in the morning. The colonel's gentle snores had been rippling around the cab for three hours, but Edward was wide awake. The sight of the eerie lines of crosses fading into the twilight had shaken him and he was aware of a faint acrid smell. As rain beat against the cab roof, he watched the dark outline of the trees moving in the wind through narrowed eyes, fearful that the face of a dead man would suddenly appear at the window.

*Does Hugh know that we are here? Do any of them? Are they waiting for us?* The thoughts went round and round in his mind and by the time one o'clock arrived he was thoroughly on edge.

He gave the colonel a nudge and said, 'Time to go, Jocelyn,' and with a mumble and a deep breath his friend came to the surface and opened his eyes. He got out of the cab and stretched, then looked around.

'Filthy night,' he observed with satisfaction, 'no danger of a courting couple being out in the fields tonight. We'd better get dressed, Edward.'

They put on the dungarees and boots and set off with no further delay. As they approached the cemetery the atmosphere in the cab became tenser and the colonel said quietly, 'Can you manage without lights? It would be better if you can.'

'Let's try,' Edward replied, and switched them off. Even though there was heavy cloud, sufficient light remained for him to pull up by the gate. A gust of wind shook the lorry and rain lashed onto the windscreen. They looked over to the rows of crosses. The nearest ones were visible, but the lines disappeared into the night.

*As if they go on for ever*, Edward thought.

The colonel held up his watch. 'Twenty past one. Let's see how long this takes us.' He looked at the man behind the wheel.

His eyes were fixed on the graves and the distress coming off him was palpable. He reached across and gripped his upper arm.

'Are you ready, Edward? This is a grim business, but our job is to do it as quickly and cleanly as we can. We are relying on each other and once we start we have to drive on through to the end, whatever happens. There can be no backing down. Do you understand that?'

His tone was deadly serious, and Edward felt the man's eyes on him. The acrid smell was quite distinct now, as though the source was closer. He shivered and took a deep breath.

'I am ready. I won't let you down, sir.' He reached out and the men shook hands.

'Right then. Good luck to both of us and tally ho.' The colonel opened his door onto the screaming night and slipped outside.

If anything the weather was getting worse and by the time the men had the crate untied and on the ground, rain had soaked through their dungarees.

'Crate first, then we'll come back for the tools,' said the colonel in a raised voice. With the wind howling the danger of being overheard was nil. They slipped the two carrying handles under the bars and with Edward at the front they crossed the ditch and entered the cemetery.

*Row sixteen, plot twenty-four*, the two numbers were engraved on Edward's memory, and he counted the rows off then they turned and made their way between the crosses. At number twenty-four they stopped, and Edward risked a brief flash of his torch. The uneven black letters were there, just as before – Hugh George Spense, Coldstream Guards.

'Okay, back we go,' said the colonel and they returned to the lorry and collected the spades, groundsheets, jemmy and rope. Five minutes later they were standing by the grave.

Edward seemed distracted, looking around and staring into the dark corners of the cemetery and the colonel decided to take command. 'We'll spread the groundsheets along each side and shovel the soil onto them, then it'll be easier to refill the hole afterwards. Come on, let's get them in place,' he said briskly.

They did so and with no further ado the colonel picked up a spade and drove it into the pile of earth on top of the grave with his foot. It slid in easily and he grunted and lifted the full load out and turned it onto the groundsheet. Edward picked up his spade and set to work. The soaking, clinging soil smelled wet in the driving rain, but it was not enough to override the harsh acrid stench. Buffeted by the wind he worked on, head down and moving mechanically, afraid of what he might see if he looked up.

But it wasn't just the smell. Since they had entered the cemetery his head had begun echoing with the sounds of battle. Men screaming, shouted commands and explosions and small arms fire. He remembered it so well and his mind reeled as the emotional bombardment grew and grew in intensity. He realised he was crying as he dug, the tears mixing with the rain that lashed his face.

As the soil piled up on the groundsheets they passed ground level and started to penetrate down into the grave itself. He risked a quick glance round and when his eyes passed over his brother's cross and out into the darkness a pulsing pain drilled into his head, and he cried out and fell to his knees.

'Are you alright?' the colonel asked.

'Yes,' he answered unsteadily and got to his feet. *When they come it'll be from there.* The thought was suddenly in his head.

They pressed on, Edward becoming so completely consumed by the cacophony in his head that he was barely aware of what he was doing. To his surprise his spade suddenly struck solid wood. He stopped and looked around, careful to keep his eyes low as a second hollow *thunk* sounded moments later at the colonel's end. The top of the coffin was about three feet below ground level.

'Right there he is, let's get the rest of the soil off and create a space round the sides,' the colonel said. 'Then we'll try and get the rope under it. At least it still sounds reasonably solid anyway.'

He looked at Edward and was not reassured. The man was as white-eyed as a frightened horse. 'We must look like a right pair of ne'er do wells.' He laughed, trying to lighten the mood, but there was no reply, so he simply bent back to his spade and worked on. Moments later he saw Edward had done the same.

They uncovered the coffin lid and then cut out two chimneys on either side of it, giving themselves a space to reach down and underneath.

'We'll have to lie down on the coffin and try to scoop enough soil out with our hands to get the rope underneath and up the other side. Then we can lift him out and effect the transfer,' said the colonel matter-of-factly.

Edward stood by the hole, his body slack and the spade resting on the ground. He was openly sobbing, and the older man reluctantly acknowledged his distress with a question. 'What's wrong?'

'It's the noises in my head, Jocelyn. I swear I can barely stand it. I can hear the moment the men died. It won't stop and it's just overpowering me.'

'I'm sorry, but we need to keep going. I don't care if you cry, but don't you dare stop working. Now get onto the coffin and start digging with your hand.' The colonel's voice was uncompromising. He had commanded men in battle, and it showed.

A long and shockingly loud crack of thunder sounded directly overhead as the wind howled in the trees on the edge of the cemetery. They both staggered and turned their faces away from the lashing rain, but as the squall eased the older man cried, 'No, wait a minute. I have an idea. Let's just take the lid off now and get Hugh out. There's no need to move the coffin at all. Then we can just put the lid back on and refill the grave.'

Edward nodded blankly as the brilliance of this suggestion passed him by completely. 'Okay then.'

The colonel put down his spade and picked up the jemmy. With one look at Edward he said, 'I'll do it,' and lay down next to the pile of earth on his side. Moments later he stood up again, his face in a grimace of frustration. 'We'll have to make more room for the crowbar to work, but I'm sure this is the way to do it. Come on, Edward, let's get to it.'

They both picked up their spades and set to work again, cutting two narrow channels away from the grave edge so the jemmy could provide the leverage they needed. After ten minutes the thing was done, and the colonel lay down again and wedged the thin end under the coffin lid. Grunting audibly he pushed it forward and then leaned down. There was a loud crack as the nails gave way and the lid rose an inch.

'There we go. Not long now. You try your side, Edward, see if you can loosen it.' He passed him the jemmy as another vicious squall drove over them and rain drummed on the coffin lid. Wordlessly Edward took it and mirrored his actions. There was another crack, and he pushed the crowbar deep under the lid and levered away.

'Nearly, keep at it,' the colonel shouted, the rain pouring down his face. Still lying prone he reached down and slipped his fingers into the gap below the lid and pulled upwards with all his strength. Edward threw the jemmy aside and reached down too and they managed to lift the coffin lid up and away.

As they did so another flickering bolt of lightning struck the woods and in its harsh light Edward finally saw his brother again.

The body was in uniform, and his cap was placed on his chest. He was still intact with sallow sunken skin and hair visible on his head. A single round hole showed clear in his forehead and Edward instantly thought, *It was quick, thank God.* And then the light was gone and in its absence the darkness in the graveyard seemed even thicker.

'He seems to be in one piece.' The colonel's voice was close, and Edward realised he had moved around the grave and was now behind him. But the next moment the acrid smell became so strong he could taste it in his mouth and a pulsing, furious voice exploded in his head.

*'What are you doing!'*

He cried out and fell to his knees as though hit with a blow. Unwilling but unable to resist, he slowly raised his eyes from the grave and looked over his brother's cross. 'My God,' he whispered.

'What is it, what can you see?' The colonel's voice was urgent.

'They're here,' he said, terrified. 'Three men in uniform standing ten feet away.' He raised his arm and pointed. 'One is a sergeant and the other two are privates. They are all dry and one of the men has half his face missing. I can see them clearly. The sergeant is carrying a rifle.'

The colonel stared but all he could see were dripping white crosses disappearing into the night. 'What do they want?' he asked, trying hard to keep his voice steady.

But Edward ignored him and spoke out into the darkness, raising his voice against the wind. 'This is my brother. His name is Hugh and we're taking him home, back to Blighty. For my mother.'

*'We know who he is. He's our officer and should stay here with his comrades.'*

'I know but I made a promise,' Edward's voice rang out. 'We both served. Please leave us alone and let me do this. We mean no harm or disrespect.'

Uncontrollable shivers ripped through his body as he waited on his knees, mouth open and rain streaming down his face. If the men chose to walk through them then they were finished. It would be light before they could recover, and it was inevitable that they would be found with the grave open. Their worst nightmare.

*'Alright. He agrees. Godspeed.'*

A wave of sweet warmth blew over him and he shut his eyes with relief. He was crying again as he called out, 'Thank you.'

'What do they say?' the colonel asked.

'They say, "Godspeed," Jocelyn. It's alright.' He looked back over the cross, but the men had disappeared. 'They've gone.'

'Right then,' the older man replied grimly, 'get up and let's press on.'

Edward climbed down into the grave and handed Hugh's cap to the colonel. Then he wedged his feet to either side before putting his hands under his brother's arms and lifting him. He was surprisingly light and to their relief he stayed complete as they manoeuvred him out of his grave.

They eased him into the crate, but it became distressingly apparent that he would not quite fit. Try as they might, they couldn't adjust his head so that it was below the level of the crate sides.

'Hell's bells,' muttered the colonel. 'Look away for a moment will you, Edward?' Moments later he heard a sharp crack and then the slam of the lid. 'That's done the trick,' he remarked decisively.

The final tasks were completed without further incident. The crate was loaded onto the lorry and covered with the tarpaulin. They replaced the coffin lid and shovelled the earth back into the hole. As the rain and wind finally began to ease they rebuilt the mound of earth as best they could, shaping it so that it looked like the others again.

'It's not perfect and the grass will look flattened for a day or two, but with a bit of luck no one will come this way. And the rain will help,' the colonel observed as they loaded the last of the tools into the truck. He looked at his friend and laughed. They both looked like visions from hell themselves, soaked through and covered with mud. 'Are you alright now?'

To his relief Edward smiled back at him and he saw that a degree of calm had returned to his eyes. 'Yes, I think I am. I can barely believe it, Jocelyn. We've got him.'

'So we have. That's the toughest part of the job complete, but we're not home yet, not by a long chalk. Let's get our dry clothes back on, then we'll put some distance between Rouville and ourselves. We want to be well away from here and on the way to the coast by daybreak.'

# Chapter Fifteen

As the two men made their way through northern France, in Great Tew Innes decided that she would visit Beech Farm to check on Nell Atkins. Despite Edward's remarks about the self-reliant nature of childbearing on the estate, she felt she would be failing in her duty if she didn't at least put in an appearance. Especially as it was the girl's first baby and there had been a long wait before she and her husband had conceived.

After lunch she borrowed the Dances' Austin and drove cautiously along Rivermead past the farms and through a little hamlet until she arrived at the turning to Beech Farm. Two minutes later she pulled up outside the handsome Georgian frontage and climbed out.

Hearing a woman's voice coming from the side of the building she walked round the corner into the farmyard. A hay wain was pulled up, its long wooden harness shafts resting on the ground as though tired from labouring in the fields, and a barn door was wide open. Just as she was about to announce her presence with a call, Nell Atkins emerged from within and set off across the yard towards the house.

'Hello,' Innes said brightly. 'I thought I'd pop in and see how you are.'

But instead of a smile of welcome, the other woman turned and stared, her eyes wide with alarm. In fact Innes realised it was more than alarm, the girl looked horrified. Then with a visible effort she collected herself.

'Dr Knox, I'm sorry, you gave me a start. We weren't expecting you today and I didn't hear the car.'

But Innes was barely listening. Nell Atkins had a neat figure and slim waist, and she didn't need any medical training to understand very clearly that she was no longer pregnant. Struggling to find the right words, she said, 'Mrs Atkins, forgive me asking but have you had your baby? When we last met I thought you told me it was due towards mid-November. Was it premature?'

The girl stood motionless for a moment, then she cried, 'There's no baby,' and broke down in tears.

Shocked, Innes blurted a series of questions. 'What has happened? Did you lose the baby? Why ever didn't you let me know at the cottage hospital? I would have come at once.'

But Nell's sobs just became louder and longer, and the young doctor instinctively reached out and embraced her. She held her tight and whispered words of comfort as the girl rested her head on her shoulder, but she was facing the wrong way to notice Nell's husband appear at the back door of the farm. Taking in the scene in one quick glance he disappeared back inside without speaking.

As the girl's tears subsided, Innes heard footsteps coming across the cobbled yard. It was Mr Atkins senior.

'Now then, what's all this then?' he asked as he took in his distressed daughter-in-law. 'We weren't expecting you today, Miss Knox.'

In a few words she explained her reason for the call, before ending with the observation that Mrs Atkins was no longer pregnant and appeared very upset about the fact.

His handsome face creased with a sad smile. 'It turns out there never was a baby, Doctor. Only in Nell's imagination. She wants one so much that she invented the whole thing. She had us all fooled for quite a while.'

'But when I saw her she…' Innes tailed off as the recollection hit her. 'Of course. You didn't let me examine you did you, Nell. What was it, a cushion I suppose?' She gently pushed the girl back off her shoulder and then said with the utmost kindness, 'Nell, you are not the first woman to suffer in this way. I am so sorry. Perhaps we should go inside and have a talk about it? If there is anything at all that I can do to help you, I most certainly will.'

Atkins nodded. 'Come on, love, how about a cup of tea and a chat with the doctor?' With that the girl allowed herself to be led across the yard to the farm's back door. Still trying to adjust to the new situation, Innes followed.

*

An hour later Innes drove thoughtfully back to Great Tew, fully absorbed by the psychological trauma that poor Nell Atkins was experiencing.

Her husband and father-in-law had both been present during the discussion and the girl was embarrassed and emotional about her failure to fall pregnant and clearly blamed herself. But Innes had been at pains to point out that it was not necessarily her failure that was the cause.

'Men too can suffer biological malfunctions, Nell, and you should not assume it is your fault.' She suggested that the couple come to the cottage hospital to discuss their fertility with Dr Hall, but this proposal was met with a flat refusal. Instead the two men demanded assurances that she would, 'Not speak of it in the village,' to which she had replied shortly that the whole matter was under medical confidentiality, and she would not discuss it with anyone.

'Not even Dr Hall?' Nell's husband insisted.

'If that is what you wish. Not even with him.' The relief in the sitting room at Beech Farm had been noticeable, and as the hedges slipped by, she reflected rather bitterly that avoiding gossip seemed to be a higher priority than care for the girl's welfare. It was also glaringly obvious to Innes that sooner or later people would start asking, 'Where's the baby?' She could only image what the impact of that would be on the girl's perilous mental state.

She decided to visit Oxford the following day and obtain a guest reader's ticket at the university library so she could do further research on the subject. Mrs Atkins was suffering and needed help, but there was no ignoring the fact that she had stumbled into an intriguing real-life case which offered an opportunity to extend her knowledge in her chosen subject.

When she returned from Oxford the maid had left an envelope on her dressing table. The contents were brief and self-explanatory.

*Beech Farm, Friday*

*Dear Dr Knox,*

*Following your visit yesterday, we have had a discussion as a family and would like to invite you to supper tomorrow night so we can talk things over a bit more.*

*If you are unable to come please send a note, otherwise we will expect you at 7 p.m.*

*With kind regards,*

*Isaac Atkins.*

Innes was cheered by the invitation and hoped that there had been a change of heart regarding conception advice. Going downstairs she informed Eve that she would not be in for supper the following evening.

As the invitation seemed to have come out of the blue the older woman was curious, and in response to her questions, Innes found herself tempted to open up to her friend. Sensing something interesting Eve suggested a walk and offered a blatant bribe to ensure the girl's agreement.

'When you confided in me about the wean I promised that I would tell you some of my secrets too, Innes. Perhaps it's time for that now. Why don't we have a stroll along Stream Cross before supper?'

They set out and after they had crossed the bridge Eve linked arms with her friend. 'Do you remember that rather unfortunate dinner when you first met Edward and he quoted Shakespeare at you?'

'"There are more things in heaven and on earth than are dreamt of in your philosophy?" Yes, I remember.'

'What do you think he meant by that?'

Innes thought for a while as they steadily climbed and the view across the Cherwell valley opened up. In the late afternoon sun the fertile landscape full of big dark-leafed trees lay at rest. Immediately below the track she could see a horse-drawn plough cutting furrows in the red earth, while further away the smoke from a steam engine rose above the hedgerows as it pulled a cutting machine across a pale yellow cornfield.

*It really is heaven on earth around here*, she thought, then said, 'As I recall I was speaking about the benefits of science and how it is improving our understanding of the world. Perhaps he was implying that science cannot explain everything. That there are things that defy understanding and maybe always will?'

Not for the first time Eve was struck by Innes's intellect.

'Yes, I think that is exactly what he was saying. Before the Christian church became established people worshipped in a different way and at particular places. That continues to this day, and I am involved. In fact I won't beat about the bush, Innes, from your perspective I suppose you would call me a witch.'

Innes stopped and looked at Eve in astonishment. 'A witch?'

'Yes, that is to say I am a practitioner of the old ways of doing things in the countryside.' She smiled at her friend and added, 'And you might be surprised at just how effective those things are.'

They resumed walking and Innes said, 'Surely you're not talking about spells and incantations? Not in 1919?'

There was a pause and the young woman thought, *Good lord, she is.*

But Eve didn't answer directly. 'People like me use the natural power in the earth. Energy runs over the land in streams and influences us in many ways. Creech Hill Ring marks the spot where two of those streams collide. The inner ring marks the exact place, but there is also a huge outer circle of stones that acts like a magnifying glass, built by our ancestors when their lives were completely entwined with such things.'

They walked on up towards the summit of Tan Hill and Eve continued talking about her beliefs. Innes was silently sceptical, but as her friend explained the accuracy with which the outer stone circle had been placed in the landscape thousands of years earlier, she realised the structure really was remarkable.

'Creech Hill Ring is a place of great power, Innes. At certain times it offers a way through into another place. A place where our souls go when we leave our bodies and from where they come back to earth as a new life when so ordained.'

'Are you talking about heaven?' Innes asked hesitantly as they approached the summit of the hill.

Her companion gave a short sardonic laugh. 'No, I am not. Heaven and hell were invented by the Romans to scare their empire's population into obedience. There is no judgement when we die. In fact we don't really die at all. Our spirits are eternal energy.' She glanced over at the younger woman and rolled her eyes conspiratorially before adding in a whisper, 'And as I say, we come back.'

Eve directed her towards a gate, and they walked through it into a grassy field. Thirty yards away a single standing stone twice the height of a man stood on the summit of the hill. They walked up to it.

'This is one of the stones in the outer ring. It has special qualities, they all do.' She slipped a ring from her finger and placed it on the vertical face of the rock. When she moved her hand away it stayed there. 'It's magnetic. Now look around.'

Innes slowly spun through a full circle. In every direction the far horizon was visible. The village of Great Tew spread out below them and she could clearly see the hall and the church and in the distance the long line of trees that marked the ride that led to Creech Hill Ring.

'They're all aligned,' she said in surprise. 'Tan Hill, the church tower, the ride and Creech Hill.'

Eve nodded. 'This is the Litha stone. If you drew a line from here through the centre of Creech Hill Ring and onwards, it would hit the Beltane stone on the far side. Turn and look the other way.'

She did so and immediately saw the tower of the chapel in Little Tew in the same line. Beyond it in the distance another church steeple rose high.

Satisfied that Innes had seen what she wanted her to see, Eve said, 'The churches are built on older sites. Waymarks I suppose you could call them. On the ridge line beyond the far church there's another stone just like this one. You can put a ruler down on the map and all these ancient places line up exactly. The line marks the energy stream, and the sites were chosen because of that, by people who understood their significance. We are standing right in the middle of it up here. In fact it runs straight down the aisle and through the altar of St Mary's church.' She smiled. 'No coincidence.'

Innes looked at her. 'I'm afraid I can't feel anything.'

Eve raised her eyebrows and dug around inside her bag. Her hand reappeared holding two thin metal rods. They were each about eighteen inches long with a right angle bend a third of the way along. She held them up, one in each hand with the longer bar protruding forward.

'Come with me.' She led Innes to one side and handed her the rods. 'Hold them like I was doing, pointing forwards, just loosely in your hands, at waist height and keep them level. Now wait for a moment.'

She walked twenty feet away, to the far side of the standing stone and turned to face Innes. 'Keep holding them loosely, parallel to the ground and walk towards me.'

'What's going to happen?'

'You'll see.'

Feeling both slightly nervous and foolish, she walked slowly forward. After three paces, to her astonishment both rods vibrated slightly and turned in unison to point at right angles directly towards the tower of St Mary's.

She stared down at them and then looked at Eve, her mouth agape. 'I did nothing. They moved completely on their own.'

'You're in the energy stream now, the rods are showing you that.'

Still barely believing it, she walked on and joined Eve, then turned and recrossed the stream. This time the rods turned in the opposite direction, but again ended up pointing at the church.

Eve spoke quietly. 'Just because we can't see something it doesn't mean it isn't there. The people who lived here thousands of years ago might have sensed these streams directly, or they might have dowsed them, like you just have. Or they may have had another way to find them that has been long forgotten. But they marked them by building lines in the landscape at a scale that made them invisible. Secret lines. And places like Creech Hill Ring are either destinations or crossroads. And to simple witches like me, they are wondrous places.'

She smiled and then laughed at Innes's incredulous expression. 'I'm not asking you to believe it all, but I wanted you to understand that there is another dimension to life. As Edward said, "There are more things in heaven and on earth…" and when he says he can see ghosts there's little doubt in my mind that he can.'

Innes nodded slowly, her eyes fixed on the hidden line stretching across the landscape towards the distant ridge. For a brief moment she sensed something, as though she had flicked past a picture page in a book.

'I was thinking how beautiful it is here as we walked up the hill,' she said. 'The sense of peace is wonderful. It does feel as though there is something else at work,' she acknowledged shyly to her friend, as though trying out the words.

Eve moved to stand next to her. 'It's more than that. The land is resting after the summer's labours and the line is easing down. Every living thing is connected and that's what you're tapping into. The noise and bustle of big cities crowds everything out. Perhaps now you are away from Glasgow the other side of your nature will develop. Who knows?'

'How do you use the ring exactly?'

'That's a very big question, Innes, and not one I can answer quickly or easily. But perhaps we can explore those things a little in due course.'

They loitered on the hilltop for some time and as they walked slowly back, Innes told her in great confidence about Nell Atkins's falsified pregnancy.

Eve was hugely sympathetic. 'The poor girl. And how awful for Isaac too, he must have had his hopes raised then dashed.'

'It is dreadful, and I had to make a solemn promise not to speak about it – which I am now obviously breaking – but I trust you absolutely, Eve, and I feel a little out of my depth. I went to the library in Oxford to read up on the subject and these are deep waters, psychologically speaking.'

Eve sighed. 'I may be able to help them myself. Without them ever knowing,' she hastened to add. 'In the meantime I presume your best course is to go to supper tomorrow and see what happens.'

Innes agreed. When they reached the bottom of the hill they met the wean and Ellie playing by the stream. After a noisy reunion they walked back to Marston House together. As they passed Holly Cottage Innes glanced at the front door and asked, 'Have you heard from Jocelyn about how the fishing trip is going?'

'No. Hopefully no news is good news. I suppose we'd have heard if either of them had drowned,' Eve said lightly.

Had Innes looked over she would have seen an uncharacteristic frown of worry on her face.

*

Taking turns to drive, the two men made careful but steady progress across northern France towards Groffliers. They stopped on a deserted stretch of road and dumped all the grave robbing equipment in an overgrown ditch, leaving just the crate and handles tied down beneath the tarpaulin.

By seven o'clock the lorry was parked in quiet countryside less than a mile from Groffliers and, as darkness fell, the two men walked into the village to quietly ascertain the location of the lane that led down to the quay at Port de la Madelon.

Thankfully there was no one around. It turned out the village was little more than a hamlet and as there appeared to only be one lane that ran in the right direction they took it. After fifteen minutes of silent walking they emerged from between high hedges to see the river L'Authie spread before them in the moonlight. The estuary was three hundred yards wide, and a small inlet ran directly towards them with a wooden quay some thirty feet long positioned on its left-hand side. A steep bank of exposed mud glistened in the moonlight on the other side of the creek.

'This is it. It must be,' Edward whispered. 'Mason said it was tidal. When the water rises the *Fair Venture* can get alongside easily I'd say.'

'We can park here, and I can turn the lorry. And there are no houses, it's a good spot,' agreed the colonel. 'Let's head back and put our heads down for a couple of hours. There's nothing to do until one o'clock, that's when we need to be down here and ready.'

They returned to where the vehicle was concealed and settled down to wait. An occasional car went past but otherwise nothing disturbed the night. At half past twelve Jocelyn eased the darkened lorry down the track and swung out into the lane.

But he had made a mistake. With the instincts of a British driver he had looked the wrong way and failed to notice an unlighted bicycle just feet away from the lorry. They heard a shout and then a thump as the front of the cab turned and hit the cyclist fair and square, catapulting him and his machine into the ditch on the far side of the road.

The two men stared at each other in the gloom as the implications of the accident hit them.

'Shall we just drive off?' Edward suggested, his pulse racing.

'We'd better check he's alright. We don't want him chasing after us into Groffliers and raising a hue and cry.'

'Good point.' They climbed down and walked over to where the unfortunate man was climbing out of the ditch, pulling his maimed bicycle with him.

The colonel listened to an exchange of French in which the aggrieved tone of the victim was all too apparent. As he watched he realised to his dismay that the fellow was wearing a uniform of some kind and this impression was confirmed as he watched him bend down and pick up a French kepi hat from the edge of the ditch and place it on his head.

'*Un moment, monsieur, s'il vous plaît*,' he heard Edward say. Then he turned to the colonel and said quietly, 'Keep smiling at me, but we're in bother here, Jocelyn. This fellow is the local bobby, and he is mightily outraged at our road manners and rather too curious as to why two Englishmen are skulking about in the middle of the night near his village. He's just asked me what's on the lorry.'

Jocelyn smiled back and kept his tone level. 'Alright. Tell him I'll have a look at his bike and keep him talking.'

Edward turned and began speaking again, his voice full of sweet reason. The colonel leaned over to inspect the stricken bicycle then casually slipped his hand into his jacket pocket and with a single stride stepped behind the policeman and hit him on the back of his neck. There was a flat *thump* and with a modest sigh their inquisitor dropped to the road.

'He's not having the best of evenings,' observed the colonel. Then he raised his hand and showed Edward a small blackjack, adding, 'A souvenir of my early days on the beat. I put it in my pocket before we set off.'

Working quickly they cut some spare rope from the crate ties and secured his hands and feet, then gagged him and dragged him back up the track into the woods. His bicycle followed.

'It's not ideal but it's late now and I can't imagine there will be much other traffic along here. We only need him to remain undiscovered for four hours at the most and then you'll be on the boat, and I'll be driving back to Boulogne,' Jocelyn said. He glanced at his watch. 'Ten to one, come on, let's get down to the quay.'

As they turned to walk back to the lorry a low moan from the gendarme indicated he was regaining consciousness. 'Will you hit him again?' Edward asked.

The older man chuckled. 'Getting bloodthirsty, aren't you? No, I think not. He's gagged and won't come to any harm. Come on.'

A few minutes later they drove down the narrow lane and parked. The colonel quietly answered Edward's next question before he'd asked it. 'Let's get the crate untied and off the lorry then move it onto the quay when the *Fair Venture* appears. With luck you'll be gone again very quickly.' He nodded towards the creek. 'The water's much higher now.'

It was true. Only the top two feet of the mud remained in view and a tongue of silver and black water now ran up the creek and gently gurgled and eddied around the wooden stanchions of the quay. Edward walked to the end and looked downriver towards the sea, hoping that the boat might be in sight already but, apart from some patches of light mist that had floated in with the tide, nothing stirred.

Turning he walked back to the lorry, and they unloaded the crate.

'Got the torch?' Jocelyn asked.

'Good point.' Edward reached into the cab. 'I'll wait at the end of the quay where there's a view downriver. Maybe you should stay at the end of the lane in case of unwelcome visitors.'

'Yes, that's fine. Try and stay out of sight, you're quite exposed down there.' And with a brief nod the colonel melted away into the dark.

Edward found a place where he was backed by reeds but had a clear view downstream. And there he stayed for two hours. A fox strolled past along the foreshore and there was the occasional splash of water as a fish rose, but apart from that all was peaceful.

The view across the water-filled estuary was wonderful. On the far side, above a wide reed bank, the wooded hillside was capped by a flat ridge that ran in both directions as far as he could see. Downriver the water swirled in the moonlight as the tide pushed in from the sea. After the tensions of the last two days the sense of peace was hypnotic and, safely concealed and feeling strangely alone, he drifted into a trance-like state as small quiet night noises rustled around him. The salty air coming upriver reminded him of the quay at Rye and he idly replayed his conversation with Jim Mason in his mind as he waited.

The view down the river was so unchanging that he was shocked when he suddenly spotted a dark shape in mid-stream and realised guiltily that his eyes had been closed.

*For how long? Thank heavens he'd woken up.*

As the bow pushed through a low blanket of mist on the water, the ghostly shape solidified into a hull, wheelhouse and mast. A single blue light showed at her masthead. He raised the torch and flashed it three times, counted to ten and did it again. The blue light flashed three times in reply then went out. Turning he walked quickly along the quay and said softly, 'They're here,' as the colonel appeared out of the shadows.

'Good,' he grunted, 'I thought I heard voices up the track a minute ago, which isn't a good sign at this time of night.'

They slotted the two carrying handles under the arms on the crate and carried it onto the quay as the *Fair Venture* appeared at the mouth of the creek, the quiet rumble of her engine just audible as she made the turn.

A sudden shout rang out behind them. They both turned and saw a figure at the mouth of the lane. As they watched he turned and ran back the way he had come, calling out in urgent French.

'This might be a close run thing,' murmured the colonel. 'I suspect our gendarme has freed himself and raised the village.'

The boat made its way up the creek with agonising slowness. As it inched forward they moved the crate, so they were in exactly the right place. Fortunately the bulwark was roughly level with the lip of the quay. Edward assumed the single figure on deck must be the mate as he could see the shadowy figure of Mason in the wheelhouse.

A chorus of shouts and the sound of running footsteps reached them over the boat's engine. Edward glanced at the lane. The cat was clearly out of the bag.

'Come on then, if you're coming,' said the man on the deck, the tension in his voice clear.

The colonel made a decision. 'I'm coming with you.' They lifted the crate and somehow managed to balance it on the bulwark and scramble over. Edward caught his foot and fell but the mate stepped forward and steadied the crate and moments later it was safely on the deck.

'Okay.' He waved to the wheelhouse and there was a clang as the engine telegraph sounded followed by the hiss of water as the engine went astern. They had not tied up; it was a touch and go call.

'What about our bags?' said Edward.

'Too late,' the colonel said shortly.

But Edward ignored him. Their passports were in the bags and those would lead straight to Great Tew. He bounded up onto the quay just as a crowd of shouting people flooded out of the bottom of the lane. The lorry was thirty yards from him and about sixty from them. He sprinted to it and hauled the door open. Grabbing both bags from behind the seats he turned and within ten seconds of leaving the boat he was running back towards it.

'Come on, come on!' the colonel shouted and gestured frenziedly, all secrecy gone.

The *Fair Venture* was now at least ten feet from the quay and moving backwards at an increasing speed. He angled his run to the very last piece of quay and as a hand brushed down his back and a voice bellowed inches from his ear, he leapt despairingly up and out into the open space above the water.

The next moment he was aware of an agonising pain in his shins and a terrific blow to his chest as he hit the vessel's side. The mate and the colonel were with him immediately and with each holding an arm they hauled him over the bulwark and onto the deck, where he lay panting, still gripping their luggage.

'You must have wanted them bags mighty badly,' observed the mate.

'I'm sure I've broken both my legs,' Edward said, his eyes watering with the pain. The colonel stood watching the gesturing crowd on the quay and gave them a friendly wave. '*Au revoir, mes amis*,' he called as his friend got slowly to his feet. Then he looked at Edward and pointed to the bags. 'Well done. Passports?'

'Yes.' The younger man stood at the rail as the *Fair Venture* reached the main river and turned downstream. The engine telegraph clanged again as she went to slow ahead. He heard the wheelhouse window open and looked up.

'Good morning, Mr Oxford.' Mason's face appeared as he called down. 'Well that was almost more interesting than we like. And congratulations, incidentally, you pulled off the finest pierhead jump I've seen in many a long while.'

'Our passports are in the bags.'

A snort of laughter sounded. 'A lesson then. Keep what you really need on your person. I thought you would have remembered that from the war. Anyway, if you go below Denzyl will sort you out with a cup of tea or something stronger if you prefer. We're alright now, don't worry. The tide is with us, and we'll be off the coast in an hour and a half. Then we can have a chat about the Candover end.' There was a pause and he added, 'You are in funds I take it, Mr Oxford?'

'Yes, that was in my pocket.'

'Well done. Take a seat and enjoy the ride.' The window clicked shut.

True to his word ninety minutes later the *Fair Venture* was butting away from the French coast in a freshening wind as the dawn showed astern. The crate was securely lashed to the deck and covered with a cargo sheet to protect it from spray which blew back from the bow from time to time. Denzyl was at the wheel and Mason was sitting with them in the saloon. There was no sign of the engineer.

'Obviously we can't make it across tonight, so we'll dawdle and go in tomorrow night. That's what you were expecting, I take it?' Mason said as he cradled a mug of tea to which he had added a generous slug of rum.

'Yes, that's ideal. We're meeting our transport on the jetty at two in the morning,' Edward replied.

The captain nodded. 'Fair enough. Two o'clock it is. I'll take the wheel again and Denzyl will sort out some bacon and eggs, and then I suggest you put your heads down on the settles here. Try not to be seasick and if you are, over the side please. Talking of which, remember, Mr Oxford, any sign of a revenue cutter showing an interest and the crate goes into the sea.'

With that he left, and the mate appeared shortly afterwards and cooked their victuals on a tiny stove in the corner. The two desperados agreed they had never had anything that tasted better.

# Chapter Sixteen

By late afternoon Bert had arrived in Rye with the lorry. He parked and found a pub where he had a good meal, and then took the truck in the direction of Candover Castle, aiming to find a spot to lie up.

Following signs to Winchelsea he left Rye and after fifteen minutes he spotted a road to the left signposted Candover. He followed the twisting tree-lined lane through the little village and as the towers and battlements of the castle appeared in the trees ahead he pulled onto the verge and turned the engine off.

*There's a turning off the drive before you get to the lodge*, he thought. That's what the colonel had told him.

He climbed up onto the flatbed and then up onto the roof of the cab and looked around. From this higher position he could see the castle quite clearly half a mile down the lane, so he assumed the lodge was up ahead. Three fields away to his left the river flowed out towards the sea. He decided that a reconnaissance on foot would be a good idea, so removing the key from the ignition, he slammed the cab door shut and strolled off along the road.

Five minutes later the gravel lane began to run through open parkland and a pair of wrought-iron park gates came into view. Just as he was getting anxious about having to answer questions from a curious lodge keeper, he reached an unmade track on the left with grass growing down the middle that seemed to lead in the right direction.

With a sigh of relief he turned down it and disappeared from view.

The high hedgerows were thick with ripe blackberries, and he stopped to eat his fill, staining his hands crimson with their sweet juice before pressing on. The track led straight down to the river and after giving the surface an assessing eye he decided it would be manageable in the lorry even with the lights off.

At the end there was a tiny tar-painted shed and a little jetty, which seemed to be in good repair. At first Bert thought it was probably routinely maintained by the estate even if it wasn't used much, but then he saw a fine cabin cruiser moored on the other side. He walked onto the jetty and gave her an admiring inspection. Her name was the *Candover Queen* and he realised that she was probably owned by the castle and used for pleasure cruising.

He looked around. Hedges hid him from the road, and he couldn't see any buildings on the other side of the river. He walked to the end of the jetty and stared downstream to the sea. A fishing boat was making her way from the choppy waters offshore into the calmer river and he stood and watched as she approached, then turned and retraced his steps.

He was satisfied. He'd stay where he was until half past one then drive down to the quay and watch for the boat with the blue light at her masthead. He had his torch and he was in the right place.

Bert Williams was ready.

*

The Channel crossing became increasingly uncomfortable during the day. The *Fair Venture* wallowed and corkscrewed in the rising swell that was feeding onto the beam from the south-west. As darkness fell a series of sharp squalls drove them from the deck back down to the stuffy saloon, where the combined smells of tar, fish and fried bacon didn't help Edward's queasiness. Nevertheless, the two men made the best of it and later in the evening when Mason called them up into the wheelhouse they were only too happy to have a change of scene.

'Dungeness lighthouse,' the captain said without preamble as they climbed up the ladder and entered. He pointed over the starboard bow and moments later they saw a double flash appear above the dim line of the coast. 'We'll just do a few big circles while we wait. There's nowhere to anchor out here and I don't want to go any further inshore until we're on the final run up the river.' He glanced at the clock above his head. 'Ten o'clock now, we'll be moving in at one fifteen to be at the quay at two. The tide will be good, it should be an easy lift up onto the jetty for the crate.'

They stayed up in the wheelhouse for some time talking about the war and then retired below and dozed on the settles until the mate came to get them.

'We're a cable off the river mouth, gents.'

Grabbing their bags the two men followed him up the ladder onto the deck. A red light flashing in a regular pattern was reflecting on the water not far ahead of them and Edward heard Mason's voice through the open wheelhouse window.

'That's Camber Beach Buoy, Mr Oxford. Time to pay the balance.'

Edward climbed up to the wheelhouse and handed over the cash, which Mason counted quickly in the light of the compass binnacle and tucked into his coat. 'Very good, sir, all there. A pleasure doing business with you. If you'd help Denzyl get the tarpaulin off, we'll be alongside the jetty in about twenty minutes.'

*

Bert drove the lorry slowly down the track to the river. The lights were off and he was glad he'd had a look earlier, otherwise he would have had his doubts about where he was going, but he reached the end easily enough and took the opportunity to turn around and leave the vehicle facing back up the track.

He peered at his watch. Dead on two o'clock. Climbing down he pulled on his coat and a knitted woollen cap, then walked to the end of the jetty, sat down on a bollard, and stared out to sea. It was cold and he hoped it wouldn't be a long wait.

It wasn't. He saw the boat from quite a long way away as she steamed through a patch of moonlight on the water. As she got closer a blue light appeared at her masthead and he grunted in satisfaction, then stood up and gave three flashes on his torch, followed by another three. The blue light flashed three times and went out.

Five minutes later the *Fair Venture* was alongside, and Bert saw Edward and the colonel on the deck.

'Well met, Bert,' Edward called quietly. With the mate helping it was easy enough to get the crate up onto the jetty. Within seconds of Denzyl jumping back down onto the deck the engine telegraph rang and the vessel started to go astern.

He didn't look up and no one said goodbye.

'Come on then, Bert, lend a hand with these handles,' the colonel said and within ten minutes the crate was loaded, lashed down and covered with a tarpaulin.

Edward felt a surge of emotion. 'Bloody hell, Jocelyn, we've done it,' he whispered wonderingly as Bert climbed into the cab.

'Not quite, but nearly. The final straight now anyway,' came the encouraging reply.

However, it turned out the final straight had one last trick to play. As they left Rye the radiator started to boil over and Bert had to stop. They conducted an inspection by torchlight and the problem was only too apparent.

'There's a hole.' Bert pointed to the final drops of water leaking out as the radiator emptied. 'That's a garage job. It won't take long, a quick weld will cover it over, but we'll have to get a tow to where we can get it fixed. Sorry, gents, but we're stuck here for the moment.'

Edward cursed but the colonel was more sanguine. 'At least we're back in Blighty. There's no reason for anyone to be the slightest bit interested in us. We'll just have to sit tight until places open up and then walk back into town and find a garage to come out and tow us back. It's inconvenient but nothing more. It does mean we won't be in Great Tew until this evening though.'

'I told the garage in Oxford it might be tomorrow to return the lorry, so they'll be fine with that,' confirmed Bert.

Edward curbed his impatience. With the prize in sight he desperately wanted to walk into the drawing room at the hall and tell his grieving mother her dead son was home again.

*

It took until lunchtime for the truck to be fixed but by one o'clock they were back on the road, heading north through showery blustery weather that signalled that the Indian summer was finally over. Jocelyn and Edward were tired and slept for two hours as Bert drove north, but by the late afternoon both men were awake and they stopped for food at a roadside inn.

'I heard your price for helping us, Bert,' Edward said with a smile, as they set off again.

The driver glanced over and grinned back. 'A clean slate with the magistrate? Well I reckon I deserve a fresh start, don't you? You'll have a word with Lord Langford then?'

'I will see what I can do. May I tell him you are hanging up your rod and snares then?'

'You can tell him what you like, Mr Edward, so long as he doesn't send me to Oxford nick if I get caught.'

And it was then that Bert's bombshell revelation changed everything.

'I've been wondering if I should mention something to you. Did I hear right that there's a question mark over Christian Freeling's death?' he remarked casually as he guided the vehicle through the outskirts of Wallingford.

Edward glanced at the colonel who pursed his lips then nodded. 'There are a couple of anomalies,' he admitted.

'Oh yes? Well I wouldn't know about those,' the driver replied, 'but I do know something about Beech Farm. It's been on my mind like.'

'What is it?' the colonel asked.

'Back in the middle of the summer I went fishing one night at Dipper Pool. All legit of course, Mrs Sutton asked me to get her some trout,' he hastened to add.

'Ah yes, that would be when Constable Burrows met you in the high street.' Edward smiled. To the policeman's discomfort, and the entire village's amusement, everyone knew the story.

'That'd be it,' agreed Bert. 'Well before I started fishing, when I was getting my gear ready in the trees, a woman came down the hill from Beech Farm and stripped off naked and had a swim. In the middle of the night, like one of those water nymphs.' He paused and then said, 'And she was pregnant. Had a belly she did.'

Edward said, 'Well I'm sure you enjoyed that, Bert, but it's well known that Nell Atkins is with child. It's her business if she wants to have a midnight swim, although a gentleman would have averted his eyes.'

'Yeah, well I didn't,' he answered without apology and glanced over and grinned. 'Very nice too.'

The colonel stirred and said, 'So what is your point exactly?'

'It wasn't Nell Atkins, it was Jane Freeling. Four or five months gone I reckon.'

*

Innes was getting ready to go to supper at Beech Farm when Eve knocked on her bedroom door and came in.

'I was expecting Jocelyn back sometime today but there's no sign yet. I must confess to being slightly anxious,' she remarked.

Innes looked up from the dressing table and their eyes met in the mirror. In the privacy of her bedroom she was not wearing her spectacles and Eve was again struck by her luminous beauty. 'I'm sure they're alright,' she replied, 'we'd have heard if there was a problem. It's only the south coast.' She noticed there seemed to be real concern in her friend's eyes and turned to face her. 'Is everything alright, Eve?'

'I'm just worried. No reason to be, you're right of course.'

'Well I hope they've caught a decent fish or two. Would you mind if I borrowed the Austin to drive over to Beech Farm?'

'No that's fine. The keys are in the drawer in the hall, help yourself.'

'Thank you. I wonder what they'll give me for dinner?' Innes said. 'Jane Freeling's doing the cooking now. She went to work there when she left the cottage, didn't she?'

'Of course she did, I'd forgotten. You didn't see her when you were there the other day?'

'No, Winnie served the tea. Anyway I doubt it'll be up to Mrs Franks' efforts here at Marston House. I must have put on half a stone since I arrived and the wean's grown an inch and a half.' She smiled at Eve and felt a warm rush of affection for the petite twinkling blonde. 'You know you really have been very kind to me and Jaikie, I am most tremendously grateful. I know I've said it before, but it's worth repeating.'

Eve smiled back. 'You are welcome, really you are. Jocelyn and I like having you both here.' Feeling the moment suddenly come upon her she seized the nettle and said, 'Do you mind if I ask you something personal?'

'I suspect we've few secrets left,' the young woman said, 'but yes, go ahead.'

Her heart beating, Eve jumped in.

'Is it completely outrageous to think that there might be a romance between you and Edward? Given what you told me I understand your cautious feelings, but you are a lovely and vibrant young woman and unless you are resigned to the life of a spinster, at some point you are going to have to consider some kind of entanglement with the opposite sex.'

Innes looked away for a moment and Eve wondered if she had taken offence, but then she answered in a reflective voice. 'I do wonder how my life will turn out. I suppose that's natural, and heaven knows, for most girls Edward is a very attractive proposition. With his position here and his good looks, I'm surprised that Lady Claire isn't organising a regular charabanc of county girls to visit the hall.'

Eve laughed. 'Oh she would, but she knows such behaviour is pointless while he is at Holly Cottage. He simply wouldn't turn up for them. It's one of the reasons she keeps plotting to get him home.'

Innes smiled knowingly. 'There you are then. In fact he has told me directly that he's not interested in romance. He said he'd seen the impact love has had on the bereaved wives and girlfriends on the estate and he…' But Eve held up a hand and gently interrupted her.

'Let's just concentrate on your feelings for the moment. For example, imagine a situation where he was interested in you and made that clear. How would you feel then?'

'You're rather cunning aren't you, Eve,' the young woman said. It wasn't a question. 'Very well, as you seem intent on backing me into a corner, I would say that on a good day, with a following wind and extremely gentle handling, it is possible I might feel able to consider his attentions favourably, but with absolutely no guarantees about where it might lead.'

The older woman grinned, relieved. 'I think there was a yes in there somewhere, wasn't there? In which case I wanted to say that, were that to happen, you should not have any concerns about the family standing in the way.'

'How would you know what my parents would think about me marrying an Englishman?' Innes replied with a smile.

Eve laughed out loud. '*Touché,* Innes,' she exclaimed gleefully, 'no doubt he would have to work at it. But Lady Claire likes you. In fact she likes you a lot. And so does Piers for that matter. That is the point I am making. As far as Langford Hall is concerned you do have a following wind. There is no expectation that Edward will marry into his class and Claire sees many qualities in you. I'm just saying, dear, so you have something to think about.'

In this her prediction proved correct. So much so that later, as she drove the Austin towards Beech Farm, Innes felt the need to pull over and sit quietly with her mind racing for quarter of an hour. Eve was right. There was a lot to think about.

\*

While this conversation was taking place, the lorry finally drove through the gates of Langford Hall. Bert guided the vehicle around to the stable yard where Fenn appeared at the sound of the engine.

'Good evening, Mr Edward,' he said, running a critical eye over the lorry. 'Might I enquire what you have done with the Alvis, sir?'

'Good evening, Fenn. The Alvis is currently in the car park of the Royal Swan hotel in Newhaven. I'd be grateful if you'd get the train down there tomorrow and pick her up.' He handed the keys over. 'You'll find she's unblemished apart from a bit of road dust,' he added with a smile.

'Of course, sir.' The chauffeur looked relieved and then pleased at the prospect of a decent solo run back in his beloved chariot.

'In the meantime, help Bert unload this crate and put it under cover, would you? Tuck it away out of sight and put the tarpaulin over it for now. Jocelyn, will you come in before you go back to Marston House? We'd better speak to my mother.'

Lady Langford was in the drawing room having a drink before supper. Fortunately Lord Langford was not yet down. As they entered unannounced she stood up and stared, her face a combination of hope and anxiety.

A loaded silence hung briefly in the air.

'We've got him,' said her son.

A shudder ran through her, and she burst into tears.

Edward stepped forward and hugged her, tears coming to his eyes as well. He spoke quickly. 'You will hear the tale, mother, but not now. I imagine Piers will be down in a moment. So just to say again, we've got him, Hugh is back at Langford. He's in a crate in the stables for the moment.'

Incapable of answering, she reached for the colonel and hugged him too.

'Thank you, Jocelyn, thank you,' she whispered. 'You are a true friend. Now everything will be alright.'

'My pleasure.' He grinned at her. 'I think I'll go back to Marston House and have a bath and a large scotch – it's been quite a couple of days.' He gently detached himself from Lady Langford and made for the door.

'Wait, I'll come with you.' Edward hugged his mother again. 'I will come up in the morning and we will have a walk. Just the two of us. Alright?'

'Yes, that would be lovely.' Lady Claire was dabbing her eyes but as she looked at him he could see that already the old sparkle was returning. It gave him a warm glow. He had done well. Then for some reason his thoughts turned to Innes. *It would be nice if she knew that I've done well too.* With this odd idea lingering in his mind he followed his comrade in arms out of the hall and down the drive.

At Marston House the conquering heroes were received with laurel wreaths by Eve who was overjoyed to see them back safe and successful.

'You've done brilliantly, both of you. Edward, will you stay to supper?'

'I really must bathe and change. I've been wearing these clothes for four days and am distinctly high.' He laughed. 'I think I'll just rustle up some bread and cheese and then go to bed, Eve. Thank you all the same.'

He turned to his friend and their eyes met. A moment of understanding passed between them. Edward held out his hand. 'Thank you, sir,' he said simply.

They shook. 'You did well, Edward. We both did actually. And the thing is done, that's what matters,' the colonel replied. He walked his friend to the front door and said quietly, 'That thing that Bert mentioned about Jane Freeling. We need to look into that.'

'I quite agree, we'll let the dust settle for a day or two then we can meet with Innes and Burrows and decide on a course of action,' Edward replied.

And with that they parted.

True to his word, Jocelyn disappeared into the bathroom with a large glass of something comforting and reappeared half an hour later, sweet-smelling and resplendent in his Chinese silk dressing gown, matching hat and slippers.

'I'll just eat and head up to bed, Eve. Don't worry, I'll tell you all about it, but not tonight if you don't mind.'

'Very well, I'll let you off this evening.' She smiled.

As they ate they chatted about various bits of gossip and Eve was tempted to tell her husband about Nell Atkins's problems at Beech Farm but decided not to. She was therefore surprised when the subject came up in conversation anyway.

'Bert told us something interesting. Keep this under your hat but apparently he saw Jane Freeling having a midnight swim in Dipper Pool and he swears she's pregnant.'

Eve looked at him in surprise. 'Jane Freeling is pregnant?'

'He reckons she must have been three months gone when Christian Freeling came back from the war.' The colonel raised his eyebrows. 'Makes you think, doesn't it.'

As the reason for Bert's curious questions became clear to her, the colonel saw his wife flicking her eyes towards the sideboard where Ellie was preparing the main course for serving and he addressed her. 'Ellie, as ever, you keep what you hear to yourself. Being the maid in the chief constable's house is a big responsibility. You know that, don't you?'

She turned and looked at him. 'I do, sir. I'd never speak of anything to anyone.' She paused and then added, 'Not like that Winnie at Beech Farm.'

Something in her tone of voice alerted the colonel. 'Meaning what exactly?'

'At the Ploughman's Ball she was sitting with me and Laura Bessing and she'd had a cider or two. She said that a lot of the time Mr Atkins senior's bed isn't slept in much. When she goes up in the morning to do him, it's like he's been sleeping somewhere else most of the night. She reckons it's been going on since Mr Freeling was away at the war.'

She paused and added, 'Well hearing you say Jane Freeling's pregnant…' She shrugged as if the thing was self-explanatory.

'Good lord,' muttered the colonel, 'her and old Mr Atkins?'

Ellie continued, 'Her husband's out of the way and she's living in the big farmhouse, cuddled up with a gentleman farmer. She's gone up in the world hasn't she, sir.'

He looked at his wife who was looking stunned. 'What is it?'

'There's something else. Nell Atkins isn't pregnant. She's been pretending.'

'Really? How odd.'

Eve gestured wildly, her head full of cascading thoughts as she tried to fit the pieces into place. 'No no, Jocelyn, it's not odd. Not when you have the full picture. Jane Freeling is having an affair with Mr Atkins senior and falls pregnant. Suppose she doesn't want the baby, but Nell and Isaac do? They can't conceive. So what if Nell announces to all and sundry that she's with child, and mocks up with a cushion, with the intention of passing off Jane Freeling's baby as hers when it's born?'

There was a silence while her husband thought about this, then said, 'It's possible they could get away with it, I suppose. The farm's on its own over there and no one's expecting to see Jane Freeling out and about while she's in mourning.'

'It's just Mr Freeling coming home from the war isn't it,' said Ellie, now fully absorbed in the conversation. 'That would be the only problem with that plan.'

Another silence filled the room. Then the colonel spoke quietly, almost to himself. 'Good God, Jane Freeling killed her husband to get him out of the way. Or maybe Atkins did. Either way they're all in on it.'

As the reality hit them Eve gave a wide-eyed gasp of horror. 'Innes told me that the Atkinses were obsessed with keeping the fact that Nell wasn't pregnant a secret. They absolutely insisted that Innes promise she wouldn't tell anyone else.'

'She told you,' he observed with a smile.

But his wife wasn't laughing. 'They don't know that. As far as the Atkinses are concerned, only Innes knows their secret and if she keeps quiet they can still get away with it.'

'Well I know now, and I can assure you that they won't.'

She shook her head frantically. 'But they don't know that, do they? They think Innes is the only one who knows Nell's secret. And Innes is at Beech Farm now. They invited her to supper. She thinks she's going to help Nell with a psychological problem, but what if they've decided to make sure, doubly sure, their secret is safe?'

In her anxiety she jumped to her feet and said, 'Jocelyn, what if they're planning to kill her too?'

Adrenalin rushed through his body as he stood up too. Ellie gasped, her hand to her mouth. He turned to her. 'Ellie, run and get Constable Burrows. Tell him to come here immediately. I'll get dressed.'

'Innes took the car,' his wife cried.

'Right. Run up to the hall and turn out Fenn. Police business, he's to bring the Austin to Marston House at once. Tell him it's an emergency. Ellie, when you've been to the hall go and get Bert Williams too.'

# Chapter Seventeen

Innes drove onto the gravel turning circle in front of Beech Farm with a feeling of nervous anticipation. While Nell's mental condition was a little daunting she was hopeful that she would be able to help her come to terms with the issues that underlay it and knew that if she planned to develop her career in psychiatry then she must not duck opportunities to gain practical experience.

She climbed down from the Austin just as the front door of the farm opened and Clayton Atkins appeared. 'Good evening, Dr Knox, it's very good of you to favour us with another visit at short notice, we're all very grateful.'

His handsome face was split with a genuine smile of welcome and with the usual pleasantries observed he led her down the stone-flagged hall and into the drawing room. A fire was burning to keep off the evening chill and Nell and Isaac were waiting for her. She also noticed Winnie standing by a tray of drinks.

'Now tell me, what's your poison, Doctor?' Mr Atkins asked. 'And please call me Clayton. I'm sure we're all on first name terms amongst friends here.'

She smiled back at him. 'Then I am Innes, to you all. And I'll have a brandy and soda please.'

'And for me, Winnie,' Isaac said. The maid took the rest of orders and busied herself with bottles and glasses.

'I think you'll enjoy supper, Innes,' Nell said with a smile, 'it's rabbit stew. Mrs Freeling's speciality.'

'Ah good, is that what we're having?' Isaac said. He looked over at Innes. 'It's become my favourite since she started cooking it for us. Plenty of parsley with it, that's the secret.'

'You know you're right, son, parsley does set it off. Winnie, ask Mrs Freeling to do a little pot for each of us,' his father said as the maid served his drink.

'I will, sir,' she replied and disappeared through the door.

Isaac spoke up. 'Innes, we've asked you back because we've had second thoughts about getting some help conceiving.' He looked embarrassed. 'It's not easy for us, we're private people but Nell and I thought we could have a talk with you after supper. If that would be alright?'

'Yes, I'll make myself scarce and you can have a heart to heart,' his father said.

Innes nodded. 'Of course, I'd be glad to offer what advice I can. And maybe we can have a chat as well, Nell, just the two of us? Would that be alright?'

The girl smiled and nodded, and with these arrangements agreed the conversation moved on to other matters in the village and on the estate. Innes drank her brandy and then at the farmer's insistence had another one before, an hour or so later, Winnie announced that supper was ready.

Mr Atkins walked her into the dining room, with Nell and Isaac behind. A large soup tureen was steaming fragrantly in the centre of the oak-panelled room and Clayton rubbed his hands together and said, 'Aha, that smells like mushroom soup. Just the job for an autumn evening.'

The soup was excellent, and Innes enjoyed it. Winnie cleared away and then re-entered bearing a bowl of stew and various vegetables. She placed them in front of Mr Atkins who served each person. She also passed him a small tray bearing five little pots of finely chopped parsley and he handed one over to each of them. Innes noticed they all used their fingers to spread plenty on and though she wasn't keen on parsley, it was clearly expected that she would do the same, so she obliged, being as sparing as was polite.

'Well then.' Mr Atkins beamed at her. 'Tuck in.'

The rabbit was delicious, and Innes reflected that Mrs Freeling might have found her métier as a cook. She really didn't like the parsley but got some down while pushing as much as she could to the edges of her plate.

As they ate Innes sensed a tension in the room that had not been present before dinner. In fact the easy chatter of earlier had almost dried up completely when a thunderous knocking on the front door echoed down the hall and into the dining room.

'Who the devil's that?' said Mr Atkins. 'Someone in a hurry and no mistake.' He got to his feet as the others looked at him in alarm. Or rather Isaac and Nell did. Innes was suddenly feeling rather ill. She was starting to shiver and had developed an unpleasant burning sensation in her stomach.

Feeling increasingly detached from the scene she heard Mr Atkins meet Winnie out in the hall and moments later a loud voice which she recognised. *The colonel's here, he must be back from fishing*, she thought vaguely as a convulsion pulsed through her and she realised that she couldn't move her arms.

As raised voices carried through from the hall she saw Isaac rise and leave the room. To her surprise Nell reached over and picked up her pot of parsley, then walked quickly to the window. She watched helpless as the girl pulled up the sash and threw it outside. It seemed the next moment the colonel was in the room and bending over her, his face close to hers. Burrows and Bert were there too.

'Innes, can you hear me?' The colonel's head was close to hers, his face a mask of concern. She tried to speak but couldn't form the words as another strong convulsion ripped through her.

'Taken ill, has she?' said Atkins. 'She mentioned her tummy was sore a minute or two ago didn't she, Nell.'

'That's right,' his daughter-in-law confirmed, frowning with worry.

'I don't like the look of her at all,' the colonel said. 'We'd better get her back to the hospital at Great Tew straight away. Lend a hand, Bert.'

With the colonel attending to Innes, Burrows had been standing back observing the scene while keeping an eye on the two male Atkins. He studied the room, particularly the table. What did the manual say? *When inspecting a crime scene an investigating officer should look for inconsistencies or unusual elements.*

So he did. And he noticed something.

'Where's Miss Knox's parsley pot?' he asked quietly, almost to himself. Then suddenly confident he repeated himself louder. 'Where's Miss Knox's parsley pot? Everyone else has one, why doesn't she?'

Clayton Atkins turned and looked at him. 'She doesn't like it, Constable. We all enjoy a bit of parsley with rabbit stew, but she didn't want any.' He shrugged. 'Up to her really.'

Burrows looked at Innes. Her eyes were rolling in her head but for a split second she managed to meet his glance. It was enough. He was sure Atkins was lying.

'Never mind the parsley, Burrows, come on, get her arms,' the colonel said impatiently. But the constable ignored him and walked round to the end of the table. *Yes, there, faint but clear enough.* The round mark of a pot like the others showing in the starched tablecloth by her water glass. He leaned over and picked up Nell's pot. Exactly the same mark showed underneath it.

'No,' he said firmly. 'She had a pot by her place too. There's the mark. Now why would it have disappeared, I wonder?' Everyone in the room stared at him as he remembered a conversation with the farmer's wife at West Lea Farm. Her amused remark came back to him word for word.

*'It might look like parsley but it ain't. It's hemlock, bless you, and deadly poisonous.'*

He looked at the colonel and then at Innes. 'I think they've poisoned her. With hemlock. They've all had a pot of parsley with their stew, but she's had a pot of hemlock. It looks just the same when it's chopped up. That's why it isn't on the table any more.'

'Hemlock poisoning?' Atkins said incredulously. 'Are you out of your mind? The woman is a doctor. She's helping my daughter-in-law.'

The colonel stared at him and then made some quick decisions.

'Right. Bert, carry Innes out to the car and drive her to the hospital in Great Tew, quick as you can. Raise Dr Hall and tell him it's suspected hemlock poisoning. Then go to my house and tell Eve to telephone to the police station in Banbury. They know her there. I want their car and four officers here as a matter of urgency. Have you got that?'

'Yup,' said Bert and with marvellous economy of word and movement he lifted Innes up in his arms and removed her from the scene. Within less than a minute there were five of them left in the dining room.

'Have a seat would you, Atkins? We're going to have a bit of a wait now I'm afraid,' the colonel said. 'You too, Isaac.' He nodded at the younger man standing at the end of the table. 'We may be barking up the wrong tree of course in which case we'll clear this up, but for now I'm inclined to believe my officer.'

Moments later the three Atkinses were sitting at the dining table again while the colonel stood by the door with Burrows at his side. The constable looked around. The pot couldn't be far, there hadn't been enough time. *Where would you hide it in an emergency?*

'I'll just have a look around, sir,' he said and walked over to a large dark brown dresser on the far wall and began to systematically open every drawer and cupboard. It took him five minutes to rummage through and he found nothing.

'Satisfied?' asked Nell.

He studied the room. There was nowhere else to get rid of it. Then he noticed the window. *Yes, that was it.*

As the others watched in silence, he crossed the room and pulled the curtain aside. It was a broad single sash window and the light from the room spilled out onto the cobbled yard outside. At the edge of the pool of light something gleamed. He grunted and raised the sash.

'Here we are, sir,' he said in satisfaction. 'I can see the pot. Someone's thrown it through the window.'

'Really? Well and good. Just leave it there for now, Burrows. We can collect it in due course,' the colonel replied, not wanting to draw attention to the rather obvious fact that if it came to a scrap it would be three against two. And if Burrows was in the farmyard his chances would be slim. He wished he hadn't had to send Bert away, but the girl's life was in danger and there was no avoiding it.

As if reading his mind, Atkins stood up. So did Isaac and Nell.

'Sit down again would you?' the colonel said with more calm than he felt. 'No one's going anywhere until the police arrive from Banbury.'

As he finished speaking he noticed all three Atkinses were looking over his shoulder and a split second too late he realised his mistake, as the cold steel of a double barrel shotgun pressed against the back of his neck.

'Oh I wouldn't say that, Colonel Dance,' said Jane Freeling.

As they all stared, Burrows spun around and threw himself out of the window. One moment he was there, the next he was gone.

'Damn. Leave him for now. Well done, Jane,' said Atkins. 'Colonel, it's your turn to take a seat now if you please. At the end here will do.' He pointed to the chair he had just vacated, and Jocelyn silently sat down. As he looked up he had clear sight of Jane Freeling. She looked quite beautiful and was clearly heavily pregnant.

He said conversationally, 'You killed your husband didn't you, Mrs Freeling? After finding you were pregnant with Clayton Atkins's baby. You must have been hoping the Huns would do the job for you.'

'That'll do. Isaac, take the gun from Jane, and Nell, find some rope to tie the colonel up,' Atkins said.

But the chief constable persisted as he worked things through in his head. 'I see now, our mistake was to believe you when you said you'd seen your husband leaving the cottage the morning he was found dead. And of course the Atkins family backed you up, meaning we trusted what you told us. Very clever I must admit, but

I'm guessing that Christian Freeling had been dead for a while by then. No wonder no one saw him walking to the yew. Am I right?'

But no one chose to answer him and five minutes later Jocelyn was gagged and bound hand and foot to the chair.

'What do you think Burrows will do, Dad?' asked Isaac.

'Well he's a long way from any help. It'll take at least half an hour for the police to get here from Banbury, more like an hour probably. We've time enough to get clear. My guess is that he's probably lurking outside somewhere so keep your eyes peeled and if you see him, shoot him. No hesitation. Right?'

'Oh yes.'

'Nell, you wait and keep an eye on him. Holler if you need us.' Atkins's voice faded as he, Isaac and Jane walked quickly out of the room.

*

Outside Burrows, nursing a painful bruise on his knee, had gone to ground in the smaller of the two barns on the far side of the farmyard. He could see the dining-room window clearly and watched as the colonel was tied up.

He racked his brains as to the best thing to do. The manual was rather short of instructions in situations like this, so he would have to improvise. He didn't think his chief constable was in any immediate danger. It would serve the Atkins family no purpose to shoot him in cold blood, especially as Burrows was free to tell the police what had happened when they arrived.

As he pondered his next action brisk footsteps sounded on the cobbles and moments later Isaac strode past in the gloom and entered the other barn. He heard the whine of a self-starter turning and then a car engine firing into life. The vehicle appeared and nosed its way out of the farmyard and round to the front of the house.

Keeping to the shadows, Burrows followed. As Isaac parked, his father came out holding two suitcases which he placed in the boot. The constable wormed his way under a shrub as the two women appeared wearing travelling clothes and also carrying suitcases. Isaac took them and loaded them into the boot as well. It struck Burrows that there was no panic. All four of them were calm and methodical in their actions.

*They've talked about this before. What to do if things go wrong. They have a plan.*

*

In the darkness Edward peddled frantically along Rivermead towards Beech Farm. Alerted by Eve but with no car, he had accepted the offer of her ancient lady's bicycle. Five minutes earlier he had met Bert carrying a stricken Innes in on the back seat of the hall's Austin and had been horrified at her condition.

'Very sorry, Mr Edward, but she's dying,' Bert had observed gravely. 'Hemlock doesn't take prisoners. Dr Hall will do what he can but…' He shrugged and tailed off.

Bert had seen cattle die of hemlock poisoning. There was no antidote.

'What can I do?' Edward said desperately.

In a few sentences Bert had outlined the situation at Beech Farm and suggested Edward cycle there to see if he could assist. 'You can't help Miss Knox by standing at the end of her bed, Mr Edward, sorry to say. Now I can't wait,' and with that he drove off.

So now, heart pumping and gasping for breath, he drove the bicycle up the hill and onwards towards the farm. At last he reached the turning and swung round onto the track that led down to the farmhouse.

As it came into view he could see the front door was open and in the light that spilled out a large car was visible with figures standing by it. The boot was open, and Clayton Atkins was putting a suitcase into it.

The cycle rattled noisily over a series of bumps on the track and as the group turned to stare at him he cried out, 'Stop, stop all of you! Where are the colonel and Burrows?'

He saw Isaac Atkins move apart from the group and raise a shotgun to his shoulder. There was a loud pop and muzzle flash, and he felt a thump in his chest as a mysterious force pushed him backwards off the bike and into the ditch.

There was no pain and as he lay twisted up in the long grass, the last thing he remembered was thinking, *I've finally been shot, and it wasn't even by a bloody German.*

Appalled at what he'd seen, Burrows burst from cover truncheon in hand and, roaring defiance, charged towards the car. He saw Isaac calmly turn and raise the shotgun again.

*It's too far. He's got the other barrel, I'm going to die.* As the sickening realisation flashed through the policeman's mind, he thought, *I should have kissed Laura Bessing.*

A small black-clad figure burst out of the front door at a sprint, skirts raised. She was carrying a rolling pin and she threw it at Isaac Atkins. The improvised weapon hit him on the shoulder just as he pulled the trigger and Burrows felt the wind of the shot pass his face but no pain. Then he was upon them, but Nell stuck her foot out and as he stumbled, Isaac raised the butt of the shotgun and landed a vicious blow on his cheek.

As his consciousness faded he saw the struggling, kicking figure of Winnie the maid being overpowered and pushed to the ground.

*

Bert Williams obeyed his instructions to the letter, stopping outside the cottage hospital and leaving Innes on the back seat while he ran next door to turn out the doctor. As he banged on the door he heard the bell of St Mary's chime ten o'clock.

In a few words he explained what had happened and with a muttered curse Dr Hall called his wife, who was the nurse and walked quickly to the car.

'Let's get her inside, Bert. There's precious little we can do with hemlock, but I can pump her stomach and put her on oxygen. Then it'll be up to her I'm afraid. It all depends on how much the poor woman has ingested. I will telephone to the hospital in Oxford in case they have any ideas.'

Satisfied that she was in the best hands that Great Tew could muster, he ran around the corner to Marston House and banged on the front door continuously until both Ellie and Eve arrived at the same time.

'You were right,' he gasped breathlessly. 'They've poisoned Innes with hemlock. I've brought her back now. She's with the doctor. The colonel says you're to call the police station in Banbury and tell them the chief constable wants the car and four officers to Beech Farm as soon as possible. It's an emergency.'

With commendable aplomb Eve did not query this direction or ask for any further details. She just said, 'Right,' and disappeared into the study to use the telephone. Standing in the hall with Ellie he heard his instructions being relayed. She emerged shortly afterwards.

'They say it will be at least half an hour before they're there. I'm going to see Innes. What will you do, Bert?'

'Get some help and go back to Beech Farm I reckon. If things get unruly the colonel and Burrows are outnumbered.'

'Good. Thank you. Do you want a gun?' she asked calmly.

'Yes, I reckon so.'

Eve walked briskly down the hall and reappeared less than a minute later with a double-barrelled shotgun and a handful of cartridges.

Thanking her, Bert ran back around to the car and drove up the high street to the Black Horse, the car's engine whining in pain as he pushed it to the limit. He burst in and saw Stanley Tirrold and a farmhand called Dent conversing at the bar. Laura Bessing was pulling a pint for a wizened pensioner sitting in a battered armchair. There was no one else.

Everyone turned to look at his dramatic entrance.

'The colonel and Burrows are up at Beech Farm. They're in bother and need help. Quick as you can. Turns out the Atkins are bad 'uns.'

They all stared in silence, frozen like a tableau.

'Come on then,' he roared. 'Oi mean now!'

There was a rush of feet across the flags and the next minute Bert was back in the car with Dent next to him in the front. He heard a happy cry of acknowledgement from the old man in the pub as Stanley Tirrold shouted, 'Look after the beer, Joe.'

He turned round and peered into the back. The publican was on one side and Laura Bessing, looking remarkably determined, was on the other. He looked at her.

'Burrows needs me.' She said it so fiercely that Bert turned without comment and accelerated away back down the high street towards Rivermead.

During the drive he explained as best he could what had happened and said he had left the colonel and Burrows in command. 'I just hope that's still the way it is,' he concluded, and the rest of the journey passed in silence as he pushed the Austin to its limits along the narrow hedge-lined lane.

They swung into the farm track with a slide of the wheels and then Bert slowed the vehicle and dowsed the lights as they nosed down to the house, passing a bicycle on its side on the way.

'That's the bike Mr Edward was on,' he muttered to his passengers.

They came to a halt and climbed out. Bert stared at the silent, darkened house. 'I'll have the gun, Mr Dent,' he whispered, then led the way to the front door. He pushed it open with his foot. The flagstone hall ran away from them into the gloom. Nothing stirred, but there was an all-consuming feeling that something was wrong.

'Have they got electric?' Stanley Tirrold whispered, the chief inspector from the pub firmly grasped in his hand. In answer Bert reached out and felt for the switch by the door and a moment later the hall was flooded with light.

'Colonel? You there?' he called as they made their way cautiously inside.

A faint noise came from the drawing room down the hall. Bert advanced and taking a deep breath he opened the door and turned on the light.

'Jesus.' The landlord's exclamation served them all well enough.

Burrows was lying in the middle of the floor, bound hand and foot and gagged. A pool of blood surrounded his head, and he was clearly unconscious. Next to him Winnie was equally restrained but was wide awake and wriggling and mewing at them as she rolled her eyes.

Laura cried, 'Burrows,' and pushed past the men to get to his side. They followed and quickly had Winnie untied.

'Are you alright?' Bert asked with an anxious glance at the policeman who now had Laura bending over him.

'They got away. Jane Freeling had a shotgun. I hid in the scullery and then they overtook the colonel and tied him up. He's in the dining room. Burrows escaped but when they shot Mr Edward he charged them, and they got him too. Knocked him down. Then they tied us both up and drove off.'

There was an appalled silence for a second.

'They shot Mr Edward?' Bert said.

'Yes, took him straight off his bike. He must still be outside in the ditch,' she sobbed.

'You find the colonel, Winnie,' said Bert urgently and with that the three men ran back down the hall and out into the night. 'Over there by the bike,' he called and to their horror they saw a dark figure hunched up in the long grass.

'Mr Edward, sir, are you alright?' Bert cried, putting the shotgun down and climbing into the ditch. 'Try and find a torch or a lantern, Mr Dent,' he added. The farmhand ran back towards the front door, his boots thumping noisily on the gravel.

In the gloom both men bent over Edward. He was unresponsive and Bert felt wet on his hands as he ran them over his front. 'Chest wound,' he muttered to the publican. 'What was the range d'you reckon, if they were by the front door?'

Stanley Tirrold stood and looked over. 'About forty yards?'

Bert grunted. 'Not point blank but too close.'

Running footsteps on the gravel heralded the arrival of Dent with a lantern, closely followed by Winnie and the colonel. In the light the clothes on Edward's chest were stained dark with blood.

The colonel said, 'There's nothing we can do here. Somehow we'll have to get him and Burrows into the car and back to Great Tew. And Innes is already there with hemlock poisoning. Ye gods, what a mess.'

They all looked up as headlights showed in the sky and moments later shone across the hedge at the top of the farm track. 'Right, that's better news,' he continued. 'I'll bet that's the officers from Banbury, in which case we'll commandeer that car as well.'

This proved to be the case and after a short conference with the new arrivals, arrangements were quickly put in place.

'Sergeant, you and the men stay here and search the farmhouse thoroughly. There's a china pot and some scraps of hemlock in the farmyard below the dining-room window that's wanted for evidence for a start. Be careful not to get it on your hands. Then you're looking for anything that indicates where they might have gone. I'll go back to the village. There's no telephone here and I need to put a national call out to watch the ports.'

The policemen carefully carried Edward into the police car. Then they went into the house and reappeared with Burrows who was still out cold, accompanied by a tense Laura Bessing. He was eased into the Austin and without further delay the convoy set off for Great Tew with the colonel driving the police car.

The sergeant turned to his men. 'Right, lads, let's get cracking.'

# Chapter Eighteen

B y eight o'clock the following morning news of the shocking events at Beech Farm was spreading quickly through Great Tew and villagers gathered in clusters to discuss what they had heard.

Edward had been taken to the Radcliffe Infirmary in Oxford in the Banbury police car. Having examined him, Dr Hall had pronounced that he had neither the operating facilities nor the blood supplies that would save his life. The wounded man had arrived at the Radcliffe at half past three in the morning but the surgeon, woken at home by the hospital following Dr Hall's call, was ready and he had been rushed into surgery where he was transfused with four pints of blood while forty shotgun pellets were removed from his chest.

'He'll need more blood yet and if he makes it, it will be because his coat saved him,' observed the surgeon to a theatre nurse and indeed the thick army greatcoat that Edward had thrown on as he ran out of Holly Cottage had absorbed some of the force from the cartridge.

Lady Claire was at his bedside, driven there in the middle of the night by Piers in a borrowed car. She would not leave him again until she knew, one way or another.

As the wards slowly came to life the surgeon came and sat with her. 'We have done all we can, Lady Langford. He was unconscious due to blood loss, but we have replaced that, and he has a fair chance now I believe, although I must warn you that he is not out of the woods yet. We must hope for the best.'

Innes Knox was in Great Tew hospital, where her condition was grave. True to his word Dr Hall and his wife had pumped her stomach and put her on oxygen and she now lay in a coma in a single room.

Again, using the telephone in the middle of the night Dr Hall spoke to a physician at the Radcliffe whose advice was sympathetic but chilling.

'There's no point in moving her to Oxford. You've done the right things, Dr Hall, but hemlock attacks the body in different ways at the same time,' he said. 'She may well suffer respiratory or renal failure, paralysis or acute depression of the central nervous system. If she has ingested a significant quantity of the plant then she will die. I'm telling you this with no obfuscation as another medical man, but of course what you tell the family is up to you. The prognosis is not good though, I'm very sorry. Keep me informed, would you?'

The only brighter piece of news was that Burrows had regained consciousness in the car on the way from Beech Farm to the village, coming round to find himself cradled in Laura Bessing's arms. Although third in line for treatment, Dr Hall had got to him in the end and pronounced that he had a broken cheekbone and concussion, and prescribed bed rest and painkillers.

With Laura on one arm and Bert on the other they had walked him slowly the short distance from the hospital to the police house. Opening the door she had led him inside and then turned to Bert.

'That's fine now, thank you. I will look after him.'

On the doorstep Bert hesitated. 'You sure, Laura? He'll need putting to bed and the like. I'll get my missus if you want?'

But the pretty dark-haired girl had just smiled at him and gently shut the door on the outside world.

*

As dawn showed through the window of Great Tew hospital, Eve sat in silence next to Innes's bed still struggling to come to terms with the appalling events overnight, but thankful that at least now she had time to think. She wondered how Edward was. If he left them, then the impact it would have on Lady Claire was too dreadful to think about.

*Hold on, Edward, hold on*, she reached out across the miles and willed him to keep trying.

Her husband was now in bed upstairs at Marston House, exhausted by the last few days. Dr Hall had also retired for a short rest, and she was alone with her friend. She took her hand in hers and was struck by how cold it was.

*Like she was already nearly gone from here.*

Dr Hall had said she was in a coma because her body had shrunk its functions back to the most basic life-supporting systems as it fought the poison. The last desperate vestiges of self-defence in action. She had two hot water bottles nestled under the blankets and the oxygen mask hissed faintly, reassuring Eve that Innes was still breathing. She moved her other hand to the bed and sandwiched the girl's palm between hers, pressing to maximise the contact, then shut her eyes and began to speak quietly. In the silence, her voice was barely audible.

She let her mind open and drift upwards, ever higher, far beyond the reach of earth and into the high white places. Her rhythmic words, not spoken in English, followed her. They were known to few people and fewer still understood their power.

It was a summoning spell. As ancient as the gods themselves.

Eve was calling down the light.

She continued for fifteen minutes, her eyes closed, steadily repeating the same words time after time in a lilting cadence, as she bathed Innes in a pure white light that pulsed and shimmered as it ran through her.

At last she tired and respectfully spoke the closing words, then slowly brought herself back into the room, opened her eyes and refocussed on the girl.

She squeezed her hand. It was warmer now and she felt the faintest of responses. A slight movement of her fingers.

\*

'What on earth has gone on up there, Wilkes?' Evans asked his reporter as they met in the newsroom. 'Actually, go and find a coffee for us both and come into the office. I want to hear the details.'

'Right you are, sir,' Wilkes replied. 'It's quite a tale.'

When they were settled, one on either side of his desk, the editor said, 'Alright then, spill the beans. Once the rumours started you drove to Great Tew. What did you find?'

Wilkes reached into his briefcase. 'When I got back last night I drafted an article, sir. Perhaps it might be easiest to have a shufty at that? Then you'll get things in the right order as far as I understand them.' He offered the piece of paper over the desk and Evans took it.

The draft was written in Wilkes's usual economical style.

### The sensational Beech Farm murder as it happened

*After our initial report on events near Great Tew on Monday night, the* Times *can now bring readers up to date on the case following an exclusive interview with Colonel Jocelyn Dance, the Chief Constable of Oxfordshire.*

*When Christian Freeling, a twenty-four-year-old labourer at Beech Farm, was found hanging in an ancient yew tree on the Langford Estate all the evidence pointed to a tragic suicide, driven by the horrors of the war in France. There was great sympathy locally for his attractive wife Jane Freeling aged nineteen to be so bereaved after seeing her husband return safely from the war.*

*But things were not what they seemed. With the instincts of a natural policeman, Colonel Dance led discreet enquires designed to elicit the truth behind the death.*

*Following some fine detective work it was discovered that Jane Freeling was three months pregnant when her husband came home from the war. She had managed to conceal this fact from him, but clearly could not do so for much longer. This established a motive for Mr Freeling's death and, convinced he was on the right track, the Chief Constable accelerated his enquiries concerning the people living at Beech Farm.*

*Although they hid the truth very skilfully the police established that, if readers with forgive the salacious details, Mrs Freeling and*

Mr Clayton Atkins, the widowed tenant of Beech Farm, had become secret lovers when Mr Freeling was away with his regiment. The evidence suggests they acted together to murder Christian Freeling so they could enjoy a life together.

In an extraordinary twist to this story the childless son of the accused, Mr Isaac Atkins, and his wife Nell, who also resided at the farm, planned to present Mrs Freeling's unwanted baby as their own when it was born. To this end Mrs Nell Atkins announced that she was with child and presented herself to the village as such, using a cushion to fabricate her condition.

Miss Innes Knox, a local doctor, was cruelly hoodwinked by the couple when she visited the farm to provide medical assistance to Mrs Atkins, in the belief that she was near her time. Sadly for her she stumbled on the reality of the plot and was poisoned with hemlock under the pretence of a supper invitation.

Fortunately Colonel Dance was hot on the trail. He arrived in the nick of time and personally prevented her from taking a fatal dose, but even as you read this, Miss Knox lies in Great Tew cottage hospital, hovering between life and death. The other casualties are Mr Edward Spense, youngest son of the Dowager Lady Langford of Langford Hall, who arrived at Beech Farm at the height of the crisis to give valiant assistance and was fired upon by Isaac Atkins with a shotgun. His life was saved by the expertise of a surgeon at the Radcliffe Infirmary, and he too is now in the cottage hospital under the care of Dr Hall. He is expected to make a full recovery.

Constable Burrows, also in attendance at the farm, received a blow to the head in the fracas and broke his cheekbone. He is recovering at home. But the greatest casualty is of course Mr Christian Freeling, who served gallantly in the war, and then fell foul of an evil plot when he believed he had returned safe home.

Clayton Atkins, Jane Freeling, Isaac Atkins and Nell Atkins disappeared into the night while the attentions of the police were rightly concentrated on the emergency treatment of Miss Knox and Edward Spense. As readers will be aware, Isaac and Nell Atkins were apprehended boarding the SS Carpathian Star in Liverpool two days ago. There have been no sightings of the other two fugitives, and I understand from the Chief Constable that the current theory is that they *split up and crossed the Channel to France independently before their names had reached the ports. French police have been informed.*

*Readers can rest assured that the* Times *will continue to follow this story.*

Evans put the piece of paper down and whistled quietly as he leaned back in his chair. 'Good heavens, Wilkes, that's a story and a half. These remote villages, they have their moments, don't they?'

'Don't they just, sir. And of course Lady Langford was in the news back in the summer when her Legionnaires fought that pitched battle in the Strangers' Gallery at the House of Commons.'

'Of course, the War Graves Commission bill. Were there any repercussions over that?'

'No. It all went quiet. I assume she gave up on the whole thing. You'll recall her son Lord Langford was not best pleased at having to retrieve her from Westminster magistrate's court.'

Evans laughed. 'Yes, I remember. Very wise of her. You can't fight the might of the government.'

Wilkes said, 'Anyway for now Isaac Atkins is being charged with the attempted murder of Edward Spense, and both he and Nell with being accessories before the fact in the attempted murder of Innes Knox. If they can find the other two it'll be a murder charge regarding Christian Freeling, and I imagine they'll swing given the evidence. Although Jane Freeling will have the baby first of course.'

'Perhaps, but I can image a defence barrister having plenty to chew on as well. If they all lay the blame off on each other it might not be as clear cut as you anticipate. How was Freeling murdered in fact?'

'The chief constable believes that he was poisoned by his wife the night before he was found in the tree. She laced his dinner with hemlock and left it ready before going off to Banbury to see her mother. He would have been dead when she got back. During the night Atkins senior and junior took him by means unknown to the Langford Yew and hung him up there before dawn. The entire family then colluded to say that they had seen him leave Beech Farm carrying a rope that morning, leading to the assumption that the man had committed suicide.'

Evans clicked his tongue. 'You know it's funny, Wilkes, we think here in the capital we've got the monopoly on brains. It's easy to forget that country people are just a smart and just as capable.' He handed the article back over the desk. 'That's fine. Print it.'

*

It was All Hallows' Eve, the last day in October and the pagan sabbat of Samhain.

In the gardens of Langford Hall Bert Williams had been working on the hilltop at the end of the privet ride all day. He was digging a grave for Hugh Spense and the gardeners had been instructed to keep well clear of the area. Lady Claire had also contrived to send Piers into Oxford for most of the day, leaving the field clear for him to get on.

The grave was to be a classic shape. Hugh would be removed from his crate and laid to rest in the earth with no coffin. Although Edward had been moved from the cottage hospital to Langford Hall that day, he was still largely bedridden and incapable of any exertion so, after discussing the practicalities with Lady Claire, Edward had let Bert into the secret and commissioned him to dig the grave and assist with the interment.

He and his mother had also decided to keep the reality of Hugh's grave from Piers. As far as Lord Langford, or anyone else was concerned, the site would be a place to remember the sacrifice he had made, but nothing more. Although they had agreed that the truth would be formally recorded in the confidential Langford family papers and each new person succeeding to the title would be informed and charged with keeping the matter secret. The longstanding family solicitor had been briefed to this effect.

By late afternoon the grave was ready, and Bert rested on his spade. *I reckon the sexton would be proud of that*, he thought.

It wasn't only at Langford Hall that preparations were underway. Eve was also getting ready. During the day she called unannounced on people in the village and received others at Marston House. She had the same conversation with all of them and one upshot of this was that after lunch in the Black Horse Stanley Tirrold addressed Laura.

'I'll be going out about nine o'clock this evening,' he said, 'so you'll be in charge.'

'Oh yes? What are you up to?'

'A job for a friend. That's all you need to know,' he said firmly. 'Setting one or two things straight.'

And with that the ever-curious Laura had to be satisfied.

So it was that throughout the village and in the hall various people made various preparations and by the time Stanley Tirrold looked at the clock and said, 'That's me away then, Laura, I'll see you in the morning,' everything was in place.

If Laura had looked out of the window half an hour later she would have seen the publican emerge from the side of the pub wearing a thick coat and carrying a large bag on his back. He walked down the high street and as he turned into Rivermead two other figures, similarly burdened, appeared out of the shadows. With a quiet nod to each other they set off together and within thirty seconds had disappeared into the night.

At the same time another party set off in the opposite direction, crossing the footbridge at Stream Cross and heading up the steep track towards Little Tew. Finally two individuals walked out alone into the darkness. Like the others, they each carried a bag.

An hour later Eve kissed her husband goodbye and wished him good luck. 'Remember, exactly at midnight, by the chime of the church clock,' she reminded him, then let herself out of the front door. She walked up the high street and turned into the gates of Langford Hall. Passing the building where lights burned in the drawing room and three upstairs bedrooms, she made her way silently through the grounds.

Half an hour later she walked down the ride, between the two great standing stones and out into the middle of Creech Hill Ring. Shrugging off her pack she slowly turned and looked at the skyline, sensing the atmosphere.

*

At half past eleven Bert and the colonel retrieved the crate from the stables and set off through the gardens to the grave, using the carrying handles. They were joined by Lady Claire and Edward, walking slowly and with the aid of a stick. He carried a bible in his free hand.

They arrived at the end of the privet walk, passed under the arch and out onto the hilltop. It was a fine night. The moon was waxing to full and shone down on them periodically as clouds moved slowly up from the south-west.

*A good night for a bit of poaching*, thought Bert irreverently.

'Alright then, Bert, let's get the lid off and move him into the grave,' the colonel said. Then he looked over at Lady Claire and added, 'I'm sorry, this will not be very dignified, but we'll do our best.' Once the lid was off the colonel reached into the crate and his hand emerged holding Hugh's cap.

'Perhaps you would like this?' he said gently.

Lady Claire stepped forward and took it. 'Thank you,' she said. Edward could hear she was barely holding the tears in check and his eyes were watering too. *He could still barely believe they were here doing this.*

As he watched, Jocelyn reached into the crate and lifted Hugh's body out. Bert moved to assist and between them they carried him over to the grave.

'Climb in, Bert, and I'll lower him down,' the colonel said quietly. But as Bert moved Lady Claire spoke.

'Wait.' She walked forward, her eyes fixed on her beloved son. Then she slowly leaned in and kissed his withered cheek. 'Goodbye, my darling,' she whispered. Then she stood back, took Edward's hand in hers and, as tears streamed silently down her face, she took a deep breath and nodded to the colonel.

A minute later Hugh was lying in the bottom of the grave.

'Will you say something, Edward?' the older man asked.

'Yes, when the grave has been refilled,' his friend answered. 'A short reading and a prayer.'

Jocelyn glanced at his watch. In the moonlight he saw it was two minutes to midnight. 'Eve asked us to wait until the first chime before covering him. Is that alright?' He looked over to the mother and son standing ten feet away. But to his surprise they were both staring over his shoulder.

'What's that?' Lady Claire asked.

He turned and saw in the far distance a flickering light that grew in strength as they watched. Then it was joined by another and another, three bright, equally spaced points of light on the night horizon.

'More there,' said Bert, pointing. And they all turned to see three more had appeared far away to their left.

'What's going on?' Edward said to no one in particular.

It was Bert who answered, a note of wonder in his voice. 'I think they're firing the outer ring. To make a circle of light around Creech Hill. I've only heard about it, never seen it in my lifetime. Is Eve out tonight, Colonel?' he asked.

'Yes, she is.'

'Samhain.' Bert nodded, satisfied. 'And here we are doing this?' He looked at Lady Claire. 'They're making sure your son is sent on his way I reckon, Your Ladyship.'

As he said this the low deep tone of the ancient bell of St Mary's reached them. Cast a thousand years ago and still sending its potent signal out into the night.

'Alright, Bert, start filling in, would you,' said the colonel.

*

In the middle of Creech Hill Ring, Eve stood and slowly turned full circle. Eight pinpoints of bright light showed low in the night sky, entirely surrounding her.

She looked at the bonfire she had built in the precise centre of the ring, made of logs fallen from the Langford Yew. As the first strike of St Mary's echoed out across the landscape she poured a bottle of oil onto the wood, struck a match, and threw it on.

It flared and caught immediately and within a minute it had built to a strong blaze, signalling its response to the ring of fire that surrounded the ancient place. As she watched the lights in the distance seemed to gain in strength until they were clear and strong, the eight sabbats of the calendar all united and working as one, with their power focussed on where she was standing.

As the bell tolled for the final time she reached up and threw off the cloak she was wearing. She was naked underneath and as the light from the fire glowed against her skin she picked up the silver dagger and holding it high above her head she started to chant, strange ancient words that commanded and shaped the energy that crackled around her.

She felt the rough grass beneath her bare feet and the heat of the flames on her skin. The bonfire was burning blue and unworldly now and roaring like a blowtorch, fuelled by forces long forgotten but still lying ready for those who could use them. On and on she chanted until her entire body was fizzing with ecstatic energy as she channelled the ancient streams into the fire.

Her name was Eve Dance, and she was a witch.

At last she sank to her knees, exhausted and unable to maintain the focus for any longer. Suddenly cold, even in the heat of the fire, she reached for her cloak and stood up, draping it over her shoulders.

The bonfire was dying down now and giving off a strong acrid smell. She looked up and saw the outer ring was fading too. She stared into the embers.

*Had it worked?*

The acrid smell got stronger and stronger, and she instinctively turned to look backwards towards the two sentinel stones that guarded the entrance to the Creech Hill Ring.

*There he was*. Hugh Spense was walking towards her, in uniform but bareheaded, his gaze fixed on the bonfire. She stepped aside as he passed, but he made no eye contact.

As she watched he walked straight into the bonfire.

It flared up strongly, burning blue and orange and she saw the entire outer ring rise and burn again in unison. Then a single flash of fire pulsed out from Creech Hill, sending a thin disc of burning light in every direction. It continued past the outer bonfires and up into the night sky. At the same time she heard a human cry. Not of pain, not of anger. It was a cry of thanks and release. Then it was gone. She closed her eyes and shuddered.

*She had done it. Hugh was in the other place.*

Quietly speaking words of thanks, she picked up the empty bag, then turned and walked slowly with bent shoulders away from the smouldering embers, between the entrance stones, and back along the ride.

She was tired. So very tired.

# Epilogue

*Great Tew, Christmas Eve 1919*

I t was a cold, still day and in bright winter sunshine Eve and Jocelyn Dance walked under the lychgate of St Mary's and followed the path up the slight rise to the church where Edward Spense was waiting nervously by the door. As the couple stopped they could hear excited chatter from the crowd who were packed into the church.

'It sounds like a full house. You look smart. Good luck.' Eve smiled at him.

'Yes, good luck, Edward.' The colonel leaned over and shook his hand. 'Bound to be a little nervous, big day and all that.'

The third son of the Dowager Lady Langford shifted uneasily from foot to foot. 'I must confess the nerves are getting to me now. My brother's inside with the family but I thought I'd get a breath of air for a moment.'

The colonel stepped back and looked up at the clock high above him. 'Five to eleven. You'd better take your place now, before the bride arrives.' He met his eye and smiled. 'Don't you think?'

As he spoke a clatter of hooves sounded and an ornate closed carriage, polished and prepared by the Langford Hall staff and pulled by two fine matched horses, appeared by the market cross at the far end of the high street.

'Yes, come on, Edward,' Eve said firmly, 'here she comes.' With a not so gentle nudge she propelled him through the church door, then she and her husband followed him down the aisle. They sat down in their reserved seats and watched as he reached the front row.

Five minutes later the familiar bars of the wedding march echoed through the ancient church as the veiled bride accompanied by her grinning father proceeded slowly down the aisle towards the altar.

Edward stepped forward, suddenly confident. He was ready. As the bride came to a halt and her father stepped back to the front rank of chairs, Edward smiled at the happy couple and his voice rang out.

'Ladies and gentlemen, we are gathered here on this bright and joyful day to celebrate the marriage of Laura Ellen Bessing and Socrates Lysander Burrows…'

*

It had taken a great deal of persuasion for Edward to don the ceremonial robes of a Church of England vicar once again but, exhibiting the same dogged determination that she had displayed in the pursuit of her beloved Burrows, Laura had finally backed him into a corner from whence there was no escape and he had reluctantly agreed.

'It is a one-off though, Laura. I shall not be resuming the cloth and I must warn you that my personal faith is non-existent,' he told her.

Laura's reply was gloriously offhand. 'Oh don't worry about all that, I just want you standing there rather than Tukes. And so does Burrows, don't you, Burrows?'

'Yes.' Her fiancé had obviously been well drilled – as he would always be when things were important to Laura, Edward suspected. *But there was love there in abundance on both sides, it was plain to see.*

All three of them went to see the Bishop of Oxford to obtain permission for his temporary re-instatement, and they arrived at the cathedral during an ecclesiastical convention. As they entered and walked down the aisle, the cavernous space was thronged with men in clerical robes wherever they looked.

'Canons to the left of us, canons to the right of us, watch out, Burrows,' Laura muttered out of the corner of her mouth and Edward was still smiling as they announced their arrival at the episcopal offices.

The bishop was happy to give his blessing and attempted to engage Edward in a conversation about returning to the fold but was politely rebuffed. Accepting defeat gracefully he asked, 'How are you anyway, how is the chest?'

'I'm scarred but on the mend, thank you. They picked rather a lot of lead out of me.'

'Yes, I heard. What about you, Constable Burrows, you had a blow on the head I believe?'

'I did, my lord, but I am back on duty, and all is well.'

The bishop nodded and then his tone changed. 'And Miss Knox? I heard it was touch and go for a long time.'

Edward said, 'Yes. She remains very weak but is out of danger. She is being nursed at Marston House by the Dances. Frankly, the doctors are amazed that she survived. Hemlock is not a merciful poison.'

'Indeed. I prayed for her, as did many others. Faith and belief, Edward, that is the thing. We must give thanks for her survival.'

'We must, my lord,' he replied, although he didn't add that the firm feeling in the village was that Eve Dance had pulled the girl back from the brink, and that the protective umbrella of Marston House was by far the best place for her.

'And they never found that fellow Atkins senior or Jane Freeling?'

'No. There were reports of a heavily pregnant woman travelling alone on the Southampton to Cherbourg ferry the morning after the trouble, but she disappeared into France. There was simply no trace of Clayton Atkins at all. One assumes they are reunited and living incognito somewhere, presumably with a young baby. Isaac Atkins and his wife are still awaiting trial.'

There was a pause and then the bishop said, 'Well, Miss Bessing, Constable Burrows, I wish you a long and happy marriage. Edward, you may of course officiate, and I grant you permission to use St Mary's for the service. My secretary will write to you, so you have the necessary paperwork.'

As the happy couple expressed their appreciation and thanks, he turned to Edward with a smile.

'What about you then, dear fellow? Any nuptials on the horizon? I'd be happy to marry you, you know. Here if you like. And I imagine your mother is getting impatient.'

Edward looked back at him, suddenly aware that Laura and Burrows were staring at him too. The question hung in the air as the cathedral clock chimed the quarter. He thought about the grief he'd witnessed in Great Tew as the telegrams had arrived and the misery that had followed in their wake. But then he glanced at his friends and saw the radiant happiness that shone from them as the stood holding hands.

*A happy future? Do I deserve that? Maybe I do.*

He pictured Innes Knox lying on the settee at Marston House and the way their eyes had met when, at Eve's insistence, she had finally taken off her glasses. The thump in his chest had been striking.

*Here I am then*, she'd seemed to say.

In a sudden tumbling rush of thoughts, things became clear in his mind. He looked at the bishop and smiled.

'You never know, sir.'

**THE END**

# Author's Note

*T*he *Ghosts of Passchendaele* is a work of fiction but, behind it, lie some truths.

At the end of World War One there was a great national debate about what to do with the fallen and plans for the huge military cemeteries in France and Flanders we are familiar with today were very contentious at the time. Remarkably, there really was one grieving mother who did not accept that her son would be buried in France and contrived to rob his grave and smuggle him home. When the army came to move his body from its temporary resting place to a new permanent cemetery they dug up the coffin and found it to be empty apart from two knuckle bones.

The landscape of Britain is peppered with places like Creech Hill Ring. Some stand alone, many others connect and interlink, often at a big scale. They were built thousands of years ago by people who were deeply attuned to the natural forces that surrounded them and that power is still there. Modern urbanised humanity has become detached from the essential nature of our world and lost the ability to recognise and understand what our ancestors knew only too well.

The supernatural aspects of the story mirror my own experiences. When Edward Spense sees Randall's soul leave his body at Ypres, it reflects exactly what I saw at the scene of a tragic rock climbing accident. Light hazes, ghosts and astral drifting have all been part of my life since my teenage years, along with a profound relationship with the hidden landscape. There is another dimension to our existence, and we all have within us a pulse of bright energy that transcends our physical being.

Finally, at a ruined church not far from here, you can dowse for the energy stream that runs down the aisle. It will turn the rods as you walk through it. Proof enough, if it were needed that, as Edward tells Innes, 'There are more things in heaven and on earth than are dreamt of in our philosophy.'

Thanks for reading the book. If you enjoyed it, a favourable review on Amazon is always appreciated. Also, you can follow me on Facebook and Instagram, where I post regularly on paganism, the hidden landscape and other themes that run through *The Ghosts of Passchendaele*.

We will hear more from Great Tew.

Frederick Petford

Somerset, England. 2021.